C

To Macy, the C... friends. As a clockmaker, before ... been all but unknown. Now, not a resident of Fortune did not know her name. Every day, for years now, they had seen her walking the haunted streets, or heard her voice, singing:

> *Horses, hoops, and dancing jacks,*
> *Treasures here for girls and boys.*
> *Baubles, trinkets, key-in-backs,*
> *Come on out and buy my toys!*

The peddler set a toy upon the ground. It marched away, with a wonderful ticking and whirring and clashing. "My name is Macy. I know some of the street children. Tonight, I will ask them if they know anyone named Kaz."

"How will I know the answer?"

"I will find you, Ash of Ashland. It is my gift." As Macy turned away, one of the jacks dangling from the pack glanced at Ash with an insouciant grin as it kicked its striped-stockinged feet.

"Wait," said Ash. "How much for a dancing jack?"

"No more than you can afford."

"Three pennies."

"Fair enough."

Ash unpinned the dancing jack from Macy's pack, and handed over her pennies. Macy took the money solemnly, and followed her clockwork toy down the street, unhurriedly, letting it lead the way. The dancing jack Ash had purchased seemed oddly heavy, now that she held it in her hand. One foot stood firmly planted, and the other kicked gleefully out. One hand hung limp, empty-handed. The other was lifted, holding out a star. Ash's heart felt pierced.

"Ghost Dog," she said, shaken. "What have I done?"

DANCING JACK

LAURIE J. MARKS

DAW BOOKS, INC.
DONALD A. WOLLHEIM, FOUNDER
375 Hudson Street, New York, NY 10014

ELIZABETH R. WOLLHEIM
SHEILA E. GILBERT
PUBLISHERS

First Printing, November 1993

1 2 3 4 5 6 7 8 9

DAW TRADEMARK REGISTERED
U.S. PAT. OFF. AND FOREIGN COUNTRIES
MARCA REGISTRADA,
HECHO EN U.S.A.

PRINTED IN THE U.S.A.

This book is for all who are still
straining
to hear the voice
of a dear friend
who was stolen
from us—
senselessly, suddenly,
and much too soon.

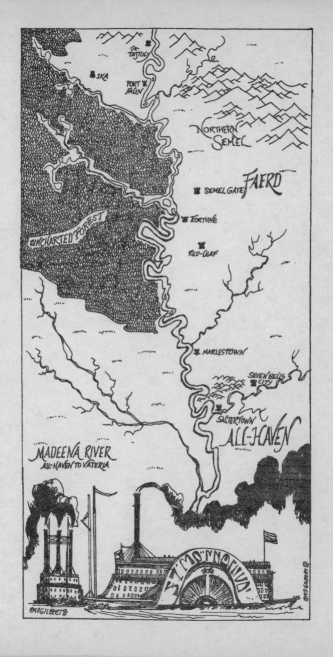

Prologue

A bitter winter held the land of Faerd in thrall that year, with heartstopping cold and snowfall deep enough to crush a barn roof under its weight. Whole flocks of sheep were lost in the snow; a late winter ice storm shattered the orchards; babies died in the cradle; old people froze beside their hearths; stone walls cracked and crumbled; chickens fell from their roosts like stones. When the thaw happened at last, late but sudden, the farmers of Faerd came out of their stone houses to stand in the watery sunlight and listen, amazed, to the sound of the ice breaking in the river. Spring had come.

At the heart of Faerd, within a day's journey of the great Madeena River, Seven Bells City huddles in the shelter of rolling hills. Here, where shepherds follow their sheep, and farmers in wide-brimmed hats walk the vineyards, the Queen of Faerd holds court in a many-towered palace. Three ancient trade roads converge upon Seven Bells City. The city has no walls, and anyone who wishes to see the queen may walk up to her front door.

The city is built of gray stone. At twilight, the bells ring, and the streets fall suddenly into shadow.

Alone in a many-windowed tower, Queen Lynthe fretted over the view below. Six years past, plague had beggared the once prosperous land, emptying the cities and leaving the countryside to fall into ruin. Now, the aftermath of this cruel winter had left the survivors floundering once again. The queen's coffers were empty; she had not been able to collect taxes since the plague's first deadly visit, six years ago. The pleas came in for funds to repair the roads and bridges, feed the people in the poorhouses, and replace the farmers' oxen, but she had no money to spend.

The lingering effects of the plague, which left the survivors blighted, had surely caused as much mischief by now as the plague itself. Not entirely immune herself to this second plague that followed so hard upon the heels of the first, the queen paced wearily from window to window in the octagonal room. Within the panes, she saw the city, the hills, the distant river: a barren, twilit land. She paused at last, and leaned upon the sill.

They did not call her the young queen anymore. Her hips heavy and her waist thick with childbearing, she wore trousers for comfort rather than pride in her figure, and a long, threadbare robe over these to block out spring's damp chill. Her hair straggled from its pins, for she had no patience with maids who fussed over her appearance. She gazed upon Seven Bells City now. Gradually, her attention focused upon the slate rooftops of one house in particular. It was a fine townhouse, nearly a palace in its own right, the home of her cousin, Diggen Elbie, a rich man by all accounts, and the queen's own friend. Not an hour ago, she had given the order for his arrest.

She knelt at the window and rested her forehead upon her folded arms. Elbie's lands she would deed to another governor, but all of her cousin's other holdings could be converted to cash, enough to replace a good many oxen. She was the queen; she did what she had to do. If she wept, alone in her tower, that was nobody's business but her own.

In the streets below the queen's tower, a wild lad scurried, one hand clutching his cap to his head, the other pumping in a fist at his side as he ran heedlessly through puddles of water and patches of mud. A startled storekeeper made a grab for him, thinking him a thief. The boy tore loose and ran on, breathlessly exhorting himself not to slacken the pace. From the gray sky an icy rain began to fall, extinguishing the last rays of sunlight.

Panting and clutching his side now, the lad passed a cluster of lordlings climbing into a carriage, and a servant too lightly dressed for this weather, who lit the lamp at the entrance with a shivering hand. The great houses of the city loomed over the wide boulevard, huddled shoulder to shoulder like shepherds around a fire. At one of the proud gateways, the boy paused at last, clutching a gatepost for support as he sobbed for breath. As soon as he could stand again, he tottered up the walk, wobble-kneed, and all but fell through the ostentatious front door, which a careless servant must have left unlatched.

Fat cherubs, illuminated in their beclouded ceiling, beamed down upon the vaulted and gilded entry hall. Furniture of ebony and velvet gleamed in the parlor beyond, where a great fire blazed in the fireplace, unattended. The boy crossed the hall and started grimly up the grand staircase, where a herd of horses milled, driven by the north wind, laughing in his chariot.

"Hey there!" someone cried. "You can't just go up there!"

"Have to see Lord Diggen," muttered the lad, dragging himself up the staircase by the banister, leaving behind him a distressing trail of black mud and water. The housekeeper descended, wrathful and astounded at the dirty boy's audacity, but the lad, inspired by the nearness of his doom, slipped out of her grasp, mounting the stairs full tilt and leaving her shouting in his wake.

Diggen Elbie lifted his head from his silk pillow and murmured, "Now what?" The beautiful woman who lay beside him, fondling him in the wake of their lovemaking, whispered something soothingly. Her hair floated around her in a tangled black cloud. Her skin smelled like roses. Her flesh was as smooth as ivory. Elbie lay back with a sigh, considering, even as she pleasured him now, how he would pay her this time. She had hinted lately that she wanted a house of her own: not the modest apartment where he kept her now, but her own establishment, with servants and a stable out back. Well, and why not? Certainly, he could afford it.

The faint sound of scuffling and cries continued out in the hallway. His smiling mistress offered him a glass of wine. "What the devil," he said, sitting up. "I'll go see what the racket is all about. Have yourself a glass, sweeting."

A high, hoarse child's voice shouted rhythmically in the hallway, as if reciting a poem. Baffled and oddly chilled, Elbie wrapped himself in a silk robe. The child's shrill shouts were overmastered by the angry cries of a serving man, and Elbie could not quite understand the words. He jerked open the door, already cursing. "What's all this racket?"

The manservant held a skinny, muddy boy by the collar, his hand firmly clasped across the lad's mouth. Nearby, the housekeeper struggled up out of her sprawl, red-faced, and gave a sloppy curtsy. "Begging your pardon my lord, this boy—"

The serving man gave a yelp and jerked his hand away, bleeding from the boy's sharp teeth. The lad shrieked, "A cold storm brews, my lord!"

Elbie reached blindly for support, cracking his knuckles upon the doorpost. "What?" he breathed. But he had heard. The serving man lifted his fist to cuff the boy's ears, but Elbie stopped him with a gesture. "No. Let him go."

Released, the lad's trembling legs could support him no longer, and he fell in a gasping heap to the floor. "Take him downstairs and feed him. Give him cake, wine, anything sweet. Put him out on the street as soon as he can walk; tell him to go on home."

The housekeeper gaped, then paled as her lord gestured impatiently. The serving man scooped up the lad and handed him to the housekeeper, who tucked him under her arm, much as if he were a weaner pig just bought at market, and huffed off downstairs, muttering to herself.

"My lord," said the serving man calmly, wrapping a

handkerchief around his bleeding palm. "Are you un-
well?"

Elbie grasped the doorpost more firmly. "Minter
Hughson, you have been a loyal servant to me, but this
night your loyalty will be put to the test. Send to my
rooms all the house servants who have not yet gone
home. I require their assistance. And have my carriage
sent round, and my best team of horses."

He shut the door decisively and leaned upon it,
breathing heavily. But the queen was a softhearted
fool! She would never—

"Come on back to bed, loveling," called Ursul from
the candlelit bedchamber. She toasted him with a lumi-
nous glass.

"I think not," said Elbie impatiently, but immediately regretted his discourtesy. His lady's life, too,
would lie in ruins before this night ended. He went into
the bedchamber and took the wine glass from her hand.
"I think you should get dressed," he said gently. "I
doubt you will still want to be here when the queen's
guard comes to take me away."

PART I:

Counting the Changes

Chapter 1: Ash

The day Ash of Ashland first considered ending her long exile, winter's melancholy voice still keened among the barren trees. For some time now, the sun had been melting the frozen fields to mud by evening, though the ground froze solid again during the night. Among the trees, snow still lay upon the ground. Even where the snow had unraveled to reveal black soil, the sledge runners glided as though across ice. With Ghost Dog running before her, Ash walked through the forest carrying a hatchet in her hand, collecting fallen wood for the kitchen fire.

The world had changed three times in her lifetime. Each time, the change had taken something away from her: first her youthful passion, then her adult desires, and finally her hope for the future. Her heart was restless now, but this period between winter and spring was the impatient time of year: a dangerous time, fraught with foolish risks, sudden passions, and premature beginnings. She had best be on her guard.

She sat upon the sledge to rest. "Planting early is just a waste of good peas, my mother would say."

Ghost Dog looked at her sideways. He had found a sunny place, where he lay on the frozen ground, his eyes like polished stones.

"Dig in your shovel, she'd say, and you'll find ice. The sun is like a slow oven, and the earth is the bread being baked. When it comes time to plant, you'll know by the scent, just like you know by the scent when it comes time to take bread from the oven."

Ash breathed in the subtle smells of the winter wood turning its slow way toward spring. "I smell ice, and snow, and the tree branches warming, and nothing more. If I planted now, the seed would just rot away."

She turned back to her work. Dark chips flew from her hatchet to litter the dirt-flecked surface of the melting snow. Like every day, this one was too short for all that needed to be done. Other chores awaited her: fences to mend, bread to bake, animals to feed.

Yet as she worked hastily to outrun the coming twilight, sometimes she heard a silence, in the moment between lifting a fence rail and placing it upon the next, and in the moment between filling the bucket and lifting it up to fill the trough. In that silence, restlessness fluttered, new hatched, eager to lift bright wings under the pale sun. The things of spring have never heeded winter's harsh lessons. If they did, then nothing would ever grow, where once snow had fallen.

Ash lived in the company of ghosts. They told stories on the long winter nights, and sang lullabies to long dead children as they rocked them in cradles that had long since gone to dust. Once, Ashland had been the hub of Semel's wheel, and many a friend and stranger came up the track to the farmhouse door, seeking succor. Now, the forest had so overgrown the road it could not be found anymore. Once, Ash had been known by another name, a name spoken even in the lands across the sea. Now, she toiled through the seasons: alone, barren, grief-stricken. Her sorrowing heart could not seem to mend. She belonged with the ghosts and did not mind their company.

Ashland Farm came first, and then the forest had grown up around its meadows and fields, enclosing it in the silence of trees and the sweet cries of the birds. A stone farmhouse crouched at the upper end of the meadow, its slumping stone walls patched with red and green lichen, the thatching weathered to a nondescript gray. At the lower end stood the barn, also built of stone. A path led to the lower meadow, the potato field, and the hay field. Within these boundaries Ash had lived for ten years now.

This spring, she watched the gray days slip from ice

to melt to ice again, as they always had done. The thaw retreated and then advanced, until slowly the season looked more like spring than winter. In the same way, her heart's restlessness retreated and then advanced, until, at sunset one day, as Ash stood on the doorstep knocking the mud from her boots, she said to Ghost Dog, "Take a journey with me."

The following afternoon, with a sack of squawking chickens slung over her shoulder, Ash slogged through mud churned up by passing sheep, threatening the ox she followed with a switch whenever he slowed his lumbering walk. The sky contained more blue than gray for once. That morning, as she cleaned the spoiling apples and vegetables out of her root cellar, she had noticed that the seed potatoes were finally budding.

The path crossed three hills and jumped a stream running cold and clear on washed stones. The stumps of trees, harvested for fuel or lumber, marked the border of Katleree land. Up ahead, the trees broke away, where Ghost Dog and six bleating sheep waited for Ash to open the gate to the Katleree's lower meadow. The gate was freshly painted, and turned silently on oiled hinges. The earth within still bore the marks of autumn's grain harvest: the wheel ruts of the thresher and the crescent hoofprints of the horses. Panicked by Ghost Dog's glare, the sheep crammed through the gate.

Up the muddy cart path, outbuildings and barns clustered around a two-story stone and wood farmhouse. The remains of the original farmhouse had thriftily been used to build the new. Some of the stones were still smoke-stained from the fire that had forced the entire Katleree clan to winter at Ashland one fine year. Thirty years ago that had been, and still the Katleree house was considered new.

Ash emptied her sack of chickens onto the ground. Evie's senior husband and an older daughter waved from the smithy, where a patient horse stood with his hoof on the daughter's knee. Atop the kitchen steps,

Ash slipped her heel into the boot jack. "Ghost Dog,
you're too muddy to come in." He glared at her, as
though she would panic like the sheep.

Within, an out-of-tune voice rather impatiently sang
a traditional lullaby. A fretful infant wailed a descant
disharmony. Ash walked through the door and across
the kitchen floor, through puddles of sunlight and
shadow, to the cradle by the fire. The woman rocking
it with her foot, her lap full of a harness she was mend-
ing, glanced up without surprise as Ash picked up the
baby, a twitching and fretful bundle wrapped in a faded
quilt. Pink-faced, the baby stared at Ash, then opened
his mouth in a toothless grin. "Hey," said Ash, "you
remember me."

"Thanks be to every god, known and unknown,"
said Evie. "Screaming since daybreak, he's been. Did
you hear him all the way over at Ashland? The child's
got a set of lungs on him!"

"Aren't you the sturdy lad, though," said Ash, as the
infant kicked vigorously against her grip, still grinning
as though the two of them shared a fine secret.

"By the good queen, he ought to be!" Evie gestured
toward her shirtfront, where buttons strained against
swollen breasts.

"A weak and scrawny little thing he was at birth.
Are you certain you're feeding him milk, and not butter?"

"Could be butter, I suppose, with All-Red's cooking.
Look at me, round as a dumpling. Now Ash, no farmer
stands when she could be sitting."

"You'll stay to supper," said All-Red, Evie's junior
husband, as Ash pulled up a chair. A brawny, muscular
man, All-Red seemed built to be a blacksmith or a
house builder. But Evie's senior husband tended the
forge, and Evie herself did all the carpentry, while All-
Red turned his large hands to the delicate tasks of child
rearing and pastrymaking. He stood at the work table
now, mincing meat, his long red hair tied back with a
strip of blue calico. It was no trick to tell which father
had sired the red-haired baby in Ash's arms.

All-Red turned his head, eyebrow raised, when Ash

did not reply to his invitation. She said belatedly, "I'd eat every meal here as you well know, if it didn't take so long walking back and forth. But I can't tonight."

Evie said, "Then you're the only one in Semel who has something to do besides wait for planting season. Have your chickens started to lay yet?" Still rocking the cradle absentmindedly with her foot, Evie launched into a lengthy catalog of the changes since Ash's last visit, before the thaw.

When Evie paused to take a breath, All-Red, his meat and vegetables minced into a paste, asked, "And what are the changes at Ashland?"

"Actually, I brought all my stock over with me, hoping you folks can look after them for a few days. I put the sheep and ox in the lower meadow—you'll be grazing there this year, won't you? And the chickens in the yard. I lost the rooster to the cold, so there shouldn't be too much commotion."

All-Red stood rubbing dried herbs between his hands and letting them fall in a green snow onto the mound of minced meat. Evie's hands, which had been busy splicing new leather into the old harness as she talked, lay still upon her patched knees now. "And when were you going to tell us?" she scolded suddenly, and jerked the lacing tight with her teeth. "And where do you think you're going, Ash of Ashland, with your fields unplanted?"

Ash frowned down at the sleeping infant. She and Evie had grown up together, and sometimes Evie forgot that they were no longer children.

"You're going to Fortune, aren't you? Six years it's been since the plague took your brother's children, and still you're waiting to hear that they survived somehow."

"How could I not know that they are dead? Do you think I do not dwell on it every day?"

"Then what kind of good will it do, to go looking for them? Haven't you heard what Fortune is like now? Death fires, day and night, corpses moldering in the streets . . ."

"I've seen worse," Ash said.

Evie did not seem to hear. Having used up her own objections, she had now begun to repeat, word for word, the cranky prejudices of her father, old Riber, against whose iron rule she had rebelled so strenuously in her younger days. "Trouble begins in Fortune: the thievery and drunkenness and misery. Why would you want to go there rather than staying where folks are civil? You'll get caught up in it again, like you did before."

Ash could not argue with a woman who considered a trip to the next farm to be dangerously long. "Still, I'm going. I'd consider it a real favor if the Katleree folks could care for my animals while I'm gone."

"Of course we'll look after your stock." All-Red, leaning on the table as he peeled the onions, frowned at Evie.

Perhaps his look reminded her of how often Ash had loaned them her ox, brought them great crocks of her pickles, and traveled regularly to Katleree, through storm and frost and summer heat, to teach their children, one by one, how to read. Evie said, "Of course we'll look after things for you. But the Ash of Ashland belongs at home."

"You know as well as I that the old days are gone and will never return. No one will come looking for me." Ash stood up and put the baby in the cradle. "I'll be back by planting time. Ten days at the most."

"Hold on." All-Red opened his pie cupboard. "Meat turnovers I've got, and good hard rolls. Take some food for your journey."

"It's not so far to Fortune," Ash said as she followed Ghost Dog down the path home. "Three days' journey, maybe four, depending on the weather. We used to go there every year when the potato crop came in."

Ghost Dog trotted ahead of her, a shadow dog, listening to what she could not hear, seeking things she would never see. The trees crowded the hillside, their heads tilted to gaze wistfully at the setting sun. Their white skin glowed, pale and cold in the gathering shadows. Soon the trees would be veiled in green, and ferns and flowers would cover their feet. Time would stand still as the children of Katleree ran through the forest, though to their elders the summer seemed to begin and end between one breath and the next.

In the twilight Ash crossed the stream with care. Ghost Dog waited for her on the opposite shore, his head wreathed in the pale mist of his breath. On her own land now, Ash paused, desolate, shivering, jamming her numbed fingers under her armpits. The still, bone white forms of the trees reached into shadows.

"I will bring the children home."

Ghost Dog turned his head sharply.

"I surprise you? You think I can't bring home the ghosts of my own kin? Maybe there're things about me that you don't know. You and Evie both."

The leafless trees sighed in a wind that had been honed sharp on the whetstone of winter. "I suppose they think I've gone mad. Oh, but Evie is right about one thing. Trouble begins in Fortune, sure enough." Hunching her shoulders, Ash started down the path again. Ghost Dog hurried impatiently ahead. The wind hunted through the bones of the forest in their wake.

When Kyril's widow, Hala, left to take Ash's nephew and nieces to Fortune to live with her family, Ash had closed up all the bedrooms and hallways of the old farmhouse so that its echoing silences would not keep her awake at night. She lived in the kitchen, where dishes painted with violets, upon which many a festive meal had been served, sat in their rack now, dusty gray and garlanded with spider webs. A forest of barren twigs hung from the rafters: the remains of herbs collected long ago.

Ash built up the kitchen fire to beat back the worst of the chill. Carrying a lantern with her, she searched through the cupboards along the wall.

Amid the skeins of wool, knitting needles, broken tools, tin dishes, broadloom cloth, boxes of ornaments and bangles for Winter-turn, carving knives, wooden bowls, and playing cards, Ash found a few things she needed for this short journey. She opened a door and went into the freezing bedroom where she used to sleep. There she took a plaid woolen blanket and an old leather satchel from the chest and carried them back to the warmth of the kitchen. Ghost Dog, half asleep on the braided rug by the fire, raised his head as she came back in.

"I know, I do not go into those rooms anymore. But I could not take a journey without this." She took out of the satchel a plain wooden box with leather hinges and a latch made of bent wire. "A winter carpenter might make a box like this to practice dovetail joints before using the good wood. The stories that were told about it! Well, those who long for change see omens everywhere."

Ash rubbed the box with a cloth until its oiled finish shone dully. "I'm not the only one to carry it journeying with me; it was scarred and battered long before it came into my hands. Grandfather Ash gave it to me the day I told him I was leaving. Do you want to see inside?" She opened the lid and held the box so the dog could see its contents. "It is full of ashes. This farm's first crop was planted in the ashes of a fire that burned the forest to the ground. These ashes."

She put the box on the table beside the other small items she would be taking with her on this journey. She could think of nothing else she might need, except for a few coins from the crockpot under the table. She set a pot of water on the stove to heat for washing, and sat down to mend the satchel's shoulder strap, so that she could pack tonight and be ready to leave at dawn.

Ghost Dog laid his head down upon his paws. A long time he watched her, with firelight flickering across the surface of his polished eyes.

᠊ᢟ   ᢟ   ᢟ

The winter after Kyril died, kicked in the head by a spirited horse he had unwisely tried to break to the plow, Ash and Hala and the children observed Winter-turn in the customary manner: with green boughs hung over the doorways, a dozen red candles burning on the tabletop, and three cooking pots set outside the door for Old Woman Winter to fill with gifts for the children. Ash kept the Long Watch alone, her head garlanded with mistletoe, a sprig of holly in her hand, pacing a slow, sun-wise circle around a single candle burning in the snow, singing all night the old songs that her grandfather had taught her.

The Long Watch was a silly business, Hala said, and refused to allow young Kaz to participate, though he had been learning the old songs at Ash's knee since autumn. At eleven years old, he was old enough to argue with his mother, who had never understood country ways, but not old enough to win the argument. He went to bed in tears, deaf to Ash's assurance that one sentinel would be enough.

The next day, or the day after, Hala told Ash she would be taking the children to Fortune as soon as the snow melted.

That was the last time she kept the Long Watch. By next Winter-turn, plague had made its first ravaging pass through Faerd, and Ash knew that her brother's children were dead. She did not greatly care whether or not winter made the turn toward spring, so she slept on her pallet on the floor as she would any other night, and did not even leave a candle burning. At the spring moon she did not journey, garlanded with flowers, to dance by starlight with the women in the woods, and bring back to Ashland a seedling to plant, to guarantee the fertility of the land. A forest of trees Ashland women had planted over the years, but Ash could not endure the risqué merriment of that starlit dance.

She had not cared for the land as she should have. This neglect lay heavy upon her as she followed the fence line through the woods shortly after dawn. Ice crackled underfoot as she struggled through the undergrowth. By the time the thicket released her onto the worn cobblestones of the Queen's Road, the ice had melted into a thousand rivulets of water flowing between the stones. Sunrise had cleared the sky of mist. The road was clear, except for a few twigs and branches scattered there by the most recent storm. It was a good day for a journey.

Though her passage through the woods had left behind a wreckage of broken branches and trampled earth, the saplings closed the way behind her now, and she could not see anymore where she had broken through. Ash centered the bedroll upon her back and started down the road. Ghost Dog, his head wreathed in mist, trotted steadily beside her.

By nightfall, they had entered the border country of Southern Semel, where the forest was punctuated here and there by rocky hilltops, and the farms began to draw closer together, as though seeking each other's company. Ash hailed a farm husband on his way to the barn for milking, and offered to help with the chores in exchange for a night's lodging. When she came into the kitchen with the milk buckets, she found that a place had been set for her at the supper table. Two husbands and two wives shared a dozen children between them. The youngest started up at the sight of the guest and crowded around, harassing her with questions.

Ash said, "I travel to Fortune to seek word of my kinfolk who used to live there."

The oldest woman tutted over the soup pot as she served its contents into bowls. "No one goes to Fortune any more. I was surprised when my husband told me you are from Ashland. Word around here has it that Ashland has been abandoned ... six or seven years, now."

Ash sat in one of the rush-bottomed chairs. She had not brought Ghost Dog in with her, for the kitchen was crowded enough. One of the older children placed a bowl of soup in front of her, and those of the family who had not yet eaten sat down around the table.

The woman said, "There is no longer an Ash either, we hear."

Ash tasted her soup. "I am the last of my line, and it is hard to argue with tradition. So I am called Ash, though the name never was conferred upon me. This is a fine soup."

She looked up to find a dozen gazes fixed upon her. "My brother-son Kaz might have become an Ash like those of old, but he died in the plague. I am just a farmer, and a poor one, at that."

"That's too bad," one of the farmers said, and passed her the bread basket. The conversation never did recover from its awkwardness, though. Simple people, they did not know what to make of her. They tried to make her sleep in a bed, but she insisted on sleeping in the barn like any other traveling stranger.

In the morning, she emerged from the barn into the mist, her satchel already on her shoulder and her bedroll slung across her back. Ghosts lurked in the vaporous haze, dancing with strange, jerky motions just beyond the limits of Ash's vision. She rubbed at her eyes, disquieted, and climbed the kitchen steps to say her good-byes. Only one of the farm husbands was awake, but he gave her a bowl of porridge.

"I gave your dog some porridge, too," he said. "Fifteen rats he'd laid out on the doorstep, neat as a shop window. More like a cat than a dog, to display his kills like that."

"Tell me, how near is Semel Stronghold?"

"I could point it out to you, if not for the mist: a big, broody wrack on the hilltop, overgrown by thickets."

"The Battle of Semel was fought nearby, then."

"On this very ground. My grandfather used to plow up the bones of the dead. He'd toss them over to the edge of the field, and once a year or so he'd load up a wagon with them and take them up to the stronghold and dump them inside the gate. They'd died trying to get there, he'd say. Let them fight on, if they need to, but not in his field."

"There're still plenty of ghosts here."

"Well, what old farm doesn't have its ghosts?"

Ash put her empty bowl on the tabletop. "My thanks for your hospitality."

"Think nothing of it. Stay longer, next time. Maybe that dog of yours will wipe out the rats entirely."

The mists, still cluttered by struggling ghosts of the bloody past, hung thickly around Ash and the dog as they once again started down the mucky road. But the sun quickly burned through, revealing a sky of won-

derful clarity. Soon she spied Semel Stronghold brood-
ing over the mist-wreathed forest, still keeping watch
over the road it had been built to protect. Of its six
towers, four had fallen and the other two were crumbling. Trees and bushes choked the proud boulevard
that once had led to its ramparts.

Ash passed between the ruined standards of the
Semel Gate. Some of the old people still told the tale
of that battle, though it was the memories of their
grandparents that they recounted. The border wars had
ended a hundred years ago. The hurts of a war-ravaged
land had healed under peaceful rule, so that even the
fiercely independent folk of Semel, forgetting the oaths
of their conquered great grandparents, now called
themselves Faerdites first, and Semelites second. Only
the ghosts gave importance to these old borders anymore.

At noon, Ash and Ghost Dog shared All-Red's good
meat turnovers as they sat in the sun by the side of the
road, and drank from a clear-flowing stream that
flowed under a neat stone bridge. As the sun began its
decline in the sky, they rounded a curve in the road and
found themselves abruptly at the edge of the Madeena
River. The road plunged straight into the water, where
a half-dozen muddy children played at the water's
edge. A boy plying a skiff off shore promptly brought
it to land at Ash's hail.

"Two pennies if you'll row me across," she said.

"And a penny each for the dog and your baggage,"
said the enterprising lad, shooing nonpaying passengers out of his boat. They scattered, barefoot on
ground that had to be as much ice as mud.

"Half penny each, you thief. I'm the only passenger
you'll have this day."

"That dog won't take alarm and tip the boat?"

Ash snorted with amusement at the idea. Ghost Dog
got in and stood sturdily in the center of the leaky boat
while Ash picked up a can and began bailing. "You
should pay me," she grumbled, keeping one hand on
her pack and bedroll so they would not tumble into the
water that seeped in as fast as she could bail it out.

The boy shrugged. "Catch a packet boat, then."

"Don't think I wouldn't like to! How long has the river been flooded?"

"Five days now."

The boy rowed briskly, showing off. Ash ceased her bailing to trail her fingers in the cold water. A long time it had been, since last she sat in a boat.

At the end of the tree-lined corridor, the road emerged once again from the quiet water. Here the boy expertly backed into the bank, and Ash, laying the boy's wage upon the seat, stepped onto shore without ever getting her feet wet. "Thank you kindly."

He gestured dismissively and set his boat bouncing across the water once again, toward the calling voices of the other children.

As Ash walked the flat and winding road, the flooded river disappeared and reappeared to her right, first nearby and then farther away. Sometimes, the afternoon sun gleamed upon its swollen surface. Other times, the barren shadows of the trees interlaced across it like the cracked glaze of an old plate.

She had to peer through overgrown trees to catch sight of the richest farmlands in Faerd. The fields were already covered with the vivid green of new grass, but the fences were falling down, stock ran wild and unattended, barn roofs were caving in, houses were falling to ruin, and plows had been left to molder in the fields. Many of the farms seemed completely abandoned.

As twilight approached, Ash stepped into a shabby roadhouse, where the ill-fed yard boy looked at her as though he had never seen a stranger before. She took a cheap room above the wash house, from which she could look down into the cluttered yard if she cared to open the shutters.

She found the tavern crowded but silent, except for one drunken woman who shouted shrilly at the others now and again. All the others sat glumly over their ale and suppers, grim and silent as the carved statues in a Homan Din temple. They turned to stare at Ash as she walked in with Ghost Dog at her heels, and even the

drunken woman ceased her witticisms to listen as Ash
ordered a supper that she hoped would be too plain to
be spoiled by an incompetent cook: bread and cheese
and ale and pickles. She begged some bread and broth
for Ghost Dog, and took their suppers up to her room.

When Ash was a child, the journey to Fortune had
been a joyous event, a four-day celebration punctuated
by fortuitous meetings with old friends and new.
Perched atop a wagonload of new potatoes, she and her
siblings hailed passing farms as gaily as if they owned
the road, the river, and all the boats that steamed upon
it.

Every traveler's tale Ash heard, and every newspaper she read, told her that Faerd had been broken by
plague. But still, the shock of what she had seen this
day left her heavyhearted and silenced, as though she
stood in the presence of someone newly, tragically
dead. She set aside her supper only half eaten, and lay
awake, staring into the darkness, long after the last
drunken farmer had exited the tavern to reel down the
road toward home.

In the old days, it used to be said that the streets of
Fortune are paved with gold. If this is so, the native
rock that intersects the shallow soil, or which hides in
wait to dull the farmer's plow, this native rock is also
gold, for it is what paves the winding streets. The
walls, the buildings, the roads, the entire city is built
with it: a coarse, soft stuff, easy to cut and shape but
quickly wearing away in the rain. From a distance, the
city seems to be made of butter softening in the sun, its
edges rounded, its walls slumping gently.

Another day's journey southward had brought Ash
to where the buds had cracked open to allow green
leaves and blossoms to explode into bright sunshine.
From afar, Ash saw that Fortune was abloom with
riotus spring, its sloping hillsides decorated with vivid
color. She eagerly entered the unlatched gates of the
city, but stopped there, taken aback.

Roof slate lay shattered in the once pristine streets.
Stones, fallen from crumbling garden walls, formed

disorderly piles where they had been cast aside to clear
the road for the wagons that still passed here. The lush
gardens ran wild, untended, spilling over walls, uprooting the cobblestones, and shattering the windowpanes. At least no corpses lay moldering in the streets,
but neither did any living people walk there, though
the smell of wood smoke and sewage suggested that
the city was not entirely abandoned.

She walked with Ghost Dog past villas turned to
mausoleums and parks returning to woodland. At the
heart of the city, the merchant's district used to crowd
upon the steamboat landing, where a shouting chaos of
goods, travelers, stevedores, and deckhands could be
found, day and night. There the pilots used to gather to
warn each other of the river's moods and changes.
Now the landing was deserted, scalloped with debris
from the receding floodwaters. Not a single boat plied
the river.

In the merchant's district, she encountered people:
gray-faced and weary in the wreck of their lives, old
beyond their years and dragging an occasional young
child impatiently by the hand. The swaggering rich and
the groveling beggars had disappeared. Everyone
looked the same now. Everyone wore despair like an
old shirt, unremarkable and going to rags. The plague
had done what all the cant and poetry of the revolution
could not: it had leveled the city.

Broken stone littered the poet's corner where once
she had paused to listen to a young man weave fire
with his words. Nearby, an old man squatted with his
back against the wall, drinking from a pottery jug and
coughing between swallows. A ragged woman sat on a
doorstep, a ragged baby in her lap. She held a brightly
painted toy over the baby's head and pulled the cord to
make it dance. The baby uttered a shriek and reached
eagerly skyward. Nearby, a group of listless and oddly
dressed strangers leaned against a crumbling wall in
the sunlight. All five of them had black hair hanging to
their waists. They watched Ash pass, their hands limp
at their sides, their faces grief-stricken.

She left the merchant's district to follow an aban-

doned street up the hillside. The road, pock-marked by
water-filled potholes, its cobbles churned up by frost,
might have proven impassable to someone less agile.
From one desolate wynd to the next, Ash climbed to
the city heights. One building after another had collapsed before the cataclysm. Young trees had rooted in
the roof tiles, and ivy twined around the gaping window frames. Birds who had followed spring this far
north built nests in fallen chimneys. Ash saw fox
spoor, and Ghost Dog started a rabbit.

Hala had not forbidden Ash to visit. But the house
no longer resembled the description she had given six
years ago: doors facing the street had long since been
stripped of their paint, debris covered the colorful tiles,
and the gardens had overrun the walls and walkways.
Discouraged by the prospect of breaking into a dozen
houses on the chance she would recognize something
within, Ash sat on a low wall. She had see no one of
whom she might ask her way.

She shut her eyes. Instantly, ghosts surrounded her:
passive and incurious as the living dead nearer the
docks. Unburied, unmourned, they were stranded between life and death, doomed to wander these abandoned roadways, as purposeless and hopeless as those
who had survived.

Ash took the knife from her belt, pricked her finger,
and let the blood drip to the ground. The ghosts
pressed forward eagerly to touch their ghostly fingers
to the blood and taste it with ephemeral tongues.

"My brother's wife, Hala, and her children, Kaz,
Dyan, and Lisl, lived on this street. Which was their
house?"

A dozen ghostly fingers, stained with Ash's blood,
pointed toward the very house upon whose garden wall
Ash perched.

The walkway had long since disappeared under a
tangle of plants. Ash plowed through to the stoop,
where a fat toad huddled. Shreds of green paint clung
to the splintering surface of the door, which hung ajar,
frozen open on rusting hinges. The hinges squawked
and dirt came cascading down as Ash forced it open.

Within, a fine carpet still lay upon the floor, with wild grass rooting in its pile. The rats and mice had raided the upholstery of the settee, and the door of a fine cupboard had warped in the damp.

Dim light coming in through cracks in the closed shutters illuminated a fiery blizzard of dust kicked up by Ash's slow passage from sitting room to kitchen, and from there down the hall to a dining room that opened out onto the garden. With her shoulder she forced open a sticky door and found herself in the nursery.

Dust swirled away from her feet as she entered. The floor was scattered with tiny pearls that crunched like eggshells under Ash's heavy boots. Pale netting draped Dyan's small bed and Lisl's crib. Within these ragged shrouds, the children still lay.

Ash crossed the room to unlatch the shutters and lean out the window. She looked upon a narrow alley, where a child's toy wagon lay abandoned in a ditch, half buried in earth, with green sprouts growing between its wheel spokes. The air was fresh, though beginning to chill as the afternoon advanced. She filled her lungs, shivering.

The massacre at Ika had bereft her of more than her man, or even her cause for living. The return home to Ashland at first seemed to give her only more of the same: both her parents and her sister had died during the previous two years, and word of their deaths had never reached her.

She did not remember how long it took before she noticed the children: days, perhaps months. Soon, Dyan, into everything, always in trouble, enemy of housecats and terror of the chicken yard, ran to Ash for haven when she had incurred everyone's wrath. And Lisl, her mother's bane, from the day she was born would only be silent within Ash's arms. Hala had hated her for it, Ash knew, and had taken vengeance in the only way she could, by taking all the children away.

Ash turned to face the shrouded beds again. First at one, then the other, she held aside the insect netting to look down at all that remained of the children she had come to call hers. Frail, fragile constructions of yellowing porcelain, they seemed too little to sustain the energy that had once moved within them. They had become bones, wrapped in rotten nightdresses and the shreds of blankets, lovingly covered and left to sleep in their cradles.

The earth of Ashland resided in those bones. Ash would take them home and plant them, like seeds, between the roots of the trees. She drew the netting closed and left them there, closing the window once again and closing the door behind herself as she left the nursery. The house had held them safe all these years, it would keep them safe a little longer.

Entombed in other rooms lay the remains of strangers, Hala's relatives whom Ash had never met. Hala's bones were scattered on the floor beside the rumpled bed where she had collapsed.

How it must torture her to have died mid-step like this, with whatever task or errand she had set herself destined to go forever incomplete! Ash knelt on the floor. "Were you thirsty? Did you get up for a drink?" She listened to the shadows. No, they told her, the pitcher lay at her bedside within reach. "Did you go to check on the children?" They had been dead, the shadows said, for several days.

"To sweep the kitchen floor?" Yes, the shadows said. Ash let out her breath in a half laugh. "Hala, you always were in such a panic about your sweeping. I will do it for you, if that will give you rest."

She went back to the kitchen and found the moldering broom standing in the corner. She swept the floor the way Hala used to sweep. After so many years, she could still remember every fussy turn of the broom, the relentless cleaning out of all the corners. Two and three times she swept the floor, until not a speck of dust remained. She opened the kitchen door and swept the debris out into the street, not forgetting to clean off the steps as well. Breathing unsteadily, she surveyed her work, to make certain that even Hala would approve of her thoroughness.

Ghost Dog appeared suddenly around the corner of

the house and stopped short. A woman stood in the alley, watching Ash in astonishment.

"My brother's wife never could abide a dirty kitchen floor." Ash went inside to put the broom away, then came back out again, firmly closing the door behind her. The handkerchief with which she wiped her face came away gray with dust. Her tear-tracks would have been impossible to miss.

"That is a ghost house," said the woman on the street. A crowd of brightly painted dancing jacks dangled from the pack upon her back. A fantastic clockwork creature stood beside her, frozen mid-step.

"Did you know the people who lived here?"

"I can't say I did. A few thousand people lived in this city once."

"Is it possible one of the children survived? Kaz his name was, son of Kyril and Hala. He was my nephew."

"Wouldn't he have come to you, if he were alive?"

"All the way to Northern Semel? It's no short journey for a boy to make by himself, and with the world coming to an end around him."

"There are some plague orphans. They took care of themselves, there being no one else."

"You've never heard of one called Kaz?"

"I can't say. Your name is . . . ?"

"Ash of Ashland."

The peddler rested one hand upon the sagging gate, where ivy twined. "Your presence in the city called out to me, Ash of Ashland. Not many dare practice necromancy any more. The ghosts are many, and hungry. Now that you have fed them, they will follow you like beggars, until you have bled yourself dry."

Ash put her hand upon the other side of the gate. "They will not be the first ghosts to haunt me."

"So I see." The peddler picked up the mechanical toy and began turning the key in its back. The dancing jacks jigged like festive children.

Ash said, "This is your city. It will tell its secrets more readily to you than it will to a stranger. Can you find out for me if my brother-son is still alive?"

The peddler tapped her fingers on the mechanical

toy's back. It made a faint, ringing sound, like a bell. "Something is happening in this city, Ash of Ashland. Are you here by design, or will you come and then go, like a moth blundering into the light?"

Ash said softly, "Of a certainty, I am blundering in."

"Indeed? Well, it is most coincidental that you have come on this day." The peddler set the toy upon the ground. It marched away, with a wonderful ticking and whirring and clashing. "My name is Macy. I know some of the street children. Tonight, I will ask them if they know anyone named Kaz."

"How will I know the answer?"

"I will find you, Ash of Ashland. It is my gift." As Macy turned away, one of the jacks dangling from the pack glanced at Ash with an insouciant grin as it kicked its striped-stockinged feet.

"Wait," said Ash. "How much for a dancing jack?"

"No more than you can afford."

"Three pennies."

"Fair enough."

Ash unpinned the dancing jack from Macy's pack, and handed over her pennies. Macy took the money solemnly, and followed her clockwork toy down the street, unhurriedly, letting it lead the way. The dancing jack Ash had purchased seemed oddly heavy, now that she held it in her hand. One foot stood firmly planted, and the other kicked gleefully out. One hand hung limp, empty-handed. The other was lifted, holding out a star. Ash's heart felt pierced.

"Ghost Dog," she said, shaken. "What have I done?"

Chapter 2: Rys

At the leading edge of spring, violent storms march down the winding road of the Madeena River, overflowing the banks, uprooting the trees, and grinding the docks to splinters between millstones of ice. In the midst of one such howling storm, in the black of night, someone came pounding on the Master of the Pilot's Guild's door, crying out her name over the howling of the wind. Startled out of bed, she came to the door wrapped in a blanket, lifted the latch, and let the storm wind swing the door open.

Her visitors crowded hastily into the kitchen, water pouring from their oilskins, apologizing even as they stamped mud across the polished wooden floor, tangled the floorcloth, tipped over a chair, and all but extinguished the fire in the stove as they crowded around it. Master Pilot Rys lit the lamp on the tabletop for their sake, rather than hers, and said, "What madman puts out from shore on a night like this one?"

One disentangled from the huddle, a small man with faded, clever eyes that glinted faintly in the light of her lantern. "The steamboat *Amina,* out of Saltertown."

"I know the boat and her captain, but I do not know you, sir."

"I'm the new mud clerk, Minter Hughson. Captain Garvin is not aboard for this trip, but Lindy of Airhome has the helm."

"I know Lindy. Who are these others?"

"Arin, the dockmaster's man, guided us to your door; surely you know him. And this is Ursul."

The woman slipped the wide hat back from her face; the lamplight revealed a delicate sculpture of fine bones, smoky eyes, a sensuous mouth, and a cloud of black hair that tangled across her shoulders, damp from the storm. Beauty-struck, Rys turned her face hastily away. She had been offered bribes before, but never had one come so close to the mark. Half flattered, half angered, she said quietly, "You must wait on the weather like everyone else. Come back in the morning."

The woman drew back as if surprised and unaccustomed to refusal. Minter Hughson said, "The morning will not wait. If we return without you, then we leave dock without a pilot. We have an urgent cargo."

"Well, make a hefty sacrifice to your gods, for you will never see dry land again."

"We will pay twice your usual rate."

"Much good it will do me at the bottom of the river! Goodspeed to you." Rys gathered the blanket, anticipating the cold blast of storm which would greet her when she opened the door to let them out.

The beautiful woman lifted a hand, the rain upon her skin shimmering in faint lamplight. "Let me speak with you alone, Madam Pilot. A moment only."

Suddenly she seemed closer, her skin afire. Without thinking, Rys had turned up the wick. Reminding herself that lamplight only endangers a pilot's clarity of vision, she turned it down again and set it on the kitchen table. "Come this way."

They went into the chilly sitting room, and Rys shut the door, so they were entirely in darkness. Rain rattled loudly upon the storm shutters that had been closed for nearly three days now.

Ursul seemed disoriented in the darkness, and reached for the back of a chair to steady herself. "Madam Pilot, you are not known to be a coward."

"I am not known to be an idiot, either." Rys walked away a few steps, and picked up a glass weight from a tabletop. A cleverly detailed miniature riverboat was frozen within its chilly prison. Rys could even see the buckets of the paddle wheels. "After piloting on the Madeena for over twenty years, do you think I will

give my experience no heed? Any boat goes abroad at
its peril in a storm like this."

"Well, we are forced to choose between perils. For
three days we have traveled against the current, staying
scarcely a few hours ahead of the hired hounds from Vateria who pursue us. If we can slip away in tonight's
storm, we will be safe. But if we wait until daybreak . . ."

"Do you expect me to believe this tale? Captain
Garvin would never place his boat at risk . . . unless
you stole the *Amina* from her winter anchor." The startled lift of the woman's head told Rys that this guess
had come close to the mark. "There are plenty of pilots
who will do anything for pay, and ask no questions. I
recommend that you find one. I do not work for outlaws, as you should have known."

"How you can make such astonishing assumptions,
madam, I cannot imagine. Because we are fugitives,
then we must be outlaws? I was prepared for arro-
gance, but even I have never seen the like of this."

"The way the water's surface ripples tells me the
difference between a sandbar and a shoal. Do you
think that the secrets hidden in conversation are any
harder to read?"

"Well, you are mistaken. Madam Pilot—Rys—we
do indeed have an urgent cargo: a person named
Cydna."

"Cydna?" Rys said, as though she had never heard
the name before. "Do you think me a fool? Cydna is
dead." But at the center of her heart there was a
shocked stillness, as though the emptiness that long
ago took up residence there had at last opened its
mouth to speak. Rys turned away sharply, to make her
way through the clutter of furniture to the cold hearth.

Ursul, unable to follow through the mystery of darkness, remained near the doorway, saying with guarded
sincerity, "I sat at her side not an hour ago. She spoke
to me of the love that was once between you. 'Rys will
come,' she said."

Rys spoke to the ashes and the stones of the cold
hearth. "I have never in my life heard so desperate a
lie."

"If I meant to trick you, would I not try to make it more believable?" The woman dabbed daintily at her damp skin with a shirtsleeve, apparently unaware that Rys could see in the dark. Yet her face, like her voice, gave Rys no sight-marks by which to navigate. Ursul had the unimpeachably pleasant and impersonal manners of a courtesan. Rys could not see what lay beyond the polished manner; this woman was an accomplished actor indeed.

"Then tell me the rest of it," she said, as though she were remotely amused by this late-night charade. "Why did she not come herself?"

"An assassin's blade cut her forearm in Seven Bells City. It did not kill her—the assassin had let his poison grow stale, perhaps. But although she will recover, she is still too weak to leave her bed. You know what is said about her; to try to protect her from her enemies would be impossible. Only her anonymity has kept her safe these ten years. She cannot turn to the queen for protection; Queen Lynthe would not risk a war with King Bartyn when she does not even have an army anymore. Cydna found friends to help her escape to Fortune. Not everyone's love has grown cold."

Rys turned to look once again at the beautiful woman, who supported her weight with one hand against the wing-back of a chair. She appeared wan enough to be a refugee, but something about this situation did not sit right. "Who are you, then?"

"A friend," said Ursul, pursing her mouth primly as any goodwife grousing over her cups.

"The truth is what I'd prefer to hear."

"Well, then, I'm caught up in this tangle by accident. I boarded the *Amina* in all innocence, to visit my mother in Fortune. They hijacked me along with the ship, and I was pressed into service to nurse this Cydna." She shrugged. "Why not? For once, I am not bored to tears."

Rys looked around the shadowed sitting room. She and Margo had spent many a stormy night comfortably huddled by the fire, reading the latest book or figuring accounts for the store. Rys' sewing basket sat on the table, with a half-finished shirt draping over the edge. Normally Rys would bring some sewing with her, to occupy herself in a boat trip's inevitable dull hours, but she doubted that this foolish journey would last long, once she had taken over the helm.

"Wait for me in the kitchen while I pack."

Ursul bobbed a small, overly deliberate curtsy and went into the kitchen. Rys mounted the narrow staircase toward the bedroom, to pack a duffle and tell Margo she was leaving. Fortunately, Margo was well enough accustomed to Rys' sudden arrivals and departures, or this one might prove difficult to explain.

Cydna, she thought. *Cydna is still alive.* Halfway up the stairs, she pressed a hand to her heart. Joy had so long been absent that it seemed a stranger. A vagrant stranger, she reminded herself, but her heart paid no heed.

Rys had been a master pilot for two years when plague shut down the entire Madeena River, from Tastuly in the north to the seaport town of Sandros in the south. Stranded in her home port of Marlestown, she managed the riverfolk's relief effort until plague struck her down. Only one in fifty survived the illness. Thanks to Margo, she was among them.

They had first met in the street, when Rys chanced upon her, a lone merchant defending her store against looters during the early days of the plague. Many an unlikely alliance was created in those desperate days; Margo and Rys survived the terror and desolation of that nightmare summer by clinging to each other. Rys never imagined they would remain together for seven years, but much that had once been unimaginable had since come true.

She never told Margo about Cydna. If Rys still carried a torch for a woman long dead, that was her business.

A screaming harridan of a knife-wielding wind stalked the streets of Marlestown, hurling wild flurries of rain, spear-tipped by ice. Along black, slippery streets, Rys and her escort hurried through the shuttered town, making their way by the weak light of a storm lantern swinging in the dockman's hand. Ursul, her lush hair covered by a broad sailor's hat, bent into the wild wind as grimly as any, uncomplaining and resolute.

Minter Hughson, the mud clerk, with Rys' duffle bag slung over his shoulder, slipped on icy stone and fell to one knee, cursing. The dockman dragged him to his feet again. Overhead, a shutter banged in the wind and a painted wooden sign creaked on its chains. Crouching to duck the onslaught of rain, they hurried on. The riverboats clustered at their winter docks came into sight; a swaying forest of smokestacks, all but invisible against the black water, rising above the tin roofs of the warehouses. Here, at least, light glimmered, the faint casting of lanterns as the boats' caretakers worriedly paced the landing.

As they drew near, Rys heard the groaning of bows rubbing restlessly against the pilings as the wind rocked the topheavy boats. Rys turned to the woman at her side, whose sturdiness through the wildness of the storm had surprised her. Though Ursul spoke with the over-pretentious, refined accents of Seven Bells City, her foppish ways seemed mere affectations, a mask of frailty overlaying a solid core. "It would be certain disaster to venture out in this storm," Rys said. "I am here because of Cydna, but I will advise her to wait until morning."

Ursul shrugged. "You are the pilot, madam."

"You say that she lived in Seven Bells City? That surprises me."

"Surely she will tell you all when she sees you. Many times she has asked for you."

"I never thought she would forgive me."

The wind must have snatched Rys' words away. The woman at her side said, "I beg your pardon, madam?"

"I said, that must be the ship."

The *Amina* writhed upon her moorings. Rys smelled the sharp, resinous scent of wood smoke: fat pine, for speed. Her fires stoked, her bows wreathed in escaping steam, the *Amina* stood ready to leap heedlessly into the flood. A roustabout waited at the foot of the landing stage, water pouring from his oilskin-covered head and shoulders. Money exchanged hands between Minter Hughson and the dockman, who hurried off toward the dockmaster's office, where a warm fire surely burned. The clerk gave Rys' duffle to the roustabout and led the way up the gangplank, admonishing them to hold onto the railings. As they climbed onto the boat's forecastle, Rys grasped the clerk by the shoulder. "You must not interpret my presence aboard the *Amina* as an agreement to pilot her. I will speak with your first mate."

"Madam, I will fetch him at once." The clerk hurried into the rain, across a barren deck, dimly lit by storm lanterns and occasionally crossed by crewmembers, who were caped and hooded against the rain.

Rys took the courtesan by the arm. "Where is Cydna?"

"This way." Keeping her balance easily, the woman crossed the rocking deck.

Rys pushed back her hood as her guide led the way up the main stairway to the passenger deck and into the shelter of the salon. They paused to shake the rain out of their oilskins, so the expensive rugs that covered the floor here would not be waterstained. No lamps burned here. Perhaps, for safety, the mate had ordered all flames to be extinguished, lest a lamp overturned by the rough weather catch the boat on fire. Ursul took Rys' hand to guide her to a port side stateroom. "Your friend is probably asleep, though she swore she would stay wakeful for your arrival." The damp had roused the scent from her hair. Breathless, Rys let go of her hand. Ursul turned to the shapeless figure which had followed them up the stairs. "Why did you not bring a lamp? Stand by in case Madam Pilot needs anything, and I will fetch some light so she need not talk in darkness."

Rys opened the door and went in, letting the door close behind her. The stateroom's sitting area smelled faintly of mildew and damp wood, as boats often do

after a winter's inactivity, but a small stove bolted to
the floor in the corner kept it warm enough. Faint light
leaking out from its crevices illuminated a nearby armchair and a table standing under the shuttered window.
A curtained doorway gave access to the sleeping alcove. From behind the curtains, Rys heard only silence.

She reached for the doorknob even as the bolt slid
into place, locking her in. She leaned back against the
wainscot, stunned.

No long lost friend lay sleeping in the alcove. The
cabin was empty except for her. The shutters prevented
her from seeing out into the storm, but the vibration of
the engines and the faint echo of deckhands' shouts
told her all she needed to know. The riverboat had
been released from her moorings, and was backing
away from the wharf and into the grasp of the howling
storm.

By her pocket watch, half an hour had passed when
the key turned in the lock once again, and the stateroom door was opened. She had added more wood to
the stove, and sat with her feet crossed before it, letting
her damp boots dry. She scarcely turned her head when
she heard the door being unlocked, but she fixed a cold
glare upon the small, lamplit procession which entered
the narrow room. One woman, her oilskins pulled back
to reveal pistol, sword, and an array of knives attached
to her belt, carried a lantern which she hung carefully
on an overhead hook. Its steeply angled light illuminated the hats but not the faces of Rys' captors. One
hat, bejeweled and fur-lined, which had been carelessly
allowed to be stained by the storm, informed her in detail about its wearer, a shapely and overconfident man
at the head of the procession.

He swept the hat from his head and gave a neat bow.
The revealed hair swept his shoulders, its curls rather
tangled by the wind. "Madam Pilot," said the man with
the hat, "I beg your forgiveness."

Rys had hung her oilskins upon a hook to dry. Her
woolen uniform of pilot's blue would be nearly black

in this light, but the flattened oval badge of the Pilot's Guild glittered upon her shoulder. Words would only have diluted the message of her cold stare.

"Of course," continued the man lightly, "what we have done is unforgivable; beyond description; the very height of river piracy. I shall not compound the sin by rudeness; therefore allow me to introduce myself. I am Diggen Elbie. My brave Ursul you have already met—" he gestured into the midst of the procession, where a sailor's hat once again covered his mistress' opulent hair. "And these, my merry crew, well, you shall get to know them soon enough."

Rys uncrossed and recrossed her feet. "You waste my time, little man."

"Diggen Elbie," the man said again, gently enough, though his face had gone cold as river ice.

"Lord of Carterain, Governor of Corbenton, the queen's own cousin, and a fool for all that. A brave boat will go to the bottom this night because of your idiocy. And you will go down with it."

Even as she spoke, she heard the faint thud and vibration of a drifting log striking the wooden bow of the ship with a glancing blow. Though the flotsam which fills a river at spring flood posed threat enough to a night-traveling steamboat, it was the wind rocking the boat so vigorously which most concerned Rys. Whoever piloted the *Amina* now was having a beggar's time of keeping her nose into the wind so it would not simply turn the boat over.

"The brave boat will not go to the bottom once you are at the helm, madam. Shall we go?" The gesture with which he waved her toward the door had an element of violence in it.

"I will not pilot this boat."

"Oh, but you shall, madam, or perish."

"I shall not perish alone, sir."

"Indeed, you shall not." The queen's cousin showed his teeth; perhaps it was meant to be a smile. Desperate enough straits he had to be in already, to be fleeing like an outlaw in a ship that surely he had stolen from its moorings, and at least part of its crew along with it.

His response to her obstinacy would tell her much about what kind of man she dealt with.

"Come with us on a tour of the boat, Madam Pilot. We wish to show you something." He gestured to the woman-at-arms, and she stepped forward, bristling.

Rys got lightly to her feet. "Certainly." Faintly, she heard the ship's bell, ringing with the rocking of the boat. The armed woman looked as though she were more in the mood to hang her head over the ship's rail than to escort a recalcitrant pilot about the boat. It made no real difference; if Rys decided to make a run for it, where would she go? Into the river? Only if suicide appealed to her.

The nobleman's retinue made a disorderly exit from the stateroom. Leading the way, with a lantern in her hand, Ursul unlocked and opened another stateroom door. She held high the lantern, to reveal a half dozen faces, white as ghosts in the lamplight, their faces stiff with fear: a woman, a man, and four small children. The woman sat in the armchair, with two of the children in her lap and a third at her feet. The fourth knelt in the corner, vomiting on the floor, with the man holding her head. After a moment, Ursul shut and locked the door.

"At least bring them a basin," said Rys. "A mint draught would help settle the children's stomachs; there will be some in the galley."

Ursul ignored her and continued down the length of the central salon. Behind one locked door after another, she revealed her prisoners: another frightened family; an angry man who came shouting out of his bed; an old woman, shawl-wrapped, dozing by a cold stove; a defiant, well-dressed boy who had occupied himself in captivity with systematically destroying his prison's furniture and curtains. Rys counted some twenty people in all.

"As you see," said Diggen Elbie, when they had finished exhibiting their prisoners, "you will indeed be in good company when the ship goes down."

"Who pilots her now?" asked Rys.

"Her mate, Lindy Airhome, who brought her up the river from Seven Bells City."

"Then he has been at the wheel for near a day and a night without respite? Indeed, sir, you have a madman's luck to have safely journeyed as far as Marlestown."

"You cannot mislead me, madam. It is no great trick to navigate a flood, I am told. We will be safe enough."

"No great trick? Then why did you not leave me warm in my bed?" She turned her back to him, the mule-headed imbecile, and told the man beside her to fetch her oilskins and try to find out what had happened to her duffle bag, while he was at it. Though he could have been another of the queen's respected advisors for all she knew, he promptly set about doing her bidding. Beneath their silks and furs, every member of the little party smelled of fear, except perhaps Ursul, who absentmindedly jingled the keys in her basket. "Set your passengers free from the cabins," Rys said to her. "At least they will have half a chance should the boat go down."

The man reappeared with her oilskins. Ignoring the armed woman at her elbow and the nobleman's entourage that trailed her, Rys strode across the salon toward the stairs that would take her to the pilothouse on the upper deck.

Lindy Airhome hung half out the pilothouse window as he peered into the tarry darkness, trying to see anything at all through the rain and spray of the storm-tortured river. Rys tapped him on the shoulder to get his attention, and then turned to shout angrily at the dimwit who had brought a lighted lantern onto the deck with him. "Put out that flame before I hang you between the stacks for the crows to eat! I'll take the helm, sir. You're about to plow the *Amina* into a stand of trees."

The exhausted mate gave way gratefully, and stumbled across the pilothouse to collapse onto the bench. Rys put her mouth to the speaking tube and shouted at the engineers below, "Half speed on the port engine!

Full stop on starboard!" Then, feeling the engines slow, she wrenched the wheel around. The wind struck the boat broadside, and the nobleman and all his attendants went reeling crazily across the pilothouse, clutching at each other in a frenetic dance.

"You're going to tip her over," muttered the mate, through lips stiffened by cold. "Captain Garvin will have our hides."

Rys hung all her weight on the wheel, cursing under her breath. The stool on which she might sit on a calmer night flipped over and fell with a crash. The armed woman groaned and hung on the doorsill for support. The half-submerged trees on the flooded bank slipped past, invisible to all except Rys. She grabbed the speaking tube, shouting, "Full ahead, both engines!"

The boat leapt forward, bravely fighting the current now, though the wind continued to tip her sideways. She felt a little sluggish; no doubt she had taken on some water in the course of that desperate turn. The wind buffeted her again, and then seemed to catch its breath.

They had slipped behind the shelter of the Onstring Bluffs, against whose steep sides the river had been worrying for hundreds of years. Rys ordered the engines slowed, until the boat just barely held her own against the current, and sent the exhausted mate below to oversee the pumping out of the boat's hold.

She turned to find the queen's cousin clinging to the windowframe of the pilothouse for support, with his fine fur hat now hopelessly ruined by the blowing rain. "You're blocking my view, sir," she said.

"I thought the best pilots didn't even need to look at the river. Pilot's Sight, is it called?"

"Move out of the way, or be moved, sir. It's your choice."

"If there are some in the Fellowship of Thieves who have this ability, no doubt they call it Thief's Talent. A mighty useful gift it would be, in their profession." Lord Diggen stepped aside, so he no longer blocked the window, and gave Rys a mocking bow. Like a true gentleman, he meant to make her suffer for his discomfiture.

Well, now that he had seen firsthand the danger in which he had placed the boat, perhaps he could be convinced to tie in to shore. The lightless river swept an uprooted tree down upon them, like a spear raised to puncture the boat's fragile skin. Rys turned her aside at the last moment, so the tree broadsided her harmlessly, sending a hollow thunder reverberating through the boat. She let out her breath heavily and leaned gently into the wheel to nose the *Amina* into the current again.

"Sir, you are a landed man, so I doubt you know this river as I do. He has a vexatious personality, changeable as a boy at puberty. On a dry summer day, his water level may rise; on a wet spring day, it may sink. He is forever changing his course, and sometimes his water level will sink so low that even a little skiff can run aground. It is out of respect for the river's temperament that the boats which ply the Madeena area have shallow drafts. The *Amina*, for instance, measures some thirty feet from the water level to the top of the pilothouse, but only about four feet from the water level to the bottom of the boat. So, in a strong enough wind, she can be turned right over, easy as you please."

"We filled her up with firewood just outside of Marlestown, to give her more ballast," said Elbie. "The mate already gave me this lecture, Madam Pilot, though not a quarter so arrogantly."

"I know the *Amina* has a good ballast, sir, and still she almost went over just now. You have shown yourself to be a clever man; I must assume you abducted me because of my record and reputation. So heed my experience, I ask you. The finest piloting that ever was seen upon the river cannot control the wind. Let me tie in to shore and wait out the storm."

"Do you think I have undertaken this journey for my health, madam?"

Rys glanced over her shoulder, as if checking the view to her side. Grim and resolute as death, Diggen Elbie stood a few paces behind her, arms folded, face like stone. "No, sir, I doubt that," said Rys, taken aback. Like his mistress, this man was more than he seemed.

"Then cease your complaints and make it your business to keep this boat afloat. And I must insist that you address me properly."

"On dry land I will call you whatever you like. But when I stand at the helm, I am the ship's master and I call no man or woman 'my lord'."

The other members of the entourage, perhaps beginning to recover from their seasickness as the boat stalled for time here in the shelter of the bluffs, murmured with shocked outrage at Rys' insolence. But his lordship merely sat on the bench near the wood stove, well out of the way of the pilothouse windows.

The rain-sleeted black river muscled the boat casually this way and that. The trees that normally stood on the riverbank waded in water now, the level of which rose, even as Rys watched. The riverbankers would be keeping flood watch this night, and, come daybreak, no few of them would claim to have seen a ghost ship pass them by, laboring upriver through a storm that no sane pilot would challenge.

Rys glanced again at the sheltering bluffs. Soon, the wind would broadside them once again. Up ahead, the river took a turn which would put the boat's nose safely into the wind again and give them another respite. Never mind how Rys would pilot throughout the night; how would she get them through the next quarter mile?

She said over her shoulder, "At least let me put the passengers ashore."

"And why should I do that? They are my insurance that you will pilot the boat well."

"I have never piloted badly, sir, but if it is my word you want, I will give it. Any of this boat's crew will vouch for my integrity."

"It's the truth, my lord," said the first mate, who had just reappeared, breathing heavily, at the door of the pilothouse. "Rys' word is solid as an iron-hulled boat."

"Indeed," said Elbie. "How refreshing."

Exasperated, Rys sent the mate to bed, and told one of his lordship's servants to brew her some tea in the galley. All winter long, she had lived, as Margo put it, like a human being. She was no longer accustomed to staying up most of the night, and it seemed this night would be a long one.

❦   ❦   ❦

Halfway between midnight and dawn, Rys shouted into the speaking tube for the engines to be slowed, and began violently ringing the bell to summon all hands. Startled awake by the clangor, the armed woman straightened from where she had been propped in the pilothouse doorway, and reached for the tin cup of tea poured hours before. She seemed surprised to find it stone cold, and glanced at Diggen Elbie, as if wondering if he realized she had fallen asleep on watch. His lordship, who had himself fallen sound asleep upon the hard bench, sat bolt upright, crying, "What happened to the wind?" He set his booted feet down in the water that flooded the pilothouse floor, and crossed to the windows to stare wildly, only half awake, into the darkness.

The rain, which at times had blown through the windows in sheets, had slacked off to a drizzle. The clamor of storm had lapsed into a silence which to the newly awakened passengers must have seemed ominous, when combined with the racket of the all-hands bell. But Rys peered upward, hopeful that she might spot stars beyond the breaking clouds.

"What happened to the wind?" cried Elbie again. He still seemed confused, caught between sleeping and waking, frowning at the tree branches that loomed out of darkness to brush dry fingertips along the sides of the boat. Clearly, he was accustomed to more soothing awakenings.

A haggard young woman Rys had never seen before stepped into the pilothouse. "Madam?"

"Who are you?"

She looked around herself as if to ask someone else

to reply on her behalf. "I guess I'm the second mate.
I couldn't wake Lindy."

"It's all right. What's your name?"

"Kiva."

"I took the boat up a chute, trying to avoid a bad
turn, and now our way is blocked by tree branches.
You're going to have to take the crew out on the yawl
to clear the passage. You do have saws?"

"By our gods, madam, Captain Garvin will have our
hides if he hears you took his boat through a chute—"

"He will never believe Rys of Marlestown did such
a thing. Can you get the way cleared, or should we
throw some water on Lindy?"

"Oh, I can do it, I guess. A man who sleeps through
the all-hands bell won't be worth the salt on his skin
anyhow. With your permission, I'll light the forward
beacons so we can see."

"Go ahead. Just take care not to let your debris tangle with the paddle wheels. Send someone to mop up
this water. And is there a cook on duty?"

"I will have supper sent up to you." As the young
woman exited the pilothouse and began shouting shrill
orders from the bridge, Rys picked up the stool that
had overturned when she first took over the helm, six
hours ago, and sat down for the first time.

While Elbie's retinue sought shelter below, and
Elbie himself nonchalantly slept, Rys had run the river
as it had never been run before. She slid the boat into
every nook and cranny that could possibly shelter it
from the wind. She hugged the shoreline, sometimes
ignoring all convention and making the boat fight the
strongest current rather than crossing into the slack.
Where the river had flooded its banks, she took the
boat overland, crossing oxbows in chutes that appeared
with the flood, and once even cutting across a flooded
plain, dodging treetops and a partially submerged barn.
She called no leadsmen to take soundings; she knew
this piece of river so well that she could use the trees
as leadlines to show her the depth of the water.

Now, as the forward beacons were lit, illuminating
the dense treetops laying atop the black water, Elbie

paced from window to window, as if he could not believe his eyes. At last, he said in a muted voice, "What exactly is a chute?"

"It's a channel that can only be used at high water. Hotheads use them to shorten the distance of their run, but I've been using them to keep the wind from broad-siding us."

"It appears to me as if we are in the middle of a forest."

"Generally speaking, that's what grows on the banks of a river, sir."

By the light of the beacons, Rys watched a bunch of mangy-looking deckhands set out in the yawl. Some of them seemed mighty uncomfortable in the little boat, clinging to its sides with white-knuckled hands, and staring yearningly back at the steamboat huffing and churning as she held her own against the current. Landlubbers, thought Rys, a cobbled-together crew made up of house servants and grooms, and maybe a man-at-arms or two. No doubt they were wishing about now that they knew how to swim.

Well, experienced or not, they certainly were loyal, to follow their master on such an adventure, that promised so little reward.

The crew secured the riverboat to two sturdy trees. Rys told the engineer to cut the engines and take a supper break. A stiff, neat gentleman appeared at the pilot-house door, a covered dish in one hand and a fresh pot of tea in the other. Expecting the usual midnight fare of scrambled eggs and fried bread, Rys found she had been served a disjointed gamebird cooked in spicy sauce, which nestled in a bed of finely chopped vegetables. Out of his pocket the stiff gentleman produced two rolls wrapped in a napkin, and a spoon.

"This is the queerest trip I've ever taken," Rys muttered. She scarcely knew what to do with such noble fare. The steward, or butler, or whatever he was, poured tea for Lord Elbie and asked him diffidently if he could bring him anything to eat.

"Nothing, Grelling. Thank you." Elbie stared

bleakly after the departing servant, scratching at the beard that had begun to sprout on his chin.

"Is this the adventure you expected?"

"I don't know why," said Elbie, turning to watch the activity on the river as he brought his tin cup daintily to his lips, "but the sheer magnitude of your impertinence intrigues me."

"I have been tricked, kidnapped, abused, and forced to take actions contrary to the creed of my guild. If I react only with impertinence to these grave insults, you should consider yourself fortunate indeed."

"I do wish someone had warned me about your nasty personality. I had my choice of a dozen pilots. They are all cozy in their winter quarters, this time of year, and easy to find. Surely I could have located one who did not consider herself too good to serve a noble lord!"

"I think it more likely that I am serving a criminal. Did you steal from the queen's coffers?"

Elbie uttered a sharp, startled bark of laughter. "The queen's coffers? Oh, madam, they have long been empty."

"Well, you surely have done something equally heinous. By all accounts, Queen Lynthe holds you dear."

Rys hoped only to silence him so that she could enjoy her meal in peace. But Elbie, his back to her now, said after a moment, "I accused her husband of assassinating her brother, King Anselm."

"King Anselm? Why is what happened to him even important anymore? That was before the plague."

"Indeed, he is the forgotten king. How could his mysterious disappearance compete with a wholesale disaster such as the plague? But still, it is a pitiful ending for a man who in life suffered from such an ailment of self-importance."

Rys had been served a meal that was impossible to eat neatly out of her lap, though with the first mouthful she forgave the inconvenience. She ate straddling the bench, with the plate between her knees, using her fingers as often as the spoon. The queen's cousin continued to speak musingly, his voice swallowed up from time to time in the sound of the rain thrumming on the pilothouse roof.

"Why is it important, you say? Indeed, with the plague, the world did seem to be coming to an end. Does it then follow that no one remembers the hurts and grudges of the past? I myself have seen no evidence of such forgetfulness. Indeed, the plague has brought out the worst in human nature, as far as I have been able to see."

Rys, her mouth full, forebore comment. She did not want to encourage him. But it was hopeless. The man could have listened to himself all day.

"The king was assassinated, and the man who killed him rules beside the queen, unaccused and unpunished. This is an injustice long suspected by those who serve the queen. When I uncovered the truth, would it not have been a disservice had I failed to tell her what I knew? I would be a poor courtier indeed if I let my queen be weakened by her own ignorance. Unfortunately, she did not see it that way."

Aggrieved, Diggen Elbie paced restlessly from window to window. "Though I never thought she would accuse me of treason. I thought she would be amused, actually. A duller man than her husband never walked on this sweet earth. The whole thing is absurd."

Rys could not help but laugh at the man sulking like a spoiled child denied a new toy. He turned on her, enraged, as though to strike her, but seemed to remember that she had brought the boat to this predicament while he slept, and only she could get them safely out. She had not flinched as he briefly towered over her. He had chosen to bring a true pilot on board his stolen boat; now let him learn why the Pilot's Guild had so much power.

He turned away, muttering, "It is a hard irony, to be made an outlaw for telling the truth."

"And you had no secondary intentions? You did not hope that she would arrest him, and take you in his place?"

"Don't be ridiculous. Why would I want to rule a land of ghosts, peopled by brokenhearted fools who look only where they have been and not where they are going? No, this disaster is, in the end, all for the best. I will be warmly welcomed in Vateria, and King Bartyn will certainly have a position and purpose for a man such as I."

"The plague struck Vateria as hard as it did Faerd. You think they have no ghosts there?"

Elbie allowed Rys to finish her meal in peace, though now it only seemed appropriate that the queerest meal she ever ate on board a boat be accompanied by the strangest conversation. She wiped up the last of the rich sauce with her bread, and held her napkin in the rain until it was damp enough to clean her face and hands.

It was she who broke the silence to say, "I would like to know how you found out that Cydna and I were friends."

"I certainly do understand why you kept it such a secret. It would not do for the Pilot's Guildmaster to be known to have been lovers with the one whose curse caused the plague. I discovered it when I investigated you at the queen's behest, after you became Guildmaster. It seemed like such a useful piece of information that I kept it to myself, all these years."

"I told the queen myself, lest some busybody try to blackmail me over it. But you did not investigate as thoroughly as you should have, sir. We were never lovers, and Cydna had nothing to do with the plague."

"All the more tragic. You yearn for her still, your passion unrequited."

Rys dropped her napkin on top of the plate for the roustabout to carry away when Kiva got around to sending one to clean up the pilothouse. "I'm going to the head."

Elbie's mocking laughter followed in her wake as she stepped out into the rain and climbed down to the main deck, shadowed at a distance by the armed woman. In the flooded river, the novice crew had swarmed up the trees and now tethered with ropes the branches that needed to be cut, so that they would not float downstream and foul the riverboat's buckets. It was a strange, surreal sight: the deckhands, illuminated by the beacons, against a backdrop of uninterrupted darkness, sweating and cursing in the trees as two oarsmen worked the yawl below, and the haggard second mate shouting from the prow, pointing and gesturing like a puppeteer. That they could get through the night without losing someone to the flood waters seemed most unlikely.

Rys looked the *Amina* over from stem to stern, finding her to be in better shape than she had expected. Though Kiva had become second mate by default, she seemed to be making the best of her inexperienced crew. The few roustabouts who had not gone out in the yawl had familiar features: the last time Rys had seen them, they had been part of the nobleman's retinue. Now, they nursed the beacons and hovered at the rail, ready to throw ropes and floats to anyone who might have the ill fortune to fall into the water. Others, standing at the rail of the main deck, turned out to be the prisoners Rys had viewed earlier. She had never expected Ursul to heed her demand that they be set free.

The engineer and the firekeeper lounged near the boilers on the firedeck, the plates on the floor licked so clean they would not interest not even a rat. The firekeeper seemed to be one of Elbie's men. A rigidly disciplined man-at-arms watched over them. Rys had shared many a crew's table with the engineer, so she squatted down and chatted with him for a while, as if this were any other river trip on which they had both drawn the afterwatch. By sheer good fortune, two engineers had been on board when Elbie hijacked the boat, and they could relieve each other every six hours. Too bad the queen's cousin hadn't been so lucky with his pilots.

She returned to the pilothouse to find Elbie asleep on the bench again, while Ursul inexpertly swabbed the floor. The armed woman, shocked to find her lord's lady engaged in servant's labor, tried to take the swab away from her, but Ursul snapped irritably, "Do your own job." She fed the stove and solicitously covered Elbie with a blanket before gathering up the dirty dishes and making a dignified exit. Rys put her stool near the stove, hoping its heat would take some of the damp chill out of her bones, and settled down to watch the deckhands saw away at their tree branches.

The armed woman held a twig in the stove until it flamed, and used it to light a pipe. She sat down in the doorway, the embers of her pipe glowing, and silence descended. The voices of the struggling deckhands seemed faint and far away. A fine mist of rain continued to fall, silently, shimmering like a gilded veil in the light of the beacons.

"Is it true?" the armed woman said suddenly.

"Is what true?"

"That you knew Cydna, the Poet's Sorceress."

Rys glanced over at her guard. The woman's leather jerkin was greasy and well-worn. She kept her weapons polished, but her homely, weathered face was guileless. "I knew Cydna," Rys said, "but there never was a sorceress. What is your name?"

"Mardi, madam. What do you mean, there was never a sorceress? Everyone knows—"

"Everyone knows that Naiman the Poet could tell the most outrageous lie, and tell it so beautifully that everyone believed him. Cydna the Sorceress was one of his creations."

"What do you mean?"

"She was just a countrywoman like you. Passing her on the street, you'd never even look at her twice."

"Huh." Mardi sucked on her pipe and said no more.

Rys had been riding the river for well over half her life, now. Twenty years ago, she had been a helmsman, a pilot's apprentice. Riding the current southward, on the way home from a rare trip to Vateria, she spotted a figure on the bank waving a white kerchief to attract the boat's attention. They took the boat in and picked up a muddy Semelite farm girl lugging a big basket of food, with a satchel and a bedroll over her shoulder. She only wanted steerage, so the coppers she paid were scarcely worth the trouble of picking her up. She had never before taken a riverboat trip, and somehow Rys found herself showing her around the ship when she should have been memorizing the river.

They were both very young, and of humble station. As they sat together late that night, teaching each other the card games of the country and the city, they had spoken, as children do, of the greatness for which they were surely destined.

Within five years, everyone in Faerd knew Cydna's name. In another five years, Cydna was dead, killed by the legends she could not control, an innocent to the end. Rys, on the other hand, through running her life as though it were a riverboat, had trapped herself within the cage of her own self-discipline. She had become the best pilot on the river. The youngest Guildmaster in the history of steam travel, she had kept Faerd's artery of transportation flowing during the worst years of the plague.

She had learned firsthand what Cydna meant when she cried helplessly, "No one knows me! My life is a masquerade!"

But by the time the Poet's Revolution was over, even Cydna could not distinguish her true self from her costume, no more than Naiman could keep from being seduced by his own rhetoric. When Rys betrayed her beloved friend, it was through telling her the truth she could no longer bear to hear. Rys had not seen Cydna or Naiman for over a year when they were both killed at the Massacre of Ika.

Sitting quietly in the pilothouse, with the stink of the armed woman's tobacco making her nose itch, Rys pondered the loneliness that had so handily betrayed her earlier. She could not have been so easily tricked, had she not secretly believed that Cydna was not dead at all, or were she not secretly restless in her cozy home in Marlestown. But she doubted she would ever learn to heed the secret hungers of her heart.

A shout from the river gave her the excuse to abandon this disconcerting thought. She stood up to check on progress. The yawl darted about, collecting the deckhands out of the trees. Rys told the engineers to start the engines and go forward at half speed, to put some slack into the ropes. The second mate cut the

Amina loose, and the current carried the yawl safely back to her mother ship.

"Onward to Fortune," muttered Rys. Elbie writhed and grumbled in his sleep. The armed woman, sucking on her pipe in the doorway, didn't even turn her head.

Chapter 3: Macy

To Macy, the City of Ghosts had become a city of friends. As a clockmaker, before the plague, she had been all but unknown. Now, not a resident of Fortune did not know her name. Every day, for years now, they had seen her walking the haunted streets, or heard her voice, singing:

> Horses, hoops, and dancing jacks,
> Treasures here for girls and boys.
> Baubles, trinkets, key-in-backs,
> Come on out and buy my toys!

Every child in Fortune played with her toys, whether their parents had money or not. But she had been making dancing jacks for less than a year. Those she never gave away.

Reaching into her pocket for the key at day's end, her hand encountered the three pennies with which Ash of Ashland had bought a dancing jack. Macy paused at the top of the steps, considering what to do.

A fortuitous meeting that had been, a meeting at the crossroads. There would be choices to be made. Macy turned the key in the lock and went into her cellar home.

"What is it?" said the young man busy at her worktable. "You've come back early."

"A congruence," said Macy.

The young woman spoke without looking up from her work with the burnishing cloth. "We've been thinking, Macy, that we'd better move on. We'll be all right; we'll find a safe place ..."

"What do you mean, a congruence?" said the young man.

"I mean, a coming together of things that is too remarkable to be merely caused by chance. Look here." Macy laid the three pennies on the work table.

The young woman came over to look. The coins were not remarkably old. "What?" she said irritably.

But the young man touched a coin. He licked his fingertip and took in his breath. "Oh," he said. "Ashland."

❧   ❧   ❧

Five days before Macy met Ash of Ashland, she had interrupted her usual rounds, to return abruptly to the center of town. In the old merchant's district, where entire streets of abandoned shops had been closed down and walled off, the illusion of crowded, noisy commerce was sustained by forcing the surviving merchants into close quarters, where they might happily continue to out-shout each other by day, and share cups of thick coffee at night, under the awnings of their crowded stores. Scarcely room remained down the center of the roadways for people to make their way between displays.

Turning a corner, Macy all but ran into a pot-hung sleeping wagon, brightly painted with scarlet and hyacinth scrollwork. On the broad side, scribed in letters almost unreadably ornate, were the words "Kevin, Purveyor of Fortune." The two draft horses, engrossed in their feedbags, paid her no attention. But a familiar voice called her name, and she turned to greet a thin, graying man who walked among the market stalls, carefully carrying a tin cup in either hand.

"Cup of tea?" he said.

"How kind." Macy slipped loose the straps of her heavy pack and set it on the ground.

"That's one of your better ones," Kevin said, gesturing at the clockwork toy. "What does it do?"

"It walks. It does some other things, too, if you know how to persuade it." Macy took the cup from his hand, sipped, and sighed. "Your sign should say 'Kevin of Fortune, purveyor.' People will think you sell good luck charms."

"Sign's been the same for thirty years. No one's been confused yet."

"No one's ever come up to you and asked to buy some fortune?"

"Oh, I suppose they do. And I tell them, 'Get your fortune the same way I got mine. Make it.' Then I sell them a pot, or a pretty trinket, or somesuch." Kevin, who could scarcely be described as rich in anything other than good humor, laughed heartily and leaned his shoulder against the sleeping wagon in a familiar sort of way, as one might lean against a horse or an old friend.

"Have you just come into town?"

"Well, I've been here only a quarter hour or so, waiting for you to find me."

"Good thing for you I always know when a friend is in town. I wouldn't have expected you until nearly summer. Usually, you're just starting your northern run this time of year."

"Things are different this year. When we've finished our tea, maybe you'll get up on the driver's seat beside me, and we'll just go off to a more quiet street, where we can talk without anyone hearing us."

"Maybe I will," said Macy. "So tell me how you passed the winter."

They chatted on the street corner. A passerby bought one of Macy's dancing jacks. When the two peddlers' cups were empty, they hauled Macy's pack up on top of the wagon, and Kevin hupped to the horses, who rather reluctantly leaned into the traces and started down the street at a slow walk.

On this fine day, with the air so sweet-smelling and the spring wind so soft, one might almost forget that Fortune was a haunted place. The streets contained a market day crowd of basket-bearing shoppers, and though their clothing might be patched and shabby and their baskets more empty than full, still they hurried busily enough from shop to shop. Old men and women sat on benches in the sunshine, nodding sleepily or sucking on their pipes, and one or two even had a vigorous young charge to watch after. Freight carts from the dockyard rumbled past, whips flicking across the backs of the sweating horses. One might almost forget the nightmarish years of closed doors and darkened windows; of neighbors dying on the street, without dignity, of death wagons and orphan's cry. One might almost forget the smell rising up from the burning grounds.

Kevin said, "Think anyone will ever smile again?"

"Look there." A young woman, dressed in a much patched and mended jerkin, with holes in the knees of her trousers, strode along the walk with an infant riding on her hip and a long loaf of bread tucked under her arm. A smile of pleasure came and went across her features, reluctant and tentative as sun breaking through a winter's storm. Macy said, "I sold her a dancing jack for her little one last week. Didn't charge her much."

"Sometimes it surprises me that you can keep body and soul together."

Kevin turned his horses up a side street, where the illusion of vigorous activity rapidly gave way to the reality of vacant decay. "Now here's my tale, and you tell me what you think of it. Coming on the road north, out of Winterfair, I ran into a bad storm. Pulled over to the side of the road to wait it out, and ended up staying three days, watching the road wash out. It was a terrible storm—I would have hated to be on the river in the midst of that."

"Ay, that was bad. Ripped the shutters right off the windows, it did."

"Well, when it began to clear, I went out to check on things, and was right heated up when I realized my wheels had sunk in the mud. The last thing I wanted was to wait another two or three days, so I took out a shovel and started digging the wagon out, throwing in some road gravel from time to time, to give the wheels some purchase. I had pretty much gotten it to where the horses could drag it out, when I turned my head, and a couple of bedraggled youngsters came crashing through the thicket.

"Well, I was startled, and they seemed startled enough to see me there, and mayhap a trifle frightened at first. But then one of them offered to help me dig out if I would give them a ride to Redleaf. 'I'm on my way to Semel,' I said, but the other said that would do well enough, for all it lay in the opposite direction, and they grabbed up my shovel and set to work. I'd scarcely gotten the horses in the traces before they started shoving away at the back end of the wagon, and pretty soon, among the three of us and the horses, we had pulled free of the mud.

"Now I ain't no fool, so I had realized quick enough that the two of them weren't out on a holiday trip, and I suggested they travel in the back where it's more cozy. Soon enough, not too far down the road, I came across a crowd of Homan Din priests, running barefoot through the muck, and all of them pretty worked up about something. 'Have you seen a couple of young-sters come this way?' they shouted at me.

" 'I haven't seen anybody at all for three days,' I told them. They stepped aside to let me pass, but one of them, an old fellow with his beard wagging, shouted, 'Don't let him go until you've checked in the wagon!'

"Well, I got pretty worked up at this and I said, 'I'm a free man and this is the queen's own road, and be-damned if you think you can just poke through my things without a by-your-leave. I ain't one of your be-sotted followers, and I got business to attend to. So get your fat asses out of my way or I'll run you down.' Well, they let me pass, not that I gave them much choice, since I had my whip in my hand and my horses were feeling a little frisky after three days with nothing to do, and acted inclined to take a kick at anyone who drew too close.

"After a while I came to a great encampment in the mud off to the north of the road, a hundred or more people, it seemed, with their tents all collapsing be-cause the ground had gotten too soft to hold their stakes anymore. I hailed a fellow by the roadside and asked him what was what. He told me it's the competition for the Homan Din festival drum-dancers, and he just saw the best performance of drum-dancing he had ever set eyes on. 'But then one of the drummers turns out to be a woman,' he said. 'That one will be lucky to escape with her skin still attached, I tell you.'

"So I figured that one of my passengers was sure enough that woman, and so I stopped a little ways down the road to have a chat with them. The two of them had crawled into an empty storebox and shut the lid on themselves, and were well nigh suffocated. But one of them was a woman, sure enough, not that you could see it unless you looked the right way. Turned out they were friends of yours, and the upshot of it was that I offered to take them to Fortune. Zara, the young woman's name, and Kaz, the young man."

"And you accuse me of being too kindhearted," said Macy. "I told those two the Homan Din priests were nothing but trouble. They deserved to lose their skins."

"Well, you're right enough about the Homan Din being trouble. I don't know how the word could spread so fast, but it seemed in every town I passed there was a Homan Din priest, keeping a low profile, watching the road traffic with a look on his face like he was ready to kill somebody. The two drummers scarcely left the sleeping wagon the whole trip."

"Let's have a word with them."

Kevin drew up the horses, who seemed more willing to stand still than they had been to walk. Kevin always took good care of his beasts though sometimes it meant they ate grain while he ate beggar's bread. He would not have tired them out so with no good reason.

Macy stood back while Kevin unlatched the narrow back door. A battered brass lantern hung by a hook immediately above the dark entrance, and a tin match box had been nailed to the door, but the light shining through the open door illuminated most of the crowded interior of the wagon. The contents of Kevin's sleeping wagon looked and smelled much as if a section of the merchant's row had been neatly sliced away and put into a wooden shipping crate. Kevin had aborted his run, sure enough, to arrive in Fortune with most of his goods unsold.

At the far end of the wagon, beneath hanging clusters of sausages and biscuit tins close packed along a high shelf, two dark figures huddled in the shadows. Macy had not seen Kaz and Zara in over a year, and they were at the changing age, when the last softness of childhood gives way all at once to adulthood. They had not changed so much that she did not recognize them, though.

The two of them had been living wild on the streets of Fortune for over a year when one of them took ill and they came to Macy for help. They let her feed them sometimes and bind their hurts, but they would not let her tame them. In the end, they had not done such a bad job at raising each other.

It was Zara who over a year ago had first heard drums pounding in the court of Homan Din, where women cannot go. The foreign religion had not much caught on until after the plague. Macy knew that Zara slipped into the forbidden temple a time or two, to toss into the god's lap a mocking offering of menstrual blood smeared upon a rag. She was not the only woman of Faerd to engage in such warfare; indeed the priests were nearly hysterical over it. But today it was simple curiosity that brought her into the temple to watch the drum-dancers perform for the god.

When she spoke to Macy about it later, she had the look in her eyes of a sailor, who after a long and harrowing journey had spotted land at last. It was a rare thing that had happened to Zara when she discovered the Homan Din dancers, even more rare because most talent goes unrecognized and unrealized on the streets. If she could not resist climbing a wall when she learned the gate was locked, who could blame her?

Macy said, "Do you think the Homan Din priests intend to kill you?"

"Yes," said Zara. Then her old, fierce self flared up. "But you should have seen us, Macy! We could have drummed the stars right down out of the sky!"

Sometimes, on a moonlit night, the two of them used to set up in the middle of a deserted street and start thrumming softly on their cobbled-together drums. Macy, usually busy with her tools and paintbrush in her cluttered cellar workshop, would feel rather than hear the rhythmic heartbeat of sound.

It might be summer, or it might be the depth of winter, with the sharp-edged stars slicing the cold sky with their fierce light. Macy would hurry down the haunted byways, scattering ghosts like dried leaves in her wake. The drums would be audible by now, a rhythmic pulsing of sound, vibrating within the ancient stones of the ancient city. Macy would be all but running by the time she found the chosen street. Always, others would be there before her. Already, they would be dancing.

Girls and matrons and old women, boys and husbands and codgers, they gathered, called forth by the drums from the docks, the streets, the shops, the hearthfire and cradleside, the offices of government, the stables, the fortress, and the boat decks, where every day they worked their homely magic. Witches, all of them, a wilder magic brewed in their hearts as they danced under the open sky.

Now the drums had been silent for a year and more. Macy stepped forward, to lay a hand upon Zara's shoulder. Kaz, quiet as always, sturdy as stone, took her other hand in his. Macy said, "Why should you call down the stars for people like the Homan Din, who cannot love and will not know you? Maybe you hoped for something else, but I hoped only that you would come safely back to Fortune. Now tell me what happened."

They told her:

The priests of Homan Din held the drum-dancing competition in the rain, the old fools, because the god had decreed they must hold the competition on the third full moon of the year, no matter what the weather. Their only compromise was to cover the drumming ground with a pavilion, but the seeping water kept sneaking in through the seams in the canvas. Assaulted by the damp, the drum heads sagged, the drum-dancers drooped and slipped on the wet stage, and the senior priests made exhibitions of themselves through fits of temper. The priests of Homan Din needed to select a troupe of drum-dancers who had thunder in their hands and wings upon their feet. Instead, presented with a pathetic display of clay-footed, ham-handed, graceless bunglers, the priests sought someone to blame.

The god's failure to arrange the weather to their convenience could not be easily explained, until one priest had an inspired insight. Someone in their midst must have committed an offense which caused the god to withdraw his favor.

Therefore, in an atmosphere of suspicion and righteous rage, the old men intently watched the performers, the acolytes, and each other. Though the competition became a comedy, and the poor boys responsible for its success wept in desperation, one drum-dance troupe after another humiliated themselves upon the stage, under the unforgiving glare of the censorious and indignant priests. That the drum-dancers could perform at all, out of tune and slipshod though the performances might have been, was a miracle no one except the other drum-dancers could appreciate.

Throughout two days of competition, Kaz and Zara had seen the others unwrap their drums too early, only to suffer the ignominy of limp drumheads and sodden shoes. When their drum-master, old Diskin, was handed his red chit, he waited until the current troupe had finished their performance and begun, hangheaded, to quit the stage. Not until his troupe had carried their drums to the stage did they unwrap them, and not until they had dried the platform did they put on their shoes.

An acolyte hurried over to the priests, carrying a tray of steaming teacups. Sitting on the ground as they were, on padding every bit as sodden by now as an infant's swaddling, the priests reached eagerly for the steaming cups. Kaz and Zara's troupe had set and racked the drums before the acolyte had finished handing out the tea; never in practice had they set up so swiftly.

Fingertips together beneath his chin, Drum-master Diskin bowed deeply, first to the priests and then to the audience, which consisted solely of other troups awaiting their moment upon the stage. Other drummasters had delivered lengthy speeches in this moment of introduction, but Diskin said only his name, as was required for the records, and the names of the others. He bowed a second time, this time in homage to the image of the god which stood beyond the priests, shrouded in oilcloth to keep him from moldering. "In honor of Homan Din, we play Thunder."

Splay-kneed, he knelt before the great drum. Kaz, Zara, and the other two drum-dancers poised before the other three drums: one a double-headed senar drum, the other two the single-headed camar drums. *Now,* Zara thought, *we will show them some drumming.* Diskin lifted the beater in either hand. In a voice that carried across the pavilion, he began to count the changes.

"It was amazing," said Kaz.

"Like we were possessed." Zara pounded frenetically upon an invisible drum, to demonstrate.

"Like being bigger than the earth and the sky. Like knowing—everything there was to know."

"And then, one of the priests—he was *ancient*—struggled to his feet and shrieked, 'A woman playing the drums!' "

"We've eaten pretty well this year," said Kaz. "I guess Zara, well . . . got more shapely."

"And that's it," said Zara. "That's all there is to tell."

They could not play the drums in Macy's cellar, but it did not much matter, since they had no drums to play. Zara haunted the shadows like a wraith, and no restorative seemed able to ease her sickness of heart. Kaz, on the other hand, proved restless as a caged panther, and irritable as well. In exasperation, Macy finally gave the boy some wood, and permission to use her precious tools. He soon became engrossed in a mysterious project involving slender wooden slats, with chisel-cut tongues and grooves so delicately done that Macy could only watch him work in astonishment. His claim that he knew something about woodworking proved to be not merely the truth, but an understatement. Perhaps the year's apprenticeship to a drummaster had not been such a disastrous mistake after all.

Throughout a cold, wet spring day, they stood side by side at the workbench, Macy piecing together a dozen dancing jacks, and Kaz engrossed in the detail work of his painstaking project.

Because of the cloudy day, twilight came early. At last, Macy rubbed her strained eyes and set aside her work with a sigh. The dancing jacks hung drying from the rack overhead.

Kaz pointed to a jack with an absurd, bespangled cap, who grinned slyly but not unkindly at his beholder. "I like that one."

"You can have him for a price."

Kaz lifted an eyebrow, for Macy had always refused their money before.

"Some things have value only when you pay for them."

"What would happen if I bought him?" he asked.

"Who knows?" Macy turned away to wash out her brushes.

"What is the price, then? We still have money left, don't we Zara?"

But Zara did not answer because she was not there.

Zara

Rain washed all the color out of Fortune, turning its buildings and streets as gray as unbleached linen, and making the stone edges blur, as though the city itself were melting away in the rain. The leafing trees wept cold tears upon Zara's head and shoulders as she passed under their drooping boughs. Basins worn into the stone contained stores of rainwater, pit traps to waylay the unwary. Zara watched the sky more closely than the road underfoot. The clouds lay across the earth like a huge drumskin, upon which the gods pound the thunder.

Finding herself ankle-deep in icy water, she kicked at the puddle, wetting herself to the knees. She went dancing down the street, jumping feet first into every puddle she could find. "It's war!" she cried. "War upon the water!" And, though behind her the puddles quickly filled as before, victory surely lay just ahead of her. Dancing like a madwoman, she battled the dreariness of rain up and down the streets of the city of ghosts.

Her crazy way landed her upon the steps of a modest house, with small paned windows gray and rain-slick below the overhang of the slate roof. Here the vines which climbed the wall had budded vivid green leaves, bright as stars in the gray day. Her mad mood deserting her suddenly, Zara tapped hesitantly upon the door and waited, muddy and bedraggled and beginning to feel the chill, until a thin woman opened the door. "I've got nothing for you. This is a poor house, girl."

"I'm no beggar. I'm here to see the tanner, is all."

"The tanner! I am the tanner."

"Your man, then."

"And what has my husband to do with the likes of you?"

"He'll know me when he sees me, I reckon."

"Well!" The woman shut the door in Zara's face. Because she could hear the sound of voices in the room beyond the door, Zara waited, shivering.

In a moment the door was reopened, by a man this time. Though nearly a year had passed since the last time Kaz and Zara pounded their drums in the haunted streets, calling the witches of the city forth to the dance, he recognized her at once, and threw open the door. "Lady's Day! Come in out of the wet."

She did not know his name, and he did not know hers. She knew he was a tanner because she had spotted him, once or twice, running a cartload of tanned hides down to market.

With his hand on her arm, he propelled her past his frowning wife, into a small, cluttered kitchen where a baby slept in a cradle on the hearth, watched over by a black cat whose eyes slitted open at the sound of a strange voice. Zara, protesting rather halfheartedly, accepted a cup of dreggy tea and a slice of buttered bread. The tanner insisted she sit beside the fire, and he stood before her, watching every bite and sip until she had ceased her shivering. From time to time, his wife peeked in, as if to make sure Zara was not murdering her husband, or stealing her baby from the cradle.

It was a gray house, the habitation of gray people. But one of Macy's dancing jacks hung from the mantle, and an infection of order and cheerfulness seemed to be spreading slowly in its vicinity.

"What can I do for you?" the tanner finally said.

"We had a bad turn of luck and lost our drums. I can't pay, but I'm hoping you can spare some rawhide scraps to make drumheads with."

"How big?"

She demonstrated with her hands. The tanner left her sitting by the fire and went into the back of the house, where they had probably set up their shop. Zara heard faintly the sound of expostulation and argument, but the tanner soon reappeared, his hands full of leather, slightly flushed but calm enough.

"I didn't mean to cause any trouble with your wife," said Zara.

"There're some things she'll never understand about me. It goes both ways, I figure. Now what else can I do? You had bad luck, you say."

"Nothing that won't blow over." Zara put her cup carefully onto a nearby table: a porcelain cup, light as an eggshell, perhaps the last survivor of what had once been a complete set. Ever since the tanner put it into her hand, she had been in a terror of breaking it. "I'd best get back before dark, or my friends will be worried."

"I'll not delay you, then." The tanner walked her to the door, past the frowning, cross-armed woman standing in the front room. "I'll be listening for the drums," he said.

The tanner had given her far more leather than she needed: five large, irregular pieces, stiff as parchment. She tucked the leather inside her shirt, so the damp would not spoil it, and started home, shivering in the wind that stalked the deserted streets. Time to put a little wood into the stove in Macy's kitchen, and sit there for a while, warming her toes and watching the windows grow dark. Kaz and Macy would be angry with her for going out; but if she had told them, they wouldn't have let her go, so let them yammer. She trotted down the street, shuddering as the wind pelted her with water shaken loose from the trees.

Her journey to the tanner's house had taken her halfway across Fortune, and now the journey home began to seem a long one. Down the narrow side streets she hurried, where lamps were being lit against the gloom. In the merchant's district, the streets were deserted except for a lone lamplighter, the stalls closed up and shuttered, the goods all packed safely away. At one street crossing, Zara paused for a moment, looking up the hill toward a walled compound, its white plastered walls ghostly in the gloom. There the Homan Din would dance and drum for their god. Off in the distance, she heard voices calling, where dockworkers and stevedores stood watch, keeping a close eye on the river's rising water. Shivering, she hurried on.

By the time she climbed down the steps to Macy's cellar door, full dark had set in, and lamplight blazed from the narrow, ground-level windows. The door jerked open in her hand as she was about to open it, and Macy and Kaz all but bowled her over as they charged the steps. Kaz had a darkened lantern in his hand; Macy carried her winged, clockwork toy under her arm. "Hey," said Zara faintly, not even certain they had noticed her in their hurry. But they paused halfway up the steps, and Kaz began scolding her as if she were

a child and him her mother, so she stalked angrily
through the door and slammed it in his face.

Macy opened the door and came in. She dragged
Kaz inside, and silenced him with a frown when he
started to speak. "There's a pie on the hearth; let's
have some supper and then we'll talk like civilized
people."

"But she's hurt."

"I'm not hurt!" Zara said.

Kaz uncovered the lantern and held it up, blinding
Zara in the sudden light. "What's that on your chest?"

Squinting, Zara peered down at her shirt, where
something seemed to have sprouted between her
breasts, like a dark fungus. She lifted a startled hand to
brush it away, but Macy caught her by the wrist.
"Careful! What have you got inside your shirt?"

"Just some leather I got for Kaz. What is that thing?
I can't see it."

"It's a dart," said Macy. "No child's toy, but poison.
You didn't even feel it hit you? Well, that leather in
your shirt saved your life, for certain."

She set the clockwork toy upon the floor, and it
promptly went marching off into the kitchen, where
they could hear its joints clashing and machinery whirring as it struggled mindlessly to continue in the face
of an obstacle. With a pair of pliers Macy plucked the
dart out of Zara's makeshift leather armor, and threw it
into the stove. Zara had to sit down after that.

"You need to leave Fortune," Macy said. "You need
to find a safe place."

They ate their meal in silence. None of them seemed
very hungry.

❦   ❦   ❦

Macy

"Oh, Ashland," said Kaz, and turned away, breathing unsteadily, leaving Ash's three pennies lying on the
tabletop where Macy had put them.

Macy said, "You had a home to go to after the plague. Why did you never go there?"

"I had a good reason. Who gave you these coins?"

"Ash of Ashland."

"She is in Fortune?"

"I found her sweeping the kitchen floor of a ghost house. I suppose it was your house. She asked me if I knew whether you had survived."

"Sweeping," said Kaz.

"I did not tell her I knew you. I offered to make inquiries."

He sighed, perhaps with relief, perhaps not.

Zara found her voice at last. "Who is she?"

"My father's sister," said Kaz. "She is from Ashland, in Northern Semel."

"Well, you don't seem very glad."

"She and my mother never were friends. She was sweeping the kitchen? Well . . ." He studied the floor. "I wonder why."

"Her brother's wife could never endure a dirty floor, she said."

Kaz gave a bitter laugh, then sobered. "Why did she come looking for me now, six years later?"

Macy said, "Who am I to ask her such a question? Kaz, she seemed—a fine person, without deceit."

"Did she seem haunted to you?"

"Well, who does not?"

"She had power once."

"A little harmless necromancy—"

"Not harmless, Macy!" Kaz sat down upon a stool. "She must not find me. Those coins, take them out and spend them."

"Not unless you explain."

Kaz swept his toe in the wood shavings on the floor. "In Semel, people remember the old ways. They still keep the Long Watch at Winter-turn, and dance in the woods in the spring to make the crops grow. One of their oldest traditions, as old as anyone can remember, is the reverence of Ashland. The Ash of Ashland used to be like a priest or a king. Though the people of Semel have another ruler and have been part of Faerd for a long time, they still remember and keep their loyalty to Ashland. This is something not many people know, outside of Semel."

Kaz gazed down at his foot stirring the shavings. "If I explained about Ash, it would be a betrayal. That is all I can tell you. Please, Macy, go out and spend the coin."

Macy picked up the pennies and shook them in her hand, so that they rang faintly together. "I cannot argue with you when I do not know what it is you fear. But there is one thing you should consider, if you think you have reason not to trust her. She bought a dancing jack from me this day."

Both Kaz and Zara lifted their heads to gaze at her. "Did she," said Kaz. He folded his hands upon his knees.

Macy went out to spend the pennies on supper.

Chapter 4: Ash

The ghosts of Fortune followed Ash from the house of her dead children to a rented room near the docks, hovering like moths around a flame as she sat down to eat her plain supper. She waved her hands irritably at the dismal figures. "Oh, go away! If I can summon you, then I also can dismiss you. Beware, lest I dismiss you out of existence!"

Ghost Dog looked up from his own bread and broth supper as though he wondered whether she had lost her mind. But the ghosts fled in a panic at her paltry threat, and Ash finished her meal in peace.

After she had eaten, she took the dancing jack out of her satchel and tugged gently on its string. It danced for her by candlelight, gesturing hopelessly with one hand and offering her a star with the other. "No choice is that simple," she said. She did not like the way the toy made her feel: angry and giddy and weary with grief. She hung it from a nail, so she could forget to take it with her in the morning.

Ghost Dog did not like the cheap room's barren floor and paced restlessly until she gave him a blanket to sleep on. She blew out the candle and opened the window to look down upon the rooftops of the city. Sunset had extinguished Fortune. Its black slate roofs disappeared into the unlit streets. The only light came from the river, which faintly reflected the clear night's stars.

She leaned upon the windowsill. A black boat, silhouetted against the white light of the river, was coming around the curve of Fortune Bend from the south. Red sparks gushed from its smokestacks, and the faraway shout of its incoming whistle sounded across the water. Ash shivered and rubbed at her arms, though coarse wool covered them against the cold. "It's too early in the year for a packet boat," she muttered. Ghost Dog got up from his bed and put his forefeet on the windowsill so he could see out. "Listen: the boat will whistle again if it is going to land."

The haunting sound once again sounded across the water: a murmur rising to a hollow roar and then reducing to a murmur once again. Dogs began to bark across the darkened city, but Ghost Dog uttered no sound. He took his paws down from the sill and returned to his bed.

"I had a friend once," Ash said. She leaned one hip upon the windowsill and watched the boat come in, slipping past the loading docks and floating sweetly up to the landing. In the silence she heard the cries of the stevedores and dockworkers, called away from their suppers by the boat's summons. A host of lanterns were lit at the river's edge.

She tipped her head back so she could see stars, blurring and swimming in a liquid sky. For a second time this day, her tears took her by surprise. "Why am I here?" she asked. "Why am I here, when there is nothing left?"

In the morning, she went down to the docks to have a look at the weather-battered riverboat. Wagonloads of wood for the boilers had already begun arriving, and bakers and butchers with baskets of bread, meat, and eggs fought the roustabouts for space on the loading dock. The mates and the dock clerk, looking drawn and harassed, directed traffic. A pall seemed to lie over the spirits of the few crewmembers that Ash spotted. Of the passengers she saw no sign. In the pilothouse, only a thin roustabout stood watch.

She collared the boat's mud clerk as he hurried past her. "What is the boat, and where is she going?"

"The *Amina,* continuing north to Vateria," he said.

"So early in the year?"

"Excuse me, I have things to attend to."

"Who pilots her?" she shouted after him, but the mud clerk did not seem to hear.

During her footloose days Ash had often ridden the river, usually as a steerage passenger, with a basket of cheese, bread, and apples in one hand, and her old satchel in the other. On fine passenger boats, lumber barges, and even in rowboats she had traveled. She knew the names of all the riverfolk. She knew their fierce passions and unswerving loyalties. Once, she would never have been able to stand so long upon a quay, recognizing nobody. But that had been before the plague.

She found a place against the warehouse wall, where she could watch the activity of the crowded landing without being jostled. A wagon pulled away, like a curtain being drawn back from a window, and there stood the toy peddler of yesterday. Red cloth patched her knees and elbows. The bright toys danced behind her. "Tell me what you want with Kaz," she said.

"He and his sisters belong to Ashland. I want to bring them home."

"Why did it take you so long to come for them?"

"And who are you to judge me?"

"The one you seek wants to know."

Silence. Silence, and Ash's knees feeling oddly weak, she who felled trees and wrestled with oxen and had never, in seven years of bitter solitude, wept a single tear until yesterday. "I should have come sooner." She leaned her shoulders against the warehouse's stone wall, lest her legs give way beneath her. "Oh, I have no good reason at all for not coming, except that everyone told me the entire family was dead! He has survived alone these last six years?"

"Not alone."

The woman gazed at Ash expectantly, but she could not imagine what more she was supposed to say. She took in her breath, and picked up her satchel and bedroll. "Take me to him, then."

"He is not certain he wants to see you."

Ash pressed her shoulders solidly against the stone wall once again.

"He says he found out about something that you never told him."

"I told him everything! More than a ten-year-old should have to hear! Why did he send a stranger as a messenger rather than challenge me face-to-face?"

The toy peddler looked uneasy. "He could not come."

"What does he fear? He should know that I will not—" But Ash could not continue. "Well," she said in frustration, "he is an Ashlander, all right. I would know that obstinacy anywhere."

"He is in hiding. There are circumstances . . ."

The two women looked at each other. Macy suddenly smiled, as wryly as her dancing jacks, grimacing and grinning at the world. "It is absurd, all these secrets. I would explain everything to you, if I had been given leave. I see no reason not to trust you."

"Then I have no choice except to assume that his trust in you is not misplaced. Kaz is my brother-son, as I told you. I have no children of my own. For generations, there has always been one in my family who bore the name of the land, therefore I am now called Ash, like my grandfather before me. But my given name is Cydna."

Macy took a single, startled step backward. The shouts of the stevedores suddenly seemed loud in Ash's ears. Surely, after all that had happened in ten years' time, the Poet's Revolution had been discounted and forgotten. But the pallor of the peddler's face, and the rich color that as suddenly flooded it, suggested otherwise. Ash reached out a helpless hand as though to stop Macy from fleeing. Macy's gaze shifted. Ash's satchel had swung forward, revealing the painted toy dancing from the strap where she had tied it that morning.

The toy peddler stepped forward to grasp Ash firmly by the arm. "Do not say that name again in the city of Fortune! Do you not know what is being said about you?"

"How could I know? I have not left Ashland for ten years."

"Well, I understand why Kaz never returned to Ashland. Come with me."

"You said he is in hiding."

"I will explain as we walk."

Ash shouldered her burdens and followed, with Ghost Dog walking beside her. As they left the landing, another wagonload of wood arrived. The *Amina* certainly was taking on a lot of wood.

Ash did not expect a man. But it was a man who rose up out of the shadows of the cellar when Macy spoke his name, a man not yet as broad-shouldered nor as powerfully built as he was destined to be, but a man in height, and a man in voice. Ash stood in the light of the open doorway, so he could see who she was.

"You brought her here!" he cried.

Macy faced him square on, her fists upon her hips, her tattered white hair fraying out from her face, like flames. "You are being a fool, young Kaz, for allowing rumors and fears to become your only teacher! Did you never stop to think that what is said upon the street could be untrue?"

Ash said, "I will leave. You know the way to Ashland, Kaz."

Macy spoke without turning her head. "You stay where you are. Close the door."

To cross Macy in her home might not be wise. Ash bid Ghost Dog come inside, and shut the door.

"Now tell your aunt what you think she should have told you."

"About the box," Kaz said. "About what happened when you opened it."

There was an unresolved tension in the room, as though the two who waited here had been arguing. The woman beside Kaz glared openly at Ash.

"I don't know what you mean," Ash said.

"When you let loose the plague."

"When I what?" Ash dropped her bedroll and satchel heedlessly onto the floor. *"You're blaming me for the plague?"* She looked around blindly for a place to sit, but there was none.

Kaz continued doggedly, "They say that after the Massacre of Ika, you took dust out of your magic box and sprinkled it upon Naiman's body. They paraded his body through the streets afterward, but by sunset, everyone who had touched him was dead. By the next day, all their friends and relatives were dead, and by the next day, there was a hundred more. My sisters, and my mother—you killed them, in the end." He took in his breath. "That's why."

Ash took out the box and handed it to Macy, who took it, to her credit, without hesitation. "It is just a box," Macy said after a moment. "An old box." Kaz, or the young woman beside him, cried out as Macy opened the simple latch and lifted the lid. "An old box, full of ashes. It is nothing more than that, and never was."

"Now I will go." Ash felt dizzy, as though she had been knocked down and not yet caught her breath.

"Don't go." Kaz sounded shaken. "If it is just an old box—" He reached for it. The young woman beside him drew sharply away, hissing like a cat. He looked into it curiously, and tasted a bit of the ashes on his tongue. Her brother's face, he had, but his eyes contained the forest. "A piece of Ashland, small enough to carry with you," he said. "All those things I've heard about this box, and it's just a way to remember."

"I would have given it to you when you left, but your mother would not allow it."

"She never understood about Ashland," said Kaz.

Macy took Ash by the arm. "Come here and sit down. I'll put on the kettle."

Ash followed her, dazed, and sat where she was told. Her eyes kept turning to Kaz as though of their own will. He had closed the box and held it in both his hands, examining the puzzlework of its joinery. "Look at that," he murmured, showing it to the young woman. She never took her angry glare from Ash's face.

"A fierce child," Macy had said of Zara, as she and Ash walked together from the steamboat landing. "Always burning herself in her own fire." Now Macy said quietly to Ash, "I guess they are coming with you."

"Ashland would give them haven. But Zara will not let him go."

"What?" Macy turned to look, and saw what Ash did. Her face grew still.

Ash said after a moment, "He is growing a beard. How old it makes me feel."

"He has not yet come into his own," said Macy.

"Then I have not missed everything."

Kaz stepped forward, put a hand rather shyly upon Ash's shoulder, and kissed her cheek. "Here is your box. Aunt—"

"I want you to keep it. I am going directly home; I do not need it any longer."

"I am going home, too."

"Are you?"

"I never should have left."

"You were a child, and had no choice."

"Still," he said.

"I should have come for you."

"If even one person recognized you, you would have been killed." He went back into the shadows, to take his fierce lover's hand and draw her forward, a gesture she gave no sign of appreciating. "This is Zara."

"You will be welcome in Ashland," Ash said.

These were the wrong words, it seemed. Zara jerked her hand loose, and stalked stiffly away. Kaz looked after her, troubled. "This is the only time I ever asked her to trust me."

Ash said, "I have heard that the Homan Din will not travel by water. By chance, there's a northbound boat at the landing right now. I have enough money to pay passage for all of us, but if we are to go, we must leave immediately."

Macy took the kettle off the fire again. "May I travel with you? It has come to me that I would like to see this place."

"Did you hear that, Zara?" said Kaz. "You always wanted to travel by steamboat."

After a moment, Macy smoothly covered Zara's silence. "Better get packing, then. What are we going to do with these drums?"

Ash got a basket and filled it with the little food she found in Macy's larder, while Kaz and Macy emptied out her peddler's pack and crammed the drums into it. To leave Lisl and Dyan's bones in Fortune troubled her. She would come back for them, she promised, before harvest time.

Whenever she looked up from her work, she saw only Zara's bitter glare. *Not again,* Ash thought, as her hands packed biscuits, napkins, cheese, and apples. *Not again. Not like Hala again.*

All roads lead to Fortune, it used to be said. If this is true, then it is also true that all roads lead away from Fortune. The father of roads is the River Madeena, and upon his restless journeyway the *Amina* still rested, as the four of them and Ghost Dog hurried through the city to the landing. The boarding whistle sounded, shrill and impatient across the rooftops. Ash pulled a red kerchief out of her pocket and waved it to get the dock clerk's attention. "It's a northbound boat," someone warned.

"Yes, yes."

They ran across the landing. The *Amina*'s pilot tooted the horn once again, but Ash was too preoccupied to look up.

PART II

Pilot's Sight

Chapter 5: Rys

Gazing out upon Fortune from the pilothouse high above the landing, Rys remembered what the city had been like before the plague: a city of dreams, where prosperity and poverty lived hand in hand. Lost Fortune, the riverfolk called it now, and still checked for plague flags before coming into port.

On the landing below, stevedores unloaded the final wood wagon. Three barrels of cured meat rolled up the landing stage, and a porter hoisted a crate of squawking chickens to his shoulder for their last journey. Minter Hughson, red-faced, wagged a sheaf of papers in an angry vendor's face. Rys feared they might come to blows. Mardi, the armed woman, watched this scene with some amusement though her attention shifted frequently back to Rys.

Elbie's loyalists had unpacked their armaments as the *Amina* came around Fortune Bend, and locked the passenger hostages into their cabins. All these precautions were wholly unnecessary as far as Rys and the crew were concerned. Like a governess who chases her charge into the dangerous wilderness, they considered it their duty to bring the *Amina* safely home again. However, this loyalty to a boat was not a thing they expected landfolk to understand.

With her hand resting upon the wheel, Rys could feel the faint vibration of the doctor engine, pumping water through the boilers to keep them from overheating. The handful of passengers waiting on the quay moved restlessly within their huddle, revealing and then obscuring their disordered pile of baggage. A more motley set of travelers Rys had never seen. They wore mismatched bits and pieces of clothing which might have been taken at random from poor-bins, or stolen from laundry lines. They looked like nothing so much as a collection of children's toys, hastily pieced together out of a ragbag, but their faces and the shapes of their bodies had been uniformly cut to the same pattern: a short people, thin and sharp-boned, with thick, straight, black hair hanging unadorned to the waist. They looked longingly at the boat.

These eager passengers must have thought themselves fortunate to have found a northbound boat at this time of year. Rys had fought bitterly against Diggen Elbie's decision to take on passengers and freight in Fortune, as if the *Amina* were any other riverboat. "By your own reckoning, your warrant is at least three days behind you," she had said. "Why do you care if the *Amina*'s failure to take on passengers at Fortune Landing arouses suspicions? The city has no militia anymore; the forts are empty. They can do nothing to you."

"They could refuse to supply the boat."

"Not so long as you pay them. The merchants there would sell their own skin if they could make a profit on the sale."

"It is a risk I choose not to take," he said. "And I would thank you to keep your peace."

The two of them had been arguing with each other incessantly for five days, but the arguments had become only a ritual by which they continuously marked the boundaries of their power. Rys had lost the argument for the usual reason: that force of logic could not win against force of arms.

On the quay below, Minter Hughson tucked the crumpled supplies list under his arm, and, with a great show of reluctance, counted coins out of his pockets. He gestured to the first mate. Rys, seeing that the landing stage was clear, sounded the boarding whistle. Lindy hustled the five ragtag passengers aboard.

She leaned out the window to check that the inexperienced crew did not miss any mooring lines. "The sooner we leave, the sooner we come home again."

Mardi gestured. "More passengers coming."

Four people, burdened by baskets and blanket rolls and bags, hurried across the landing. A thing in the shape of a dog followed after them, aloof and regal as a cock upon a roof. Rys felt a constriction, or an explosion, or a sudden sinking in her heart. Witches, she thought, amazed, watching them rush down upon her hijacked boat, like paladins on a quest. The last thing this journey needed was more complications.

"Why would a bunch of clodpated farmers be traveling at this time of year? It's almost planting time." Pretending impatience, Rys sounded the whistle again, hoping that the sight of her pacing angrily from one window to the next might make the travelers pause and consider the peculiarities of this early season, northbound boat. But the business of wrestling their bulky burdens up the narrow landing stage engrossed them, and they did not even glance up.

🌡   🌡   🌡

Pilot's Sight, like every talent, comes embedded with a curse or two. In her youth Rys kept her gift a secret, for few and rare were those who could sit in comfort before her, knowing that she saw far below the skin. Perhaps it was the talent which drew her to the river, or perhaps it was the knowledge that the riverfolk would welcome rather than shun her. On the river, her talent won trust rather than mistrust.

She never knew how much trust she had earned until the winter before the plague when a contingent of pilots visited Rys in Marlestown. She was more than surprised to see them, for some of her unexpected visitors had come from as far away as Allhaven. Flustered, she served them tea and cakes in her tiny sitting room.

They politely discussed this and that, before finally coming to the point of their visit. "King Anselm is gone. Lynthe will be Queen of Faerd, however reluctantly."

"Indeed," said Rys, worrying about how she would

feed her guests supper, when she had no servants and could not cook.

"Our Guildmaster understood King Anselm, though never was there any trust between the Pilot's Guild and the Royal House. But the queen who will be, she is no warrior. The Guildmaster does not know how to speak with her without angering her. We see trouble coming for the Pilot's Guild, trouble we do not need."

Rys sat down upon a stool, clasping her hands across her knees. "Well, the queen will be queen, and that is something we cannot change."

"True. Therefore, it is time to unseat the Guildmaster. It never was meant to be a lifetime appointment."

"Perhaps you are right," said Rys.

All of her guests, relieved, reached for more cakes.

"But why have you come to me?"

"You are the best pilot on the river," one of them said.

"Do not flatter me," she said, full of impatience. "I work hard and am well paid for it."

"We think it would be best if our next Guildmaster had Pilot's Sight. Lynthe is a subtle woman."

So that was it. She stared at them, and they gazed back at her, sincerely enough. "All I ever wanted was a riverboat's helm," she said. "I am a pilot, not a politician."

That time, all their arguments were wasted. She could not say she had no ambition, but she never had aspired to live in Seven Bells City, far from the Madeena River, and play delicate games of politics on behalf of the Guild. Her visitors returned to their winter quarters, and she returned to the river, come spring.

The next time a contingent of pilots came to her, they were gray and weary with grief and fear, and they gathered at her sickbed while the death bells tolled throughout the city. "It is the end of the world," they said. "It is the end of the river, the end of the Guild, the end of steamboats—"

The Guildmaster was dead. With Faerd in agony around her, Rys traveled by ponycart to Seven Bells

City, with three bodyguards to protect her from the lawlessness that had overtaken the roads. There she presented herself to the recently crowned queen.

They showed her to a chaotic workroom, where many pallid, frantic secretaries dressed in mourning gray penned directives and shouted orders, while raw-faced messengers arrived and left at a dizzying pace. In the center of this chaos sat the queen, her hands folded across her pregnant abdomen, confirming or denying directives with only a nod or a shake of her head. Three months now, Faerd had been at war with the plague, but had yet to win a single battle. Rys, following the hasty instructions that one of the old Guildmaster's assistants had whispered to her as they waited in an anteroom, stood back respectfully, waiting to be summoned so she could make her obeisance. The queen gestured her impatiently forward. "No, do not kneel. I have no time for such nonsense. You are the new Master of the Pilot's Guild?"

"Your majesty, I am Rys of Marlestown."

"You are pale and do not look well."

"I have been ill but am on the mend, Your Majesty."

"Good. My officials die faster than I can replace them. If you have already had the plague, you will not get it again."

"That is why my fellow pilots selected me, Your Majesty."

"Not the only reason, I hope!" The queen rose heavily to her feet, and waved away the many liveried servants who rushed anxiously forward to support her. "Give me your arm, Madam Pilot. We will walk in the garden."

In the garden, roses bloomed profusely, but the walks had not been swept in recent memory and were adrift with late summer petals. The queen walked slowly. "I cannot even offer you refreshments, since I sent my house servants away to look after their families. Is it true what the previous Guildmaster said, that the plague does not distress the riverfolk? Your lives are transient by nature, your friendships last only the length of a journey, your children grow up in your absence. So the riverfolk have nothing to lose, he said."

Rys, not wanting to call a fellow pilot a fool, though she had been calling the Guildmaster one in private for years, said harshly enough, "The plague has devastated us. I had to travel here on foot. The entire river is paralyzed."

"There are no pilots to be found, I am told, or they simply refuse to go out on the river. What is the value of a guild whose members think only to save their own skins?"

"One might ask that same question of the nobility," Rys said, then added hastily, "Your Majesty."

But the queen uttered a dry laugh and sat down upon a shaded bench, patting the space beside her. "All speak their mind to me now, and it has not killed me yet. Sit here, and let me speak frankly to you in return. My brother loved battles, and he picked many a fight with the guilds. But I want to make the Pilot's Guild my ally. Let us negotiate: what would it take to get the river running again?"

Rys remained in Seven Bells City only long enough to ransack the membership records and close up the Guild House. In less than a month, she had shamed or threatened enough surviving pilots and engineers back onto the river so that most of the major boating routes kept a regular schedule again. The shortage of pilots gave her an excuse to operate the much reduced guild from behind the helm of a riverboat, though she always expected to be called away. But, although she did receive an occasional letter from the queen, and wrote her share of them in return, she never returned to Seven Bells City.

So began a new era on the river.

❧   ❧   ❧

Rys rang the forward bell and turned the boat's nose into the current. This tame stretch of river bent placidly around the hills up whose sides the streets of For-

tune climbed. Following that gradually curving route
by broad daylight seemed like child's play.

She turned up her collar and pulled on her gloves
against the cold wind blowing steadily into her face.
Mardi sat in the doorway, sucking sleepily on a cold
pipe.

Rys yawned helplessly. Good thing the boat could
practically pilot herself up this stretch of river. How
long would it take Lindy to relieve her at the helm? No
doubt, Elbie had given the mate the onerous job of in-
forming their new passengers of their situation. Rys
spotted some debris ahead and tugged the wheel gently
to turn the boat out of its path.

Mardi leapt to her feet, saluting her lord's arrival
with a sharp slap to her leather-clad chest. Soap-
scented and still languid from his dockside bath, his
damp hair curling as it dried, Diggen Elbie carried a
crystal glass of wine between his fingers. The beautiful
Ursul trailed behind him, unrecognizable in her soot-
stained work clothes, her face grease-daubed from
tending the engines, her lush hair tied sloppily with
twine, her trousers rolled to the knee. She sat down
upon the bench and held her chapped, cracked hands
out to the faint warmth of the stove.

With every passing turn of the river, her face paled
and thinned and hardened. Rys had noticed Elbie himself gazing at his mistress in vague puzzlement, as if
he knew they had met before, but he could not recall
how, or when.

"How far to Vateria?" he said.

Rys said, "It depends on the river. Three days' journey to the border, usually, but it can take longer."

"Then we have sufficient wood."

Once again, Elbie knew little and thought he understood all, a dangerous ailment upon the river. Well, he
would discover soon enough that the river's current
grew stronger the farther north they journeyed, requir-
ing an ever more profligate burning of fuel. At the
same time, woodlots would become more rare and
widely scattered, perhaps even nonexistent because of

the recent flood. With the River's Luck, they would run out of steam long before they reached the border.

Ursul, her head drooping upon her arms, seemed to have fallen suddenly and profoundly asleep. "Where is my relief?" Rys rang the bell sharply to remind Lindy of his duties. "Did you give the first mate your dirty work, sir?"

"Almost certainly." Lord Diggen tasted his wine, and grimaced. "To which dirty work in particular are you referring, Madam Pilot?"

"That of explaining to the new passengers that they have been duped into serving as hostages to a spoiled outlaw nobleman."

"Oh, that." Smiling, he toasted Rys' ill temper with his glass. "Well, I could scarcely tell them myself, now could I?" Elbie examined the color of his wine as though he were judging it at a country fair. "I haven't had a good glass of wine since the plague. It set wine-making back a hundred years."

"I am so sorry the death of thousands inconvenienced you."

"It's cold, isn't it, for such a bright day. What do you think of my stunning Ursul, the toast of Seven Bells City?"

"We couldn't run the boat without her," Rys said, speaking the simple truth.

"Who would have thought she'd turn out to be so ... competent?"

"I hate to waste my advice. But I would never be condescending to her."

"Oh, no, not that. I just wish she would take a bath."

"She's too busy saving your skin, you stupid ass."

"And a fine skin it is, too." Elbie admired the back of his hands until even Mardi began to look disgusted with him. He drained his glass at last, and wandered happily away.

Mardi said, "He shouldn't walk the decks without an escort; he might fall."

"Let him fall." Lack of sleep made Rys savage. "Any captain who would drink on board—"

Ursul lifted her head. Her mouth had a harsh,

pinched look. Rys and Mardi looked at each other, and looked away. "I don't know why he's so deep in his cups," Ursul said, "now that they'll never be able to catch us." She stood up stiffly, making no effort to right her grimy clothing and sloppy hair, though certainly she must have heard her lord's complaints. "I'll fetch Mister Airhome, Madam Pilot. You need your rest."

"You get some rest, too. This is a quiet stretch of river."

Ursul touched her fingers absently to her forehead, as though she really were just another member of the crew. "Well!" Mardi said in shock, when she was gone.

"Someone should have warned the two of them about traveling against the current. The gods take their dues."

"What gods?" Mardi anxiously patted at her flat bosom where she wore a half-dozen god-medals, for luck and protection.

Lindy Airhome soon arrived, flustered and apologetic. "How did the passengers take the news?" Rys asked as she handed over the helm.

"Those that wanted to go to Vateria anyway didn't particularly care, or maybe they didn't understand. The others, the farmers, they weren't too happy. They did go on about planting season. It's terrible, terrible."

Rys stood a moment, looking out at the bright water. She had a feeling that Diggen Elbie's latest hostages might prove more troublesome than he had bargained for.

"Come on," said Mardi. "Let's get some sleep."

Sun-dazzled, with Mardi stumbling groggily behind her, Rys descended to the passenger deck. Elbie's thoughtless comments about Ursul's need for a bath had reminded Rys of her own stink. She never knew, when she held a boat on that narrow edge between safety and disaster, that she was afraid. She only smelled it on herself afterward.

The bright brass and the scrubbed white steps blazed with light. The hostage passengers leaned against the rail, relaxed, watching the city of Fortune disappear around the gradual curve of Fortune Bend. Many of them sipped tea from porcelain cups.

Disoriented, Rys sat in an armchair at the bottom of the stairs, and waved Mardi away. "Go to bed. I just want to sit a minute."

At night, she missed the boat's illusions: the content passengers, the efficient crew, the drug of well-being that helped them all forget who they were and where their loyalties lay. Even Mardi was forgetting, to stumble off to sleep like this, as though she were a dismissed servant rather than a prison guard who had neglected to lock her prisoner into her cell. The whistle hooted cheerily. What did the newest hostages think of all this—did they wonder if everyone had gone mad?

In the passenger's gallery, the afternoon sun seeped across the painted deck, and most of the hostages had found sheltered corners in which to huddle on deck chairs, soaking up the sun, but protected from the wind. The five ragtag travelers with the matching faces all leaned on the forward rail, long hair blowing in the wind, gazing eagerly northward. Rys had never seen anyone like them; aboriginal people had been a rare sight even in her grandmother's day.

A child ran past, screaming shrilly, chased by a second child and then by a frazzled parent. No one paid Rys any heed as she dazedly wandered the decks.

Her heart recalled her to herself, as though she had been slapped awake. Its beat pounded in her ears . . . no, it was the drums. Two drummers sat with their backs against the wall, tentatively testing the sounds of their drums, like strangers striking up a conversation. One drum was earth and one was fire, and the place of their meeting was a lightning storm.

Diametrically opposing forces lay in a clutter upon the deck, festive and funereal, hopeful and despairing, brightly painted and tied by strings. Rys held herself upright by clinging to the deckrail like a drunk. Not three strides from her, the creature who was not a dog stared between the rails as though they were the bars of a cage. When he turned his yellow wolf eyes to her, the nape of her neck crawled. Two grim-faced women, their backs to the drummers, leaned on the rail. The young people burned, energy and fire. These two were heavy, heavy as stone. How many witches could one boat bear, Rys wondered, before it sank under their combined weight?

Both the women turned their heads and pinned Rys between the sharp points of their gazes. She felt as though she were falling forward. One of the women caught her by the hand and steadied her. "Rys," she said.

Rys did not remember this particular weather-scoured and sun-lined face. She did not remember these work-hardened muscles. This brown, wind-harrowed hair had been brighter once. But how could her heart not recognize its lost home?

She pressed her face upon that broad shoulder, and breathed deeply of the salty, woolen scent of that brown skin. "I always knew we would meet again."

Ash, she called herself now. The name fit her, and yet it did not. Two kinds of people the plague had left behind: ghosts and survivors. Ash, who had been Cydna, thought she was a ghost. Rys clasped her hand, and called her by the old name in her heart.

"Any moment, my guard will panic and come searching for me," Rys said. "Elbie's people must not know, must not even suspect, who you are. They lured me on board the *Amina* in the first place by using your name."

Ash did not seem to hear. "As I watched this boat come into shore last night, I thought, *that boat's pilot must have learned from Rys*. But I never imagined that it might be you. I read in the newspaper that you are Guildmaster—why are you still at a helm?"

"The Guild is different now. Listen to me; we must not be seen together. They will use you—"

"I heard you," said Ash. She looked up from their clasped hands into Rys' eyes. "Ten years."

"Eleven."

"You have become more yourself."

Rys wanted to put her arms around her. Weakly, she said, "Listen to me."

"I heard you," Ash said again. "My brother-son travels with me, my only kinsman. You know why we cannot go into Vateria. You must help me."

"There is nothing I can do. I am not in command of this boat. All we can do is make certain they have no reason to suspect . . ."

Ash stopped her. "There is always a choice."

Rys let go of her hand, and stepped away from her. "As if it were not enough to find you at last and be unable to speak with you—" She took a breath, collecting herself. Five days on double-watch, and no end in sight. She could not afford to weep. "Do not make me choose between you and the safety of the boat. I would choose the boat, and the choice would kill me."

"I have never asked you to make that kind of choice."

"You are asking now."

The hand that Rys had clasped hung empty now. "I'm sorry," Ash said. "I didn't even think—"

Rys took her hand again. She wanted to kneel at her feet. "There must be a way we can help each other."

Ash smiled a little. "Let us think on it. Rys—"

Rys bowed her head. "Madam."

"I see why you were chosen Guildmaster."

"Why did you never send for me?" Rys looked up into Ash's stricken silence. "Now I beg your pardon. Lack of sleep makes me stupid. I know why you could not."

"Then explain it to me, so we can both understand."

"Because your heart was ashes."

"Yes," Ash said. "That is the reason."

Ash did not know about the forest rooting in her. But, turning away from joy into sorrow and back again into joy, Rys knew. She saw a forest, and she saw a river, and she saw herself piloting the way through.

Chapter 6: Ash

The bright sun set, and twilight clothed the river. The black lace of the budding trees edged a diamond-spangled sky of midnight blue. The sky melted into glazed black water, until the stars drooped almost within grasp. The river flowed from sky to earth to ocean and back again into sky.

The boat traveled against this flow: counter-current, northward, from spring to winter, backward in time. It carried Ash helplessly toward her past, toward the one place she had sworn she would never return: Vateria.

She had never laid her ghosts to rest, and now they came for her: bitter Hala, the lost children, her brother's son, the massacred farmers, the plague ... and now Rys. What next? Would Naiman the Poet rise up out of his grave to wag an accusatory finger in her face?

She fisted the rail, thinking, *this is what comes of rushing too hastily toward the most convenient solution.*

When the gruff and embarrassed mate explained their situation to the boat's newest hostages, the five native people, who were returning to their home in one of Vateria's badlands, had not cared or seemed to understand. The boat's other passengers, seeing Ash's dismay, hurried up to reassure her that the boat's pilot was one of the best on the river. Once the nobleman had journeyed where he needed, the pilot intended to bring them safely to their destinations—perhaps later than they expected, but with a story to tell. It would be an adventure.

Dishes clattered in the salon, and glasses rang in a

laughing toast. How could Ash convince her fellow
hostages to band together and wrest control of the boat
from their captors? They had accepted their improb-
able abduction with resignation and even good humor.
Against this seduction of comfort no weapon could
stand.

The turning of the paddle wheels set a constant,
rhythmic vibration rumbling through the railing under
Ash's hand. The muffled patter of the drums throbbed
with the pulsation of the engines. Bowed solemnly
over their instruments, their bound hair fraying loose
in wisps around their ears, the drummers seemed
twinned beings, two halves of a whole. Macy had long
since gone indoors, saying that there was no virtue in
suffering that she knew of. Kaz and Zara did not appear to feel the cold. Riveted between the drums, the
river, and each other, they seemed enraptured. They
had no room in that circle of attention for Ash.

Offshore, in the distance, she saw the faint light of
a lamp burning in a farmhouse kitchen. They were
rounding a curve now, and the boat turned to make the
crossing. Ash peered ahead until she spotted a
sightmark faintly glowing in the twilight, a faraway
white "X" painted on a tree trunk. Steam sighed suddenly out of a release valve as though the boat were
weary. The drums fell silent.

Ash turned her head. The two young people wrapped
their drums carefully in oilcloth, murmuring together
in low voices.

"Are you going in?" she asked. "I'm sorry—this is
not the journey I planned. I have never heard of a boat
being hijacked like this before."

Kaz laid a hand upon his love's arm, cautiously, as
one might touch a half wild animal. Despite his gentleness, she shied away at what he told her, and stalked
indoors, slamming a door behind herself.

With her hands upon the rail, Ash faced the wind.
Kaz came up beside her and pressed her sweater into
her hands. "Eventually, we will get home. It's cold," he
said as though surprised.

The sweater smelled like Ashland: of woodsmoke

and earth. Ash said, "I will not put you between me and Zara, like a piece of meat between two dogs. It was bad enough, with your mother. You must wish I had never come looking for you."

"It's Ashland that has come looking for me." He leaned against the rail beside her. "I told Zara it would, someday. I guess she thought I was just telling her a story. But the land will take hold of her, won't it?"

Is that how it is, Ash wondered? *Does the land stalk us and take us prisoner?* The memory of Hala's bitterness haunted her. "Better you never come home again than see Zara tamed," she said.

"But I want to come home." Kaz gazed into the darkness of the east bank, then straightened with a sigh. "Well, aunt, are you coming in?"

"Not yet."

"Supper sure smells good."

"I'm afraid to get too comfortable—it might make me stupid. You go ahead, Kaz. I'll be in later."

She watched him go. He knew what he could survive. She envied him his fearlessness.

🍂   🍂   🍂

The *Amina* traveled northward, past trees budding with the vivid green of new spring, past quiet, half-abandoned farmlands with their walls tumbling down, and flocks of birds like ashes flying from a chimney. Winter-pale children with their thin clothing pressed against their bodies by the wind waved eagerly from shore, hoping to be rewarded by a toot of the whistle. Dogs ran and barked, then stood like proud monuments as the fearful boat fled their ferocity.

Northbound boats must take their leisure. The outlaw Lord Diggen, treading the decks of his diminished kingdom, shook his head in disbelief at the sight of his house servants scurrying to bring toast and tea to the same people they had taken hostage at sword's point not ten days past. The children, underfoot and always in trouble, went from one entertainment to the next, as though this were no prison but a traveling circus, while their parents lay on deck chairs in the sun.

Ash paced out the length and width of the boat as repeatedly and monotonously as a carpenter taking measurements. Ghost Dog hunted rats in the boiler deck and delivered their corpses to Grelling. Ash, hair tightly braided against the wind, watched the shore, and wished for earth under her feet.

The drummers played their drums. The five people returning to their homeland in Vateria often drew near to listen and dance. Ash watched from a distance, feeling herself more alien than they. Drummers and dancers learned each other's languages, both of words and of music. As two, and then three days passed by, Ash spoke only the language of silence.

She hung the dancing jack from a hook in the cabin where she slept. She did not spend much time there. Even at night, she found herself more often upon the decks, watching the moon rise and set, the stars swirl like raisins stirred in a bowl, the lace-edged river flow silently beneath her feet, countercurrent. She knew that Rys kept a double watch every night, from sunset to sunrise, with an armed guard always at her side. She thought of climbing to the storm deck, to keep her company as she had used to do, but she doubted that would be wise.

Macy soon knew everyone on board by name. "Do you know, that Ursul, who does a little of everything, she's Lord Diggen's lover. She bought a dancing jack. Paid a good price for it, too."

"Did she know what she was doing?"

Macy shrugged. "Not my business. I just make them and sell them."

"Well, it might be interesting to see what happens next."

"It might."

They stood at the rail, side by side, like old friends.

Three days out of Fortune, the floodwaters began to recede. The trees emerged slowly, water-blackened, their roots exposed or their trunks half buried in silt, many of them tilting this way or that, like toy soldiers knocked askew by a careless hand. At midafternoon, a crewmember's hail brought Ash out of the shallow doze she had fallen into, curled upon a deck chair in the sun. Peering forward into the bright glare of sunlight reflecting off the water, she spotted a waterlogged woodlot. Its shed, which had been cleverly built atop its own flatboat, rested at an angle where the receding water had deposited it. Not enough wood had escaped the floodwaters to make it worth stopping, Ash thought, until she noticed the barge full of cut fuel wood, securely tied to shore.

With a hoot of the whistle to get the woodcutter's attention, the *Amina*'s yawl promptly set forth, bearing the mud clerk, with a dole from the nobleman's bottomless coffers. Like the other passengers, who hurried out of the salon now that they had something to watch, Ash leaned at the rail, envious of the three people in the yawl who would, at least for a little while, set their feet onto solid ground.

Soon, with an officious clatter of armaments, the nobleman's strong-arms, who until this point had been indistinguishable from the rest of the crew, appeared on the deck, outfitted in hastily donned fighting gear, and carrying a bristling array of swords and pikes and pistols. The passenger-hostages greeted the weapons' appearance with sighs and groans of disgust, but passively allowed themselves to be herded into the salon, where they entered their cabins as they had been trained. However, it took both Macy and Kaz, expostulating on either side of Zara, to keep her from exploding before the door had closed and locked in her face.

Ash and Macy went together into Macy's cabin, where they could still hear Zara cursing eloquently. "It's a waste of time to try to tell her what to do," said Macy. "Kaz is the one who thinks first. Maybe he could do so much thinking he wouldn't ever get around to the doing. Without the other, I doubt that either one would have survived that first year."

"How did you meet them?"

Macy uttered a humorless laugh, settling herself into

the armchair for a long wait. "How could I not? There was so few of us left. Nine out of ten Fortuners died or disappeared, they say. No other city was hit half as hard. I would sit out on a street corner and say the names of people I knew that had died. I could talk for an entire morning and not repeat myself."

She began shuffling a deck of cards on the side table. "I managed to nurse one daughter through it, but then she killed herself, as soon as she was strong enough. All her children dead, and her husband, too." Ash's face must have showed her shock because Macy added quietly, "That's the way it was. Some of us found ways to survive, and some of us didn't. I never would have thought I'd be one who made it, myself. I went half crazy, started making toys, though there were no children to play with them. I used to be a clockmaker, but who cared what time it was anymore?"

Ash drew the curtains back from the small windows, but she could see only a stretch of sky, edged at the bottom by the frayed green of the treetops. Was Rys awake in her cabin five doors down, alerted by the whistle or the sound of her door lock driving home? "I never thought I'd make it, either," she said.

Macy's cards made crisp slaps as she dealt them onto the table. "When I was a little one, the old folks used to talk about the wars. Now, nobody even remembers a time when there wasn't peace. Someday, it'll be like that with the plague. It'll just be a terrible time that happened to somebody else. How about a game of Three-Ten?"

Ash sat down in the armchair beside Macy and accepted a hand of cards. "Are you certain you shuffled these?" she asked, after looking at her dole.

"We get what we get, Ash of Ashland."

By the time Ursul came around to unlock the doors, the sun, a molten glob upon the horizon, cast a dim orange light across the interior of the echoing salon. The released pilot stalked angrily out of her cabin, and all the nearby crewmembers began to scurry about at the sound of her voice, like ants in a stirred-up anthill. Ex-

haustion made her face pale and hollow, and her eyes
were sketched with red. She jammed her pilot's hat
upon uncombed and tangled hair and strode among the
released passengers, rebuking their passivity with a
glance. She walked past Ash and Macy, then seemed to
consider, and turned back. "What have they done?"

"Tied a wood barge alongside, is my guess."

Rys looked cold and dangerous in the twilight. She
pulled on her gloves one finger at a time. Her guild pin
glittered in the last light of the sun. When her
guardwoman came hurrying up, fretting about the late-
ness of the day, Rys waved her brusquely away. "Let
me have some peace!"

She took Ash by the arm and walked her outside,
onto the deck, where Ghost Dog, who alone of all the
passengers had not been confined, stood with his nose
in the wind. At her first breath of fresh air, Rys turned
and stared northward, frowning into the twilight.
Farmer or pilot, they both could smell coming weather.

"We'd have run out of fuel by tomorrow if someone
hadn't been so clever. Sooner, with this storm coming."
Rys pointed into the gathering twilight. "Do you see
the sightmark there, on the point?"

"Yes."

"That's Dollin Bend. It bends differently now, but
it's still more or less in the same place as it used to be,
ten years ago. Another few miles upriver, we pass
where Mason's Crossing used to be. There's a farm up
on the hills, above the floodline, Japa's Farm. I'll be
cutting along close to the east bank there because of
shallows on the other side."

She paused, to adjust the fit of her gloves and glance
casually over her shoulder. Mardi seemed to be ap-
proaching again, for Rys finished in a murmur, "I hear
the Japas are good folks. Friendly; don't mind unexpected visitors. Go straight to their kitchen fire, or the
cold will kill you. It's the best I can do."

"Of a certainty, it will rain tonight," said Ash, as
Mardi came within hearing.

"Did you get a look at those clouds before sunset?
What kind of storm do you think it'll be?"

Ash shrugged. She and Rys both knew that the storms of spring did not vary much one from the next.

Rys turned to her guard. "We're in for a long night, Mardi. Have those rudder-breakers brought that pot of tea yet?"

Mardi obligingly accepted the distraction and began shouting fit to raise the dead. Rys turned back to Ash. Her face was stark. "Think of me, sometimes."

A flustered deckhand hastened over with the teapot. Others converged, anxious about the threatening weather, begging for directions. Tongue-tied, Ash watched Rys walk away, surrounded by her swarm. Even if that final, bitter year had not happened, as Ash wished it had not, the long years apart should have sundered them. Yet it scarcely seemed possible that, in the midst of a mundane conversation about the weather, they had said good-bye.

The coming storm extinguished the stars even as their first frail light began to shine in the twilight. The wind, always unremitting at this time of year, picked up strength, plucking at the crumpled hat Ash jammed down over her ears, and feeling at her flesh with cold, insinuating fingers. A door banged. Kaz, head bowed against the raw weather, struggled across the deck to her side. "Won't you come in? Everybody says the pilot will get us safely through the storm. She's the best on the river, they say. What did she want to talk to you about?"

"She is my friend. We knew each other, before. I don't suppose Zara can swim."

"No—I always meant to teach her. But she's not afraid."

"Of course not."

He leaned on the rail, squinting into the wind. "What do you see out here?"

"We're close to Ashland now."

He looked eastward, silent.

"Your Zara will have to find a way. Every time she loves, she trades away a little freedom. Every time she makes a choice, there are a thousand things she cannot choose. Zara will have to reconcile herself to this, sooner or later."

"Unless she wants to wander forever," said her brother-son, gloomy in the rising storm.

"Well, then you will have to choose, too. But not today, I think."

"It's too soon," he agreed, though he did not know what Ash truly meant. The sly wind had begun to unravel his hair from the threads that wove it. "Did I tell you—I haven't told you anything, have I? I keep thinking I'll tell you when we get to Ashland."

"Who knows how long will it be, before we get to Ashland? What do you want to tell me?" The dark shore flowed slowly past them, the Dollin Crossing now behind them. Even if Ash could see, she would not recognize this altered shoreline.

"What it was like," Kaz said. "The way my family died, and how Zara and I . . ."

"I'm listening."

❦   ❦   ❦

"I have to sweep the floor," Hala said. "You know how dirty it gets." And then she died.

Kaz had cried for help when he found her, collapsed on the floor. But, in a city where such desperate cries for help had been sounding for many weeks now, no one paid any heed to one more. Hala died where she lay, and Kaz, too weak from his own bout with illness to lift her, could only kneel beside her, weeping helplessly.

With white-faced calm she had cared for him as he lay ill. His sisters were ill, too, she told him, but they were getting better, just as he was. "Tell me I won't die," he begged her.

"You won't die," she said. "Early on, people were dying. But now almost everybody is recovering. It was the heat wave that killed them, they say, not the illness. Now that it's cooled off a little, the worst is over. You and your sisters are all going to get better."

Hala had always been a good liar. Kaz believed her.

Having awakened in the morning from a healing sleep, Kaz wearied of calling for his mother to come care for him, and got out of bed against her orders. He found her dying. If he had delayed in bed much longer, she would have died alone.

Now it was over. Yet sometimes she seemed to move or breathe, and he would catch his breath and lean over her, watching eagerly, pressing a hand to her chest to check once again for a heartbeat. Then he would weep again. After a while, he fell asleep beside her.

When he awoke the next time, it was afternoon. Within the stone walls of the house, the air remained cool and still. When Kaz touched his mother one last time, she was cold, and her flesh felt strange: hard, inanimate. He got to his feet, staggering. He was thirsty. He felt as though something had exploded in his belly, reaming out his body and leaving him stunned and empty. He had felt this way before when his father died. But Ash had been there then.

Kaz found his grandparents, and he found his sisters, all dead in their beds. In the kitchen, he found a pot of soup sitting upon the cold stove; the fire had long since gone out. He ate a few spoonfuls, sitting upon the stoop, and he drank a dipper of stale water from the bucket. The floor was indeed dirty; Kaz had never known his mother to go to bed at night without sweeping it first.

When he left the house, it did not occur to him that he would never enter it again.

He staggered down the street, a stunned survivor in a blasted city. He could not escape the fetid smell of death. He passed bodies in the street. He saw a few living wraiths like himself, lurching like drunks through the abandoned streets. He saw a crazed woman, tearing her hair and screaming. These sights he passed by as though they were images of someone else's nightmare.

In the first days of the plague, wagonloads of household goods and crowds of frantic people jammed the streets, parting like grass before a wind at the tolling of the death wagon's bell. No death wagon rolled the streets anymore; no one bothered to burn or bury the dead.

In the park where Kaz often went to meet his friends, a woman sat wearily on the curb, her head slumped down upon her knees. Thinking to ask her a question, Kaz drew near, then turned aside when he noticed she was not breathing. He shuffled wearily up a gradual slope, and into a grove of trees. The heat shimmered across the stone streets, but here in the shade it was quiet and cool, like the inside of a temple. Kaz sat against the roots of a tree and rested for a while, his ears ringing. He got up again and stumbled on; it was not far now.

Bracken and brambles choked a shallow ravine, where a bright stream tumbled. Kaz fell to his knees and crawled into a tunnel, where thorns caught at his clothing and pierced his hands. He wormed his way through, and into a hidden cave in the side of the ravine. Here, light filtered through only dimly, and he lay, gasping, until his eyes adjusted to the changed light. Someone had been here recently. An expensive woven mat, stolen from someone's front hallway, covered the packed dirt floor. Blankets lay in a pile in the corner. On the shelves that Kaz had helped cut carefully into the walls were piled the kind of foodstuff that is taken on journeys: tinned hardbread and dried fruit. Kaz pillowed his head on one of the blankets, and fell asleep again.

When he awoke, it was night, and Zara, illuminated by a burning oil lamp, squatted on a stool in the corner, glaring at him. She was the acknowledged leader of his circle of friends, the one whose imagination gave them the most delight, and got them into the worst trouble. "This is my secret place, too," he said.

"I brought all these things for me."

"Well, I'll bring my own."

"We can't both stay here. I'm a girl, and you're a boy."

Kaz sat up, head spinning. "We can make a wall or something."

"Why do you want to be here, anyway?"

"Why do you?" he said.

For just a moment, he saw it in her face: the horror of what she had seen, the nightmare from which she had fled. Then it was gone, and she said angrily, "I was here first!"

"This is my place, too!"

"Not any more. It's mine now."

Kaz stared at her, but he was too weak to fight, and he knew better than to pick a fight with Zara anyway. Six brothers and sisters she had. She could hold her own against someone twice her size.

"I'll go away in the morning, then," he said.

But Zara screamed during the night and would not be quiet until Kaz, in desperation, lay down next to her and held her, as his mother used to do when he had nightmares. In the morning, shamefaced, she shared some of her food with him. So neither one of them moved out of the cave until nearly winter, when the cooling weather made some parts of the city livable again. They moved often after that, following Zara's whims, or seeking a place more comfortable or less haunted. Wherever they lived, they lived together; and whatever they had, they shared. They had pressed pricked fingers together, swearing an oath that neither one of them had ever broken. "I will stand beside you, no matter what."

That winter, their eleventh birthdays passed unrecognized.

🐦 🐦 🐦

A long time after Kaz had finished speaking, he straightened from the rail, shivering. "Why don't you go in?" he said again.

"I think better out here," Ash said.

"What are you thinking about?"

"The same thing you are thinking about. About where loyalty and love begin and end. I think I already understood a little, about you and Zara. But I understand better now."

Kaz kissed Ash's cheek, as though he halfway

guessed that this was a leavetaking, and went indoors.
Within the salon, a cheerful clatter of dishes began. On
the storm deck above, deckhands ran past, hurrying to
make secure before the rising storm.

The eastern shore hung like a shadow between inky
black water and stormy black sky. It grew closer even
as Ash watched. For all the long wait, the time had
now grown short. With her satchel on her shoulder, she
walked the length of the passenger's gallery to the far
side of the wheelboxes.

Ghost Dog appeared suddenly in the shadows.
Lamplight from the salon glittered in his eyes. "No, I
suppose you would not miss this," she said. "Well, you
may do what you will. Kaz will watch out for you, or
you can jump overboard with me. I would rather have
your company than not, but it is your choice."

A flicker of lightning revealed the shoreline, dangerously close now. The faint lights of a farmhouse
emerged from the shadowed trees. Ash took off her
sweater and boots and tucked them securely into her
belt. *Now,* she thought, looking down into the snow-
melt black of the swollen river. She did not feel afraid.

The cold roused her from her reverie. The lighted
windows of the farmhouse had long since slipped
past, and the boat now drew slowly away from shore.
Ash watched solid land move once again out of her
reach. In a narrow gap between cloud and horizon, the
moon appeared, only to be swallowed up by roiling
stormcloud. Thin and ghostly that pale lightship had
been; the storm could sink it on its long journey
across the sky. But its way had been appointed, and so
it plunged into the chaos.

"So," said Ash. She sat upon the deck to pull on her
boots with hands that trembled with cold. "Am I ceas-
ing to be such a fool, or am I just becoming one?"

Ghost Dog, who from a wind-sheltered corner had
borne witness to her long indecision, got up and
stretched. "I hope I keep you amused," Ash said. He
took a step forward to follow her, then hesitated.

"Would you rather go inside? Here, I'll hold the door for you."

She let him into the salon and closed the door firmly behind him. A gust of wind tilted the boat sideways and sent her reeling into the rail, then back across the deck again. Dishes shattered within the salon. A confusion of shrill voices faded into the wind as Ash climbed into the darkness of the storm deck.

The white railings glowed in the darkness. The engines huffed faintly, like horses laboring up a hill. She took a breath and tasted ashes.

Within the shadows of the dark pilothouse, a voice spoke. Like a tame and well-trained monster, the boat responded. Ash saw a figure moving within the darkness, the slow spinning of the ship's wheel, the pilot in the shadows, turning the world upon its axis.

She stepped past the armed guard, who hung half over the rail, and entered the pilothouse. She sat on the bench bolted to the floor near the stove. Rys leaned away from the wheel, using her weight to encourage the boat's reluctant rudders to turn. Her oilskins rattled in the wind, like dry leaves.

"What happened?" Rys said.

"A choice," Ash said. "I made a choice, and it was not what I have chosen before." *This is what comes of buying a toy from a stranger,* she thought, but felt no resentment.

Rys turned her face briefly away from the brewing storm to look at Ash through the darkness.

Ash rested her elbows upon her knees, and her chin upon her folded hands. Only darkness loomed beyond the pilothouse windows, but her heart burned within her. "Now anything can happen," she said. "Anything."

Chapter 7: Rys

Rys ordered the deckhands out to extinguish the *Amina*'s myriad lamps and lanterns. The predatory wind leapt at the *Amina*, and the boat heeled sideways in a panic. Rain poured into the pilothouse, sudden as a bucket overturned. Rys hung, cursing, from the recalcitrant wheel. Sluggishly, weighed down by the barge tied alongside, the boat turned and slowly righted herself.

To turn the boat into the wind, Rys had turned away from the security of the channel. She could not even guess what lay hidden below the water's wind-whipped surface. She slowed the engines and rang the bell for leadsmen. Kiva had the wit to post a man on either side of the passenger deck, to shout the marks up to the pilot house. Their deep voices carried over the howling wind, for now. "No bottom," they shouted.

"I need to speak with Elbie," Rys said when Kiva came in to report. But it was Ursul who eventually arrived in the pilothouse. Rys told her all the reasons why she could not safely pilot the boat through this storm: the barge, which prevented her from ducking into corners or hugging the shoreline for shelter from the wind; the chutes, which had grown unusably shallow with the receding flood; the danger of shipwreck, should the ropes which lashed boat and barge together begin to break. Ursul went away and came back again with a basket of food. "Lord Diggen says to continue on."

"Is he drunk again?"

Without answering, Ursul swabbed the floor, a kind but futile effort. She left, perhaps heeding Rys' command to change her soaked clothing before she died of chill, and perhaps not. Rys stared across the tortured river, watching the point of the bend drawing closer. The leadsmen's lines hit bottom, and they began singing the measurements. Rys did not like the image this gave her of the riverbed, which grew too shallow too quickly.

"That cursed barge will give us the only stability we have," she muttered. "If we sink, gods help us, not many of us will reach shore, and those that don't drown will die of exposure."

"Best eat while you can," said Ash. She came up to hand her some cheese sandwiched in a roll. Her woolen clothing gave forth a damp, earthy smell, as though she had recently sprung out of the ground, a spring seedling.

She stood beside Rys, radiating warmth like a stove, until the rain began blowing in through the windows again. She stepped back, and Rys said, to keep her nearby, "I remember every word of our last conversation, eleven years ago." Rys could not look away from the river, but she sensed Ash, standing behind her in the center of the pilothouse, rooted and stable and silent. "For years, I asked myself what I should have done differently, until finally I realized that our whole relationship had been pointing toward that conversation. Time after time, you came to me to hear the truth about your life. It was inevitable that I would someday tell you something you could not bear to hear."

Ash uttered a hushed, ironic laugh. "Long after Naiman was dead, I was out cutting wood one day, and suddenly I realized that I had done the one thing to you that you feared most: I avoided your company because I could not endure your Sight. So who was the betrayer, I asked myself, and who was the betrayed?"

The river bottom remained stable for now. Rys bit into the bread, tasting the sharp cheese and the sweet wheat blending together on her tongue. "I did betray you," she said.

"You told me the truth. My relationship with Naiman

cost me everything and gave me nothing. It was the absolute, undeniable truth."

"Oh, anyone could see that, who knew you. But it would not have killed me to hold my tongue. Excuse me, I need to listen to the leadsmen."

Ash planted herself again upon the bench. Kiva returned, to report that most of the crew had been stationed on the boiler deck, where they watched over the bilge pumps and stood by with axes, ready to cut the lashings and set loose the barge should it start to break free. Rys said, "Are the passengers secure? And the leadsmen tied down to the rails? I'll be turning her as soon as I think you're safely below; I hope the crew is ready for some flooding. That wind is blowing good and hard."

"Oh, we're ready, madam. I'll go below."

Now the battle truly began, as Rys turned the boat broadside to the wind. The gale gusted sheets of icy rain through the windows, soon flooding the pilot house. The topheavy boat struggled against the counterweight of the barge, which unbalanced her even as it anchored her. Rys fought the wheel, as sounds of chaos echoed through the speaking tube. The boat lay over sideways. Rys kicked her fallen stool aside, and clung to the window frames. Ash, bolted to the bench as securely, it seemed, as the bench was bolted to the floor, could not be dislodged. But Mardi nearly went over the rail, as she clung there, green-faced.

Somehow, the boat made it around the point without foundering, and Rys fought her nose into the wind once again. From below, Kiva shouted the expected bad news over the roar of the engines: damage, injuries, and flooding. Staring, appalled, at the river before them, Rys scarcely listened. The edifice of the east bank was collapsing. Grown trees, their roots undermined, tumbled helplessly into the current. Even as Rys watched, what had been a point a moment before became an island, and what had been an island was joined to the western shore. If she had followed the sightmarks around what had been until tonight Gelsin Bend, Rys would have run the boat aground.

Kiva paused in her report; perhaps she had asked Rys a question. "New river," Rys said.

"What?" Kiva shouted. "Madam Pilot?"

"New river," Rys said. "As far as I can see."

"Maybe we had better tie down?"

"It's too late. We have to go through. Give me half speed."

The boat slowed. For now, with the leadsmen singing no bottom, they were probably still in the channel. The surface of the river, churned up by the noisy torrent of rain and wind, told Rys nothing of what lay ahead in the newly formed and constantly changing riverbed, whether a channel or a sandbar, a snag or a boulder. Rys pressed her forehead against the window frame. The boat shuddered as it collided with underwater debris. "Gods of the River," she said, "I've never lost a boat."

"I'll be your helmsman." Ash came up behind her, uprooting and replanting herself with each step. "I drive an oxplow now, but I remember." Ash laid her hand upon the wheel, and the boat seemed to settle, like a nervous horse under a familiar hand. "This boat will not sink," she said.

Not always the simple and homely. Not always the midwife, the picklemaker, the gardener fretting over an unexpected fungus on the pea plants. Usually, but not always. A burden of witches traveled this renegade boat. Now Ash showed Rys what a witch could do.

Beneath the melting and shifting chaos of the changing river, a secret order lay. Rys, glaring into the driving rain, demanded that secret knowledge. The leadsmen shouted at her, frantically: Mark Two, Less a Half, Mark One! "Hard port," Rys said. The boat's bottom went grinding over gravel. Panicked shouts came up from below. But the rudders did not break, and the boat did not run aground.

"This boat will not sink," Ash said. And it did not.

Rys had gone out before, to mark a new channel with buoys, and post new sightmarks, in broad daylight and clear weather, after the river seemed to be finished with its renovations. It was tedious, careful work. To feel the way through storm, like a blind man walking the edge of a cliff in the midst of a hurricane, was madness. The river shifted before her eyes, falling apart and reforming. Ash, soaked to the skin, rain dripping like sweat from her face, leaned into the wheel. She breathed open-mouthed, her muscles bulging, staring fixedly into the darkness. When they hit a snag, she flinched as though her body had been pierced.

"We're coming up to an island, or what will be an island if it survives this transformation. We'll pass it on the starboard side—there'll be a sandbar at this end. Give it a hard turn to port—"

The leadsmen sang hoarsely: Mark Three, Mark Three, no bottom.

"We're in the channel again."

More debris washed down upon them. Rys did not even try to evade it anymore. She put a hand on Ash's shoulder as the tangle of logs hit the prow, and she felt the muscles bulge as if Ash were physically warding danger away. "Do you need to rest?"

Ash shook her head.

Mardi hung over the rail, like a rug hung out to air. Sometimes, Rys heard the faint sound of her helpless gagging. Ash and Rys stood ankle-deep in water. The rain needled Rys' face; she pulled her hat brim down. "Tell me about your companion, the one who looks like a dog."

Ash took a breath and seemed about to smile. "What, are we out of danger?"

"A reprieve, is all. How did he come to travel with you?"

"He came to me just before the plague. He was thin and worn; he must have traveled a long way. That is all I know. I think he studies me."

"What is he?"

Ash shook her head. "I do not know."

"I think he is a man."

"Perhaps."

"I see him, trapped, his thoughts running in circles,

only half conscious, tortured by the knowledge that something has happened to him, something is missing . . ."

"I did not turn him into a dog."

"But surely you could have changed him back again."

"No, I could not. Besides, if what you say is true, then how do we know he is not a far better dog than he was a man?"

Rys stared at her, thinking, *This is not the one I knew.*

Ash, who had always sensed Rys' gaze even when she could not see it, added after a moment, "On the blood of fifty dead farmers I swore never again to do or undo another person's destiny. There are some things more important than kindness."

"Hold on," Rys said suddenly. "Gods of the River!"

A wall of wind washed a fresh flood of icy rain into the pilothouse. The boat groaned. "More steam!" Rys shouted. She heard no answer from the engineers below. For all she knew, the entire crew had been washed overboard, and the engines churned on, unattended. She peered ahead into the storm, trying to make sense of the wind-driven waterscape which lay before her.

Ash rubbed her face on her sodden shoulder. "What lies ahead?"

"I think we need to make another crossing, but I can't read the water, it's so churned up by the weather. The wind will broadside us all the way over, and I can't see beyond the turn. I think the river might be turning due west . . ." Rys put her mouth to the speaking tube and shouted, "Status!"

Perhaps a voice shouted something in the confusion of sounds below.

"Hold her steady, Ash." Reeling with the boat's sway, Rys went to the doorway. "Mardi, get in here."

"Can't," she gasped.

"I'm going to tie down. You'll go right over the rail when we ram the shore."

"Tie down? Can't do that . . . Elbie's orders . . ." She crawled to her knees only to fall down again.

"Do I care about Elbie's orders? I have no time to argue with you!"

She reeled back to Ash's side. She could not hear the leadsmen any longer over the howling of the wind. The river swooped away to the left, and suddenly the bank loomed. No gentle beach here, sheltered by trees. This newly cut riverbed was all jagged edges and exposed rock. "Quarter speed!" Rys shouted. Someone seemed to have survived the maelstrom, for the boat slowed to a crawl. Ash leaned into the wheel, turning the wheel hard to starboard. The boat picked up speed as it escaped the current and came into the shelter of the leeward bank. Rys rather belatedly began ringing the collision warning. *Gods, I hope Ash can hold this boat together,* she thought.

The *Amina* rammed the bank.

❦   ❦   ❦

Entangled, she held Ash in her arms. Entangled, their lives, their pasts, their futures. Entangled in a groaning, screaming, howling present, in a wash of cold water, with the wind rushing in. "Gods," said Rys, in rage and gratitude. "Gods, we owe you for this."

She felt something shift beneath her: Ash's leg? She moved, and listened, and remembered that she was still pilot of this boat. She drew up her knees, and crawled to the doorway to look out. Mardi had disappeared. Below, two deckhands struggled up the steep riverbank, slipping and shouting in the mud, bearing ropes in their hands. The *Amina*'s paddle wheels churned, keeping her nose into the bank. Rys felt their vibration through the floor.

"To have my feet on solid ground," said Ash. She rubbed a shoulder.

Someone had struck the stove as they careened across the pilothouse; Rys did not think it had been her. She dragged herself to her feet. "Are you hurt?"

"Hard to tell," said Ash mildly.

Rys gave her a hand up. They both sat upon the

bench. Rys put her head into her hands. A hand pressed her shoulder. "Are you?" said Ash.

"No." Her head felt heavy in her hands, as though it would fall through the floor if she let go of it.

"Do you suppose we managed to dump Lord Diggen overboard?"

Rys uttered a hoarse, grieving caw, too bitter and harsh to be laughter. "Our luck," she said, gasping, "has not been that good. I do think we lost Mardi."

"Too bad. The lord we could have spared."

Suddenly, light flared. Someone had managed to get a flame in this downpour, and light one of the beacons. Ash shuddered in spasms, soaked to the skin, cold as ice. Rys, still reasonably dry within her oilskins, put her arms around her.

Ankle-deep in water, with sodden rolls floating past in a basketry lifeboat lined with a soggy napkin, Rys felt her own riverbanks give way before the flood. She pressed her face against Ash's wet, smoke-scented hair. Ash lifted her head, as if to ask something. Rys kissed her.

Ash's mouth was like ice. Her lips parted reflexively, as though she were starving. She said—something, and her hand came up, knocking Rys' hat into the water and pulling their bodies together, as if it was she who had been waiting, this very long time, and could not endure it any more.

Then there were voices, and Kiva frantically shouting Rys' name, and it was over.

❦ ❦ ❦

Now there were damages to be repaired, some so urgent they could not wait until morning, although the hull, at least, still seemed to be sound. Many of the passengers had been injured. No more disheveled and haggard and miserably cold than the rest of the crew, Rys went about the business of saving the boat and organizing succor for the injured and distraught.

Mardi had been dragged out of the water, half drowned, with a dislocated shoulder. Day was dawning beyond the storm clouds when Rys knelt at her side, where they had laid her out on the fine carpet of the passenger's salon, now a makeshift hospital. Rys had been through this before: the self-doubt, the recriminations, the obsessive counting of the dead. It was part of a pilot's job and would pass.

"I should have listened to you," said Mardi. All the icy water she had inhaled had made her hoarse.

"You're lucky. They never found the other two who went overboard."

"Some luck. Will the boat still float?"

"We'll see. We have to try for Port Falin. All these broken bones cannot heal straight without plastering, and your Lord Diggen did not see fit to kidnap a doctor. You'll have to lie still until then."

"Who's going to watch you—keep you out of trouble?"

"Somebody who doesn't get seasick, I hope. You get some rest if you can."

When Rys rose to her feet, Diggen Elbie stood there, white-faced. His shirt was crumpled and stained with purple. Rys had not seen him at all until now; he must have slept through the collision and only just awakened. "What have you done with my boat?" he cried.

Nothing she could have said seemed adequate. She walked up to him and hit him, hard, across the face, with her fingers curled into a fist. She found it hard to imagine that no one had ever hit him before, but he seemed stunned. She turned on her heel and walked away. Behind her there was an enraged bellow, but, when she turned, a half-dozen people held Diggen Elbie back. Most of them were members of his own household.

❦   ❦   ❦

Rys regretted a lot of things when she woke up, groaning, to someone pounding on her door: that she had not hung her wet uniform to dry by the stove, that she had not found some liniment with which to rub her stiff muscles, that she had not eaten anything since the day before, that she had not been able to even speak to Ash, though she had no idea what she would say. But she never regretted having slugged Diggen Elbie.

She had told them to wake her up if the storm looked to be clearing. Port Falin, the southernmost of Valeria's towns, lay a good two days' journey to the north. She ate a hasty supper, as the crew, many of whom had not yet slept that day, struggled in the water and the mud to rock the boat loose from her mooring. On the way to the pilothouse, she passed Ash's brother-son, happily engrossed in repairing a broken railing, his mouth full of nails, his shirt plastered to his shoulders by the fine rain that continued to fall. The load of wood had been transferred from the barge to the ship's hold, and the barge cut loose to drift downriver.

Lindy Airhome sat in the pilothouse, with a roaring fire in the stove and Kiva by his side, sharing a pot of tea. "I tried to come up and help you, when I realized the boat was in trouble," he said apologetically. He poured Rys a cup of tea.

"One of the passengers helped me steer. Have either one of you gotten any sleep?"

"Oh, yeah, yeah, a few winks, anyhow. Take a look at that river, isn't it something?"

They stood, gazing out at the unrecognizable expanse of water. Its banks and course had continued to change rapidly while Rys slept. "That's something, all right," said Kiva. "I met a pilot once who tied down to shore in a changing river. The river changed right out from under him and left his boat on dry ground, with the paddle wheels still turning. Some farmer turned the boat into a barn, and started farming the river bottom. Five years later, the river changed again, and the boat floated all the way to Maros, with chickens on the railings and a pig in the pilothouse."

"We'll need to continue to take soundings, until we start seeing some sightmarks again," said Rys.

"Has the river gotten shorter, or longer?"

"I have no idea. Maybe it doesn't even go past Port Falin anymore."

The mates glanced at each other, surprised. Not often did riverboat pilots get lost.

Rys spent the night alone in the pilothouse. She had not been left by herself since her abduction in Marlestown. She kept thinking she heard a step on the storm deck, but it was just something banging in the wind. The clouds began to break during the night, and the water level of the river, typically unpredictable, continued to fall. The next day, she sat on the bench, interpreting the river for Lindy Airhome and dozing during the few safe stretches. That night, she stood watch alone again, swilling tea and fighting sleep on her feet. Kiva came in often to check on her. "Couldn't you have that passenger come and steer for you again?" she asked.

"She's avoiding me," said Rys.

"What?"

"We're traveling countercurrent. The old unresolved pieces of the past tend to come back at you ..." She turned to Kiva. "You wouldn't understand: you're too young."

"The river," said Kiva, "has its mysteries."

Though day had not dawned, Kiva fetched Lindy out of his bed, and got a couple of the more burly crewmembers to escort Rys to her cabin. "You will go to bed. You're doing us no good here. We'll call out the leadsmen to read the bottom for us. And we won't trust the sightmarks even if we do see them. Get some sleep."

Rys was not halfway down the gangway when she heard the leadsmen's bell begin to ring. She shed her stinking uniform into a pile on her cabin floor and slept.

She awoke in the afternoon, to the singsong of the men's voices echoing and reechoing as they shouted the measurements from one deck to the next. Their voices had woven through her dreams, like ghostly guardians warning her of the dangers of the route she traveled: gravel beds, sandbars, and snags at every turn.

"No bottom!" hoarsely sang the leadsman. Like a

blind man feeling his way down the street with a cane, Lindy had found the channel once again. Groaning, Rys got out of bed.

They had crossed the border into Vateria while she slept. One more night she kept her desperate watch, until, a couple of hours before dawn, she brought the *Amina* safely into Port Falin.

Chapter 8: Ash

In the dead of night, the *Amina*'s whistle gave the thrice-thrice signal of a boat in need of aid. Ash awoke at the sound and went out to watch as the *Amina* wove among the obstacles of Port Falin: clustered fishing boats, moored to buoys in deep water, several short, ice-damaged docks, and a neat line of rowboats, bobbing on their tethers. The town of Falin lay in darkness, its high, steep roofs like sheets of black paper pressed against a spangled sky.

As the *Amina* drew near the landing, Rys sounded the thrice-thrice signal again, and bobbing lights began to appear: townsfolk called out of their beds by the racket, and dockworkers astonished by the early appearance of a riverboat from the south. They shouted up at the pilothouse as the *Amina* came sweetly in, scarcely touching the landing, but pausing there, perfectly suspended between river and land. Mooring cables snaked through the darkness.

"What is your emergency, then, if you have no plague?" shouted a portly man, his hair upended and the lantern light glimmering on his bald pate. "Your boat appears sound enough!"

Ash could hear only part of the reply from above, with the sound of the Amina's engines rattling and panting in her ears. "Bonesetter," she heard, and "Pilot's Guild." Whatever Rys said, some of the people below shrugged and went back to their beds. Others, gesturing disgust, tied down and secured the boat. In time a wagon rattled up, delivering a thin, frowning man with an absurd hat upon his head, shadowed by a youthful assistant heavily burdened by bags and basins.

Other passengers had joined Ash on the deck, wrapped in blankets or coats against the dead of night chill. "Why haven't we been locked in?" complained one woman. "They always lock us in when we come into port."

"You *want* to be locked in?" said another.

"That's just the way it's been done. Something must be wrong."

Ash glanced in some astonishment at the querulous woman, but others seemed to agree with her, and, lacking anyone else to blame, glared upward toward the pilot house.

"She punched Lord Diggen," one of them said. "Right in the face. I saw it happen—it was shocking."

"Wish I'd seen it!"

"Who does she think she is? And what would we do without the protection of a lord? Who will take care of us, up here in this wild land?"

"What, are you an addlepate? What did Lord Diggen do so far to protect us on this journey?"

"He is our natural lord. Even the gods have their lords, to whom they bow. Are we better than gods?"

Ash was relieved when the passengers succumbed to curiosity and drifted indoors to watch the bonesetter at his work. She rested her elbows upon the rail, welcoming renewed silence. The stars faded in the east. The crisp air still smelled of winter's sweet frost and woodsmoke. Sounds rang in her ears, sharp and honed by the cold. The *Amina*'s engines fell silent, but Ash never heard the heaving sigh as her head of steam was released. In the still dawn air, the smoke from the furnaces settled around the boat in a haze.

The icebreak flags were still flying in Port Falin. Wood barges crowded every sheltered cove, shacks leaking smoke from tin chimneys as the bargefolk waited for calm weather before entrusting their loads of precious woods to the river. The wood itself had already traveled far, but its journey would not end until it was halfway across the world.

The lightening sky picked out the wide, straight roads of Falintown, and threw the high rooflines into sharp relief against the plain beyond. Ash saw few trees. The forest, if there had ever been one, had long since been cleared for farming. The land had been divided into carefully measured squares, walled in by the stones cleared from the fields, cultivated by hangheaded plow horses and incurious plow jacks, who knew the edges of their exhausted land without even having to look.

Ika lay not two days' journey to the west. Ash would never forget what it was like.

Naiman knew what he wanted when he came here. He had not reckoned on the cowardice of a beaten people. He had not expected their immunity to the power of his poetry. He had never considered that the local lord might think nothing of killing his own tenants, when homeless beggars crowding every street corner would murder each other for possession of the newly vacant land. Ash—Cydna then—had understood Vateria far better than Naiman because he only imagined that he knew what farming was like. He thought that the fact that the farmers in Faerd owned their land and the farmers of Vateria did not would make no difference at all. Ash knew it would make all the difference in the world.

🦂 🦂 🦂

"Eh, this is a depressing place," Naiman said, when Cydna came in with a cup of tea for his headache. He stood at a barren, dirt-clouded window, watching the reapers stride steadily through a field of ripe grain, the proud stands falling around them. The mid-morning sky glared like copper in the sun. The air within the farm house was close, dusty with autumn, tainted by the faint scent of something rotting somewhere. Cydna had gone through enormous effort to bring Naiman the cup of tea. The cup had been dirty, the teapot half full of moldy, stinking dregs. There had been no water in the house, or soap, or tea. The steaming cup she handed him was, in fact, a kind of miracle, but he sipped it without thanking her. She did not expect thanks.

She sat on the edge of an uncomfortable, half broken chair. Her hands itched for a scythe, but she had not been invited to help with the harvest. Her menstrual period had started. Although she'd had no reason to think she might be pregnant, now she felt weary, empty with lost opportunity. "Then let us leave," she said. "I do not like this place."

"Ah, Cyd, I thought you'd love it here. Remind you of home."

"This? Is this how you think all farmers live?"

"Poor people," he said charitably. "They sow in the dust and water the crop with their tears."

"They are poor because they have impoverished the land."

"The farmers themselves wear the yoke of slavery. They do what they must to deliver the lord's tithe and still have something for their own children to eat."

"They do what they must," she said softly, "because they do not care enough to do what they should. What makes you think that people like this will have the spine to stand up to their governing lord?"

"Cyd, I am surprised at you."

"They are a discouraged people!"

"Then we must give them courage! Or are you discouraged, too, my brave Cydna?" Naiman set his precious cup of tea onto the window ledge; he could not have drunk even half of it. Cydna resisted an impulse to snatch up the cup and throw its contents at him. He rested a hand upon her shoulder and gazed down at her, his eyes overflowing with accusatory love. "Together we agreed to come here. The people of Faerd settled for too little in the end. The people of Vateria— they will show what a true revolution is all about."

"My mother always taught me never to waste my seed. Wait, she said, until the time is right. You cannot make the spring come early by planting too early. Instead, you will waste your seedcorn and get no harvest at all."

"We agreed together," he said. He had not heard a single word she said.

He had gotten too good, over the years, at getting people to do what he wanted, her as much as anyone. But she had gotten too good at seeing into his heart. It made her cruel, as though in punishing him for his own shallow self-centeredness, she could somehow eliminate her own. Looking at Naiman, she saw a man accustomed to attention, to the adulation of crowds, to the heady momentum of a movement whose time had come. But the time had passed.

Yes, the Poet's Revolution had changed Faerd, though not in the exact way Naiman had wanted. Faerd still had a king, but Anselm ruled over a people who were empowered by law to resist him. This compromise satisfied the farmers, but Naiman called them cowards, for giving up the fight. The farmers wanted to raise their children and bring in their crops, and the folk of the cities wanted to go back to their jobs. Naiman had never planted or harvested, never worked for more than two days at anything. He could not understand.

Peace made him restless, and he decided to export his movement to Faerd. He could not do it without Cydna. "You wanted this, too," he said again. "We agreed together."

"You talked," Cydna said. "You talked until I was too tired to listen anymore. Is that agreement?"

She pitied him then, for she saw the fear that came before his anger. He knew that he needed her. He knew that it was as much the promise of her power as the impact of his rhetoric which brought the people out to listen to him. Now he would accuse her of disloyalty. He would speak glowingly of the new world. She had heard it a hundred times. She rose abruptly to her feet and stalked away. She was tired: tired of him, tired of having no home, tired of the barren life they led. She was tired of waiting until next year, or the year after that, for her own life to begin. His words buzzed in her ears, like a beehive.

He followed her and put his arms around her, so she

could not walk away again. "It will be different in Ika. Thousands of people are coming."

"And if they do not, if it is only hundreds, or a handful, what will you say? That it will be different next time? What will it take to convince you that Vateria is not ready for change?"

"I know it will be thousands?"

"And if it is not."

"Then, yes, I will agree."

"We will return to Faerd."

"Yes, we will return to Faerd."

❦   ❦   ❦

As Ash stood on the deck of the steamboat, the sun had risen, round and bright and pale. The water shimmered with a restless wind. A handful of people had come from town to stand on the landing and stare at the *Amina:* merchants waiting for the mud clerk, a man who wanted to travel south, and a curious few who hung about idly, smoking pipes and speculating to each other about the nature of this riverboat's journey. The sun had revealed a bleak town, with gray, ragged streets, boarded windows, and an occasional trudging citizen, shoulders bowed. The forbidding walls of the brick buildings were streaked with black.

Macy joined Ash at the rail, and offered her some hard bread and cheese that she had wrapped in a napkin. Grelling, the impeccable steward, had seen his cooking supplies fouled by the flood of water which washed through the boat. The disaster seemed to have broken his spirit, and the passengers had been forced to ransack the boat's pantries when they were hungry.

"There is nothing to prevent us from leaving the boat," said Macy in some amusement. "Look: there is the landing stage. Not one person has walked down it."

"How would any of us get back home again? The *Amina* is the only boat this port will see for at least two more weeks. Do you want to try walking back to Faerd? It is all wilderness between here and there, and then you would have to find a way across the river."

"No, thank you. But how will we get home again without Lord Diggen's people to act as crew? Who will run the boat?"

"Rys will get us home." The hard bread had gotten soggy in the storm, and the cheese threatened to go rancid. Ash ate without complaint; she had gone hungry too often lately.

"I admit, she is something, that pilot."

Ash's hand clenched the railing too tightly. She had to breathe deeply to get her grip to release. "Some of the other passengers talked about her earlier. After what she has been through to keep us alive, they actually condemn her for standing up to that ass of a nobleman."

Macy snorted. "People! She is an old friend of yours from before, is she?"

"For years . . . until we had a stupid disagreement and I decided the friendship was over. Yet, now that chance has brought us together again, it is as if we were never separated. If anything, she is more . . ." Ash hesitated. "Naiman always was a barrier between us, though I never realized it as clearly as she. Now he is long gone."

Macy had sold all of her dancing jacks to the *Amina*'s crew and passengers. Only one remained, a grieving and courageous fellow with a rose in one hand, which Macy carried with her, dancing alone from her sagging, nearly empty pack. He swung sleepily from his tether now, back and forth, with the motion of the water.

Ash said, "Does it seem strange to you that Rys has not come down from the pilothouse to eject that man and his minions from the boat, if nothing else? Did you notice that the engineer never let the steam out of the *Amina*'s boilers? Port Falin has a militia, and I'll wager Rys is standing by to jump port, just in case they decide to inspect the boat. She's doing it because she thinks it is possible they are still looking for me here: King Bartyn is a tenacious man."

Macy said, "You must count yourself privileged to have her as a friend."

"I am afraid of her," said Ash.

Macy raised an eyebrow. "Of her?"

"Of myself, then." Ash, who had endured without complaint the predawn chill, found herself shivering now that the day began to warm. "My grandfather told me that back when steamboats were a new thing, the boats were full traveling south, but empty coming north. It was bad luck to travel countercurrent, people believed, because to travel in that direction was to travel against time. To this day, the riverboaters make charms and rituals to ward away danger when they are traveling northward."

"Hm," said Macy. Her stubby, clever fingers drummed upon the railing.

"I am wishing I could have set some wards."

Macy shrugged. "You can run, and the past will hunt you down. Or you can step forward, and the past will embrace you. It is your choice." She pointed at the foot of the landing stage where Ursul now stood, engaged in conversation with one of the loitering merchants. A woman with a basket full of eggs stepped eagerly forward. "Perhaps we shall have some breakfast after all."

Soon after the grim man in the peculiar hat had left the boat, the embarkation bell began to ring. Lord Diggen's leaderless people stood by as the other crewmembers briskly loosed the mooring lines and raised the landing stage. Ursul came rushing out, shouting, but it was too late to stop Rys from backing the *Amina* expertly out of dock. Ursul's frantic rush for the pilothouse petered out in the passenger's gallery. She watched the shoreline's steady retreat, bleakly at first, but then with a wry smile as Rys turned the boat's nose into the current.

"She is not turning southward," said Macy, astonished.

The smell of frying bacon wafted up from the kitchen. Ash leaned on the rail, smiling as crookedly as Ursul at the pilot's constancy. "No, of course not. She has passengers to deliver."

Port Falin slipped into the distance. Ash watched, remembering.

By the time they reached Ika, a hundred or more
young farmers, cajoled away from the harvest by the
hypnotic power of Naiman's voice, had joined their deliberate inland progress. Naiman, mounted on an old
nag, rode at the head of the procession like the disrep-
utable leader of an ill-planned migration. During all
the years in Faerd, Cydna had never seen anything like
the fervor of these hope-starved people. Naiman they
followed like sheep their shepherd. But Cydna they
gazed upon from a distance, in meek adulation, as
though she were a god.

"They are too young," she said to Naiman as they
lay together in a makeshift tent, constructed out of
poles and ragged blanket, with the stars shining
through the holes in the ripped wool. "Look at them.
Not one is twenty years old."

"Is this a complaint, my beloved, or an idle observa-
tion?" Naiman seemed more than half irritated with
her. He traveled in an ecstasy of confidence, and who
could blame him for becoming tired of the doubts with
which she assaulted him, day after day? "They are not
too young to resist living their lives without hope.
They are not too young to step forward bravely into the
future—"

"They are young enough to fall victim to misguided
enthusiasms. They are young enough to blindly put
their lives into the hands of their heroes."

"What has happened to you!" Naiman cried.
"Cydna, listen to yourself! What has happened to
you?"

"Listen to your own self! Is your truth now the only
truth?"

She left the tent in a rage, and spent the night on a
chilly hillside, beneath a tree that had already divested
its withered leaves to put on instead a circlet of stars.
Her anger lapsed into sorrow, and her sorrow into silence. In that silence, her own, long-avoided truths
came and spoke to her.

She had saved Naiman's life once, by causing a

bridge to collapse. The memory of this act of destruction, which had harmed only the bridge, haunted her still. Ashland's first crop, many generations in the past, had been planted in the ashes of a forest fire that burned half of Northern Semel to the ground. Now these bright-eyed converts, these world changers, when they looked at Cydna they saw a destroyer: a sorceress who flung fire. They thought she would keep them safe.

She made sure they could see her, come dawn, sitting in forbidding silence on the hillside overlooking the encampment. When Naiman came to fetch her, she refused to speak to him. Everything she did damaged him. When she met his pleading with silence, it damaged him. When her obstinacy caused him to shout at her, it damaged him. When she rose up and turned her back upon the departing procession, it damaged him.

So it was not a hundred young farmers who marched with great bravado to the Ika fortress that day. It was less than fifty. The others had abandoned him because of the obdurate sorceress who turned away, grief stricken, as her man went out of sight beyond the curve of the hill.

Fifty and more lives she saved with only one betrayal. Afterward, she did not see how she could continue to live.

       ಕ್ಠ   ಕ್ಠ   ಕ್ಠ

In Vateria, they smoke their bacon with honey and do not use any peppercorns. They brush their bread with salt water as they put it into the oven. The large, spherical potatoes that they grow have golden flesh and taste like they should be baked in a pie. They dry plums, and salt them, and eat them like candy.

Ash sat in a corner, watching Kaz and Zara nibble at salted plums and make astonished faces. Ghost Dog ate scrambled eggs at Zara's feet. Ash ate bacon sandwiched between two slices of salt-crusted bread, and consumed this peasant fare in solitude, saving the dried plums in her pockets for later. A cheerful din rose, with an undercurrent of confused speculation. The five tribespeople were absent; Kaz and Zara had brought them food where they stood watch on deck.

The people who had been injured in the last storm, relieved to be able to move freely now that their splints had been replaced by plaster casts, all sat together in the hilarious camaraderie of survivors. Mardi, sitting among them, raised her voice in a rough hale. "Silence now! The pilot wishes to speak!"

Ash had not even seen Rys arrive. She stood at the doorway now, stiff-backed and square-shouldered, pale with exhaustion. "The Danae people who travel with us have asked me to set them down at Kerlin Point," said Rys. "We will land there at mid-afternoon. Elbie's crew will disembark there as well. In the morning, we turn southward for our return journey to Faerd. If anyone else wants to be set down in Vateria, speak now."

If Ash had not already determined which of the *Amina's* residents were allied with Lord Diggen, she could have identified them now by the expressions on their faces. Dismayed, they sought out each other's gazes.

Lord Diggen had scarcely left his cabin since Rys pummeled him after the storm. Ash, with her own heart suspended painfully between the lost past and the agonizing present, felt a sudden sympathy for those who had followed their lord into exile, only to have him disappear into a bottle of wine. Love and loyalty can sometimes leave one with only wrong choices.

The people in the salon continued their silence long after the pilot had left.

᭜   ᭜   ᭜

Bare-boned trees crowded the eastern shoreline, with rocky hills beyond: a largely uninhabited, if not unexplored wilderness. Here and there Ash spotted unmelted snow, lying in ragged patches on sheltered slopes. She saw hares, and deer, and an eagle perched over the water. On the western shore, trees grew only in woodlots. The stones had been harvested to build gray walls, which snaked across the countryside, defining the fields and roads and avenues, enclosing the neat apple orchards, and the meadows which the sheep had eaten down to bare soil. The small and largely abandoned tenancies which surrounded Falintown gave way to larger and more prosperous farms. The *Amina* passed a fortress which brooded forbiddingly over the winding river, its flags flying to show that the lord of the land was currently in residence. Children ran down to the shore to wave eagerly as the boat passed by.

Cultivated lands gave way to coarse woodlands, and a trade road built upon a dike of stone wound parallel to the river. A tributary joined the Madeena suddenly: rough and white as it plunged down from the mountains which loomed suddenly near. The river veered to the east. With the sun falling down from its peak in the sky, the Amina steamed up to a tumbledown landing, and settled there, in quiet water.

Earlier, someone in Lord Diggen's household had produced a map and, along with most of the other passengers, Ash had taken a look at it. Rys had been neither kind nor cruel to her erstwhile kidnappers, for although they would be forced to walk some distance cross country before they encountered a highway, she was not, in fact, setting them down so far from Tastuly, the king's city. By boat it might take many more days to follow the river's meanderings to Tastuly, but the road would take the travelers there quite directly.

The Danae had taken no interest in the map, which probably would have made no sense to them anyway. Theirs were the first feet to touch shore as soon as the landing stage had been lowered. They carried all their gear with them: bags and boxes, strung over their shoulders by straps and ropes. Not twenty paces from the landing, they set everything they owned down onto the ground, in an area sheltered by stones which had probably been used for generations as a campsite. Minter Hughson and two others set forth soon after. They stumbled over the rough ground, unaccustomed, perhaps, to walking at all, after so long aboard the boat. Kaz, Zara, and Ghost Dog also went ashore, to splash in a running stream, examine things they spotted on the ground, and engage in a rock throwing contest. Standing on the passenger deck, Ash watched them.

"Farmer Ash."

She turned to find the pilot leaning in a doorway, smiling so sweetly that Ash had crossed half the distance between them before she remembered her own awkwardness. They were alone on the deck. Lord Diggen's people were still packing, and the rest of the passengers crowded their way to shore, unable to resist the lure of solid ground.

"Congratulations," said Ash. "You took control of the boat so neatly that I scarcely realized it had happened."

Rys gave a graceful bow. "Thank you. I just wish this journey was over."

"How long have you been awake? You must be tired."

"I needed to stay at the helm, lest Elbie's people take it into their heads to try to regain control of the *Amina*. Farmer Ash, I ask you a favor."

"You need not be so polite," Ash said softly. "We are old friends."

Rys rested her face against the doorway, as though she suddenly no longer had the strength to hold up her head. "This is good to hear."

Embrace or be chased, Macy had said. Ash stepped forward and took Rys' hand. "What do you need?"

Rys' mouth gave a quirk, as though she would have smiled again if she were not so tired. "That you allow me to sleep in your bed."

"And what is wrong with your own bed, Madam Pilot?"

"Only that I am known to sleep there. I would stay awake until Elbie was safely on shore if I could. Best I can do is make it hard for him to find me."

"This place looks pretty convenient. Why would he try to take control of the boat again?"

"There is a reason or two. In any case, I avoid underestimating people who are more desperate than I."

"You look pretty desperate to me."

Rys took her cap off her head and laid it across her breast. "Then have pity on me."

In Ash's cabin, Rys stripped off her clothing, then looked rather surprised to find Ash standing there, with her arms full of stinking clothes that she had picked up from where Rys dropped them, willy-nilly. Ash pointed at the basin of water, which she had just filled with the pitcher. "Wash before you get in bed—those are clean sheets. Use soap."

"Heaven," said Rys, her eyes already vague with sleep. She walked dazedly over to the basin, and plunged her hands into the cold water. When Ash left the room, she did not seem to notice.

Macy had not yet succumbed to the general impulse to set foot on land, although Ash found her on the boiler deck, watching people on shore wander in the barren woods, like holidaymakers on a picnic. A mother cried out, shrill and anxious, and a child gave a heedless laugh. "I never would have imagined I'd travel so far," Macy said, with a shake of her head. "Never had the itchy foot. I've never seen trees like that before, with the bark peeling off of them. And the stones are almost black. What a grim house those stones would build! Look at that." One of the passengers bent to fill his palm with white. Playful, he sent snow flying through the air. "The trees are blooming in Fortune, but here there's still snow on the ground. It gives the heart a queer feeling, sort of like seasickness."

The Danae people had gathered firewood, and now smoke trailed from the center of their circle. They sat very still, like wild animals do when they first come out of hibernation. "Where did Kaz and Zara go?"

"Off that way. I'm half afraid to put my feet on foreign ground. You must think me a silly old woman."

"Not as silly as I, for feeling anxious because those two are out of sight, after they've taken care of themselves for six years."

Macy turned her head and raised her eyebrows at the sight of the pilot's clothing bundled up in Ash's arms.

Ash said, "Rys is sleeping in my cabin—would you keep an eye on it for a while? Lord Diggen's people may try to recapture the boat, which they can't do without recapturing her."

"Another thing that gives the heart a queer feeling, that invisible war between her and the queen's cousin. Do you think he's really been defeated?"

"By his own self, maybe."

Ash heated a vat of water and washed Rys' clothes down in the galley, where the passengers, desperate for clean linens, had set up a makeshift laundry. The guild pin she polished, using salt and vinegar from the pantry, as she let Rys' smallclothes soak in soapy water that she kept hot on the stove. By the time she climbed to the passenger deck with her arms full of wet laundry, most of the explorers had come back on board, bearing souvenirs of their expedition: early blooming flowers, going limp in their hot fingers; speckled, water-rounded stones; pieces of bark; and even a dead beetle. Exclaiming with wonder, they compared their finds as though they were nuggets of gold.

Macy sat in the passenger's salon, her deck of cards dealt out among several imaginary players, muttering to herself as she played each hand in turn. "How do you keep from cheating?" Ash asked, but Macy, frowning with concentration, did not reply. The winged, four-footed clockwork toy stood at her feet. Ash had not even realized she had brought it with her. Surely the two drums had taken up all the room in the pack.

Ash hung the laundry in her cabin. Rys, unconscious in the bed, with her wet hair beginning to dry in a tangle upon the pillow, did not move as Ash built up the fire in the stove. The cool morning had given way to a chilly afternoon, and now, with the sun dropping toward sunset, there was the promise of frost.

She heard voices and the sound of several doors opening and closing. She opened her own cabin door to look out. Lord Diggen had emerged from behind the locked and guarded door of his stateroom, and, hearing his voice, all of his followers had emerged, looking at each other as though surprised to find all of them gathered in the same place. Some had exchanged their ragged trousers and oil-stained shirts for lawn blouses and jackets of velveteen, while others had donned the more sturdy cotton and leather clothing of yard servants and armsmen. One by one, they doffed their hats and bowed deeply. Lord Diggen passed among them like a prince awakened from enchantment. Ursul walked by his side, her hair floating about her face like a cloud. She wore leather riding gear, with a jeweled horn slung over her shoulder. A gold ring glinted on every finger.

Ash gawked like a peasant. Even Macy glanced up from her sprawling card game, wild-eyed as a fortune teller coming out of a trance.

"Where is Hughson?" asked Lord Diggen, as two of the servants rushed off in search of refreshments for his lordship.

"He's seeking transport, my lord. That pilot has landed us at the most godsforsaken corner of the world."

"We must be in Vateria, then," said Lord Diggen with harsh humor. "Is there a map?"

Though the sun had not set, several lamps were lit, lest his lordship strain his eyes poring over the small print of the map. He studied it long, sitting back with a sigh only when a pot of tea was brought. Ash walked quietly over to Macy's table, gathered up the cards, and began to shuffle.

"Nay, not so," he said, in response to another tentative attempt to cast the blame for their predicament upon the boat's pilot. Those who had held him back three days before, thus allowing Rys, with a single blow, to gain control of the boat, seemed to sigh with relief. Lord Diggen leaned over the map. "See here, the most direct route to Tastuly. Yes, the boat would take us there in greater comfort, but we have not enough wood to bring us that far in any case. Is that not true?"

"Yes, my lord," said Ursul, sipping delicately from her teacup.

"Well, then. As soon as Hughson returns, we shall take our leave of this old tub."

Ash began to deal the cards. She and Macy played several games of Three-Ten as the noble lord and his minions planned the remainder of their journey.

It was almost dark when Minter Hughson arrived, driving a weatherbeaten wagon sagging on its springs, pulled by two mismatched, broken-down horses. Lord Diggen's followers examined this conveyance in dismay. Most, if not all of them, would be traveling on foot. Those horses did not look as if they could pull the wagon as far as they needed to go across country even if it were empty, much less laden with all the baggage the lord's followers had managed to bring with them from Seven Bells City.

A campfire burned on shore. With Macy once again grumbling over a card game near the cabin where Rys slept, and no sign that there was even a chance of supper, Ash disembarked. She had grown so accustomed to the unsteady, rhythmic rocking of the boat, that it was the ground she could not predict: hard and sudden it felt underfoot, alien in its permanence.

The voices of the aboriginal people carried clearly through the crisp air. Peering through the shadows, Ash sighed with relief as she spotted first Kaz and then Zara, squatting around the fire with the others, their faces intent and focused as they listened to one of the others speak. Their drums sat beyond them, out of reach of the fire's heat. Spitted rabbits hung over the flames, and a pot bubbled, its contents thick as porridge. In a few hours, while the boat's passengers complained about their hunger, these people had found the fixings for a complete meal in this barren wood. Ash spoke, and stepped forward into the firelight. Heads turned.

Kaz spoke a few stumbling words in a language Ash did not understand. One of the Danae rose to his feet: an older man, wind weathered like stone. "We welcome you, aunt of Kaz."

Ash bowed awkwardly and offered the salted plums from her pocket, which were accepted politely.

"They showed us how to make snares and dig for *ankhu* roots," said Kaz.

Ash bowed again. "Thank you for teaching my children." Ghost Dog lay beside Zara, his gray fur glowing in the fire. He gazed at Ash, and then looked away, as though she were of no importance. The one who had been talking began to speak again, and Kaz whispered that she was telling a story, but he couldn't understand most of it.

"We are going to play the drums and sing after we eat," he said, when the story was finished, and one of the people stood up to spice the thick contents of the pot with herbs from a pouch. "We are all going our separate ways tomorrow."

"How far is their home from here?"

"Five days' journey. They live in a place with no soul, where crops will not grow and rocks roll across the ground under their own power. They make their camps on bare stone, and their children go hungry. That is why they went to Faerd to see the queen."

"The Queen of Faerd cannot make crops grow in stone. Why do they not move to another place, where crops will grow?"

At this question, the people murmured and made angry gestures. Kaz said, "Over a generation ago, they were driven away from the land of their ancestors by a man who cut down all the trees and brought in herds of cattle. They have waited patiently for the spirits of the land to drive him out so they could return, but when the cattle all died, he brought in sheep, and when the sheep all died, he brought in homesteaders. Now the homesteaders are making the land tired, and the Sky People are afraid the soul of the land will be dead before the homesteaders give up and move away, and nothing will be left for them."

"They did not go to their own king for help?"

"The man who drove them from their land, he acts on King Bartyn's behalf. That is why they went to the Queen of Faerd. I think ... they do not understand very much about the world. They do not understand about countries, and borders, and such. Queen Lynthe told them she was very sorry she could not help them, and they stayed at her house all winter. That is why they are so fat."

"They do not look very fat."

Kaz shrugged. "I guess their people are much thinner."

"I'm sorry to hear that the Danae have had such bad luck. What are they going to do now?"

"There is nothing left to do but fight," said Kaz. "But they are tired, too, and their magic is tired, and they are quite certain they cannot win."

"Is there another place they could go?"

"Would you leave Ashland?"

"Well—no."

"They are like you. They will die on their land, if they cannot live there."

Kaz and Zara looked somber, but the others appeared exalted at the idea of returning to their homeland, regardless of the cost. Ash passed more plums and they ate, grinning, spitting their pits into the fire. Soon the meal was ready. Unable to refuse food without discourtesy, Ash ate only a few mouthfuls, sharing Kaz' spoon, since she had not brought her own.

"Time for drums," said one man, when the pot had been scraped clean, and the last bits of flesh had been sucked from the rabbits' bones.

Ash got up, wiping greasy fingers on her pants legs. "I have an obligation to return to the boat. I am so sorry I cannot stay."

Soon after she had boarded the boat, she heard the sound of the drums. She stood at the rail, listening, and thinking about death.

🍂 🍂 🍂

Past walled fields where cattle grazed on the stubble of harvested grain, beneath a sky that had turned from blue to iron gray, shivering in a cold wind that suddenly tasted of winter, Cydna walked in the trampled wake of those who had gone before her. Naiman had thrown her things onto the ground and left them to be trampled, though not one person, not even a horse, had dared to step on them. Cydna had left the pathetic pile lying there: everything she owned was so old and worn and travel stained, it was not worth the effort of picking it up. All she carried with her were a single blanket tied into a roll and her satchel. Her burdens were not heavy; it was something else which weighed her down, so she could not have caught up with Naiman had she wanted to.

Sadness, dread, her helplessness before the horrendous rolling boulder of destiny, self-blame. They weighed down her feet like clay mud which accumulated until she could scarcely lift one foot and place it in front of the other. The sun set behind the clouds, the gray sky turned black, and she walked on in darkness unbroken by moon or starlight.

As she walked, she remembered:

She remembered a farm girl with a basket full of potatoes, stricken before the vision of a slender man, on fire in the bright light of spring's new sun. His words were fire, his hand left burning afterimages as they gestured through the air. *He will,* the farm girl thought, *be mine.*

She remembered Grandfather Ash, gazing at her steadily from his seat beside the fireplace. "Think long and hard. Every decision you make, you get the rewards. And sometimes you pay the cost, year after year, long after you have forgotten why you decided as you did, long after you have ceased to be the person who made the decision, still you pay, long after the rewards have turned to ashes."

"There is nothing else like him in all the world, and he will be mine."

"All Ashlanders are hardheaded fools," said Grandfather Ash petulantly. "You have not heard a word I said."

"I heard, Grandfather. It just makes no difference to me."

She remembered standing at Naiman's right hand, as she had stood for days, with a jug of cool water, ready to fill his cup when he began to grow hoarse with speaking. The flow of his words washed over her like a flooding river, carrying her away to a new world, a land without borders, inhabited by people without boundaries, a generous land. He turned to her, his cup empty, leaving the gathered crowd breathless, eager for the next word. She poured from the jug, as she had done a hundred times. But this time he saw her, the molten gold of her heart blazing out at him over the rounded belly of the heavy jug.

She remembered the first time they lay together, in a filthy room on a broken bed, with the king's militia seeking him in the next county, and none of it mattered, none of it at all.

She remember Rys, sunburnt, leaning on the wheel, her dark eyes cool within the blaze of her skin. "Every time I see you," she said, "it seems there is less of you. How long will it be before there is nothing left?"

A thing cannot start without also beginning its ending. Ashes are the past, and ashes are the future. It takes an act of cold courage to plant another seed in the face of such knowledge.

Day had not dawned when Cydna found him, guarded three deep by bared blades. She walked between those honed edges, feeling them cut strands of the homely wool in which she was wrapped. But the guards continued to stare outward, unable, in their rigid discipline, to see the one that walked among them, as reduced and without substance as a shred of mist.

She walked among the dead. They had been gathered together so they could be better protected against those who wanted to claim them: the lovers and mothers who must have wailed and screamed earlier, but who now huddled upon the ground, exhausted by grief. The dead lay with their faces staring at the sky, where the faintest of dawning light outlined their features. Astonishing, that they could lie in such peace, with their bodies so broken and bloodied.

Cydna stepped among them, searching their faces, careful not to disturb their rest. She almost passed Naiman by, not recognizing him, but something about the shape of the shoulder drew her down, to dab at his filthy face with her kerchief. The ground was sticky here. She still had a little water in her travel bottle; she wet her kerchief and used it to wipe his face clean. He lay still, uncomplaining under this attention. For once, he had nothing more important to do.

"Now tell me the truth," she said. "Was this the end you wanted? Is this the bright vision you saw, that burned you like fire on the poet's corner in Fortune? Are you at peace now?"

But he had left her, in the end, with their love and their hate all unresolved, and her questions unanswered. Ashes he had given her, and ashes she gave him in return, sprinkling them upon his body in the cold light of dawning day, one pinch at a time, out of the wooden box in her satchel.

She did not know that her time of grieving was only beginning.

🍀   🍀   🍀

By lamplight, Ash played a solitary game of cards in the passenger's salon. The drums still played on the river's edge, but all the passengers, with nothing to eat and a new journey awaiting them with tomorrow's dawn, had gone early to bed. Macy also had gone to bed, leaving the clockwork toy standing like a sentinel.

There were a dozen empty cabins on this boat where Ash could have slept. She waited until a door opened softly and Rys said, "Come in here."

It had gotten very cold as the night progressed, but Ash had kept watch over the stove in the cabin, and it was warm in there, and redolent with the scent of drying wool.

Rys wore one of the soft, carefully made woolen undershirts that Ash had admired earlier as she washed them. The soft cloth molded itself to shoulders squared by muscle from all the long years of wrestling with the helms of riverboats. Rys' hair tangled around her face. It was her uniform that made her so upright. Without it, there was a gentleness in her, a rarely seen thing that Ash had long relished and remembered.

"I took your bed," Rys said, as though surprised at herself.

"I could have found another."

Rys gestured vaguely, encompassing the laundry hanging about the room. "Thank you."

"I left you with nothing to wear."

"Cydna—Ash—I think I am not as disciplined as I used to be, or maybe I am just worn out. I'm sorry if I . . ."

Ash set the lamp down, and the cards. "How long have you . . . been so disciplined?"

"As long as I've known you." Rys sat on the edge of the bunk. "Listen, it doesn't matter. I am your friend, first."

"Nine years you watched me breathe my every breath for Naiman? And never said a word? No wonder you lost your patience in the end!"

"I know I could outlast him," Rys said.

Ash looked up at her, asking herself what she had done to earn such extraordinary constancy. Rys took in her breath, and turned her gaze away.

"What do you see?" Ash said.

"That if I stand up right now, you will come to me."

But Rys did not stand up, and Ash could not seem to move without that small invitation. Rys spoke after a moment, though she still seemed unable to look Ash in the eyes. "Ten years ago, I might have still believed my heart's desire could come so cheaply. Ten years ago, I still would have been dreaming that somehow I would rescue you from grave danger, and you would fall in love with me at last, and come keep house for me in Marlestown . . ."

Ash made a sound like laughter, but laughter never hurt like this.

"It *is* ridiculous," Rys said heavily. "But after twenty years of loving you, how can I settle for being a thing that happens accidentally?" She looked directly at Ash then. "You have been alone for ten years, and this journey is awakening your heart. Suddenly I kissed you in the middle of a shipwreck, and you realized you were lonely. But I have not been waiting all these years just to assuage one night's hunger. I want to be chosen. I want you to consider, and know the cost, and make a choice that you will not unmake again."

The years had harrowed Rys, but the things Ash had admired in her in the past had only become finer with age: the vision that she turned upon herself more ruthlessly than anyone, the unshakable integrity, the wry humor. And, of course, that unflinching grasp on the hot coal of truth. Ash said, "I can't make a choice like that tonight."

"Neither can I." Rys looked away again. "Now that I have cut my throat, let's see if I can also stab myself in the heart. Six years ago, I rescued a shopkeeper named Margo from grave danger, and she saved my life in return, and now she keeps house for me in Marlestown. I never meant to hide this from you, Ash; we have scarcely had time to talk at all."

Ash sat down in the armchair. She could not bring herself to laugh again. "I'm glad."

Rys covered her eyes with a hand as though to blind her sight. "You lie!"

Indeed, if there ever was an hour that Ash could have hidden her face from the Pilot's Sight, this was the hour she would have chosen. "What am I to say? That I feel like a fool? That I hate your Margo, whom I haven't even met?"

"Gods of the River, if I had known you were alive—"

"What? You would have come to Ashland and become a farmer's wife? I belong in Ashland, and you belong on the river. Changeable and restless though the river may be, he will never go by my door!"

Rys' face was stark in the firelight. "It does seem unlikely."

Ash started to rise, and then sat down again. Throughout her long watch she had never once felt her weariness, but now she felt exhausted and emptied. She had been awake, she remembered, since long before dawn.

Rys stood up and knelt at Ash's feet. "Come and sleep."

"I don't think—"

"I would rather sleep with you than with despair."

It seemed like little enough to ask. They lay down together in the narrow bunk. After ten years of sleeping alone, Ash felt crowded and restless. Then Rys put her arm around her, and there began to be a warmth. Rys said, "I have to tell you, I cannot seem to entirely give up hope." Her voice was a murmur, but the wry humor had returned.

Between one breath and the next, Ash fell asleep.

❧ ❧ ❧

For many years after King Anselm was crowned, he and King Bartyn had feuded over boundaries and transportation rights before finally establishing a tentative treaty. The fragile peace between Vateria and Faerd was only a few years old when the Poet's Revolution began in Faerd. Never suspecting that this was one battle he could not win by force of arms, King Anselm had seemed at first to welcome the uprising. He called his army out of idleness and rode before them, magnificent and dashing upon a white horse. He conferred with his generals, and there was a great, self-important rushing back and forth of messengers bearing his proud banner.

But this was no pitched battle between magnificent armies, punctuated by ritual parleys and private feuds, with festival tents and the snap and crackle of banners carried by the cavalry. Here the enemy, which neither knew nor cared about archaic chivalries, appeared and disappeared like smoke. The true battle was not a matter of muskets and swords, but of ideas. It was the end of an age, and even a king could not stop the incoming tide of history.

King Bartyn, watching with not so secret glee the travails of his rival king, with whom he had more in common that he cared to admit, had plenty of opportunity to learn from Anselm's many, devastating mistakes. When Naiman came to Vateria, King Bartyn did not gather his forces, call together his generals, and confer at length about what to do. He immediately called forth a small, elite division, generaled by an ambitious and ruthless noble lord, and ordered the peasants slaughtered. Who owns nothing is nothing in Vateria.

He never thought it would be as easy to kill their leader, Naiman the Poet, who with the help of his sorcerous lover had for nine years easily evaded King Anselm's increasingly desperate attempts on his life. King Bartyn sent his own diviners, mages and occultists: an army of them, to capture if not kill the great sorceress. But he feared that even these would not be enough to overcome Cydna, whose fame preceded her like a long shadow in the setting sun.

He killed Naiman and killed the insurrection. The time had not yet come for the new age to arrive in Vateria, as Cydna had known and Naiman refused to hear. The mark of a great leader is the ability to know which battles can be won. In Faerd, Naiman became a martyr. In Vateria, he was not remembered fondly.

The practitioners of secret arts that Bartyn called together never found the great sorceress they sought. They were not looking for a plain, unassuming, grief-stricken woman, who stepped into roadside ditches to let their proud horses pass by. They did stop and search her once, but the only thing of interest that she carried was a plain wooden box full of ashes. It was the ashes of her dead children, she told them. She seemed half crazed, and they let her go.

❦   ❦   ❦

Sometime during the night, the drums abruptly and suddenly fell silent.

Chapter 9: Ghost Dog

They play the drums. The sun has set. In darkness they play. In shadows and darkness they play the drums.

Sparks from the fire! Like birds they rise. The heat of fire, the cold of the night.

They sing:

> *Aha, aha!*
> *I know the truth.*
> *I know what things are*
> *At their secret heart.*

They sing:

> *My pain is fire*
> *My pain is hunger*
> *My pain is my children*
> *Dying in my arms.*

They sing:

> *Tomorrow I set forth*
> *Tomorrow I go out*
> *Tomorrow I journey*
> *To the home of my soul.*

They dance, left and right. They circle around. The sparks fly up. The night claps its hands. The night wraps around them, like a blanket a child. They sing: Aha, aha! The birds cry out. The night is silver. Their breath is clouds. They cry: Tomorrow! Their whistles blow and rattles shake. The tassels fly upon their sleeves. They spin, and spin, and spin again.

They beat the drums. They make the thunder. They are the heartbeat. They know the truth.

They sing: Aha, aha!

The dog lifts his head. His eyes are gold ingot. His feet are the wind. He opens his mouth and sings in the silence. He sings in the heartbeat. He sings in the thunder. He sings:

> *Aha, aha!*
> *I know the truth!*
> *I know what I am*
> *In my secret heart*
>
> *I am a king.*

Chapter 10: Rys

The night had fallen silent. Rys lay awake with her love in her arms. She held her love in her arms, like a beacon, a sightmark, a ripple in the water, showing her the channel. Home port disappeared behind her, ungrieved.

She rose before first light, and dressed in stiffened clothing that smelled of river water and flower-scented soap. She dragged Ash's comb through the tangle of her hair, and tied it at her neck with a thong. She pinned her guild pin upon her shoulder. She put on her cap, and built up the fire in the stove so that Ash would not be chilled in the crisp predawn. Her stomach rumbled. She could ignore her own hunger, but the children on board the boat needed to eat. Half her crew would be disembarking today. There was much to consider, many problems to solve.

At the cabin door she turned and went back to Ash, to the muscled square warmth of her, the weathered face and the squint lines radiating across her cheeks. She looked down at her. "I swear to you, the day will come," she said.

She went out, closing the door softly.

The frigid night had clothed the *Amina* with ice. Alone in the silent darkness, Rys walked the length and breadth of the boat, surveying the condition of the engines, the fuel supply, the chaotic galley, the storm damage, neglect, and disrepair which had begun to make headway since the collision. Ice crunched underfoot; she climbed stairs cautiously.

From the pilothouse she watched day dawn. Smoke trailed from the campsite on shore, and voices murmured on the still morning air. The *Amina* tugged at her tethers as though impatient to be on her way. The two horses lay like slumped boulders among the stones. As the sun rose, the ice began to glimmer. One of Elbie's servants shuffled down the landing stage, to mumble over the sleepy horses and bring them grain and hay.

Hearing voices below, Rys went down to the passenger deck. The lord's followers had begun to pile baggage outside the cabin doors. Rys collared a member of the *Amina*'s crew and sent him to awaken the others. As they appeared, she put them to work, loading baggage into Elbie's wagon and preparing the boat for embarkation. The clamor of voices rose to an anxious din. The noble lord's followers had packed their jewelry and fine furs away in their trunks. Leather-dressed, Ursul walked among them, a threat lurking behind her smile.

It must have taken an entire day just to get the grease out from under her fingernails. She stepped up to Rys, baring her teeth.

"Good day," said Rys. A servant pushed past, carrying a pot of tea. "This is the day you begin your new life."

"This is the day you can flee back to safety."

Rys smiled, thinking of Ash. "I do not think so. But it is kind of you to wish me well, madam."

"And why should I not? You have performed your duties adequately. I am sure my lord will reward you."

"I trust he knows better than to attempt such a thing. Do you anticipate a warm reception at the court of King Bartyn?"

"Oh, I think his highness will be more than delighted to see his lordship. Some of the great houses stand completely vacant since the plague, without even a by-blow to carry on the family name or manage the family lands. I think King Bartyn will find a place for a man of Lord Diggen's talents."

"And what about you, madam? Will there be a place for you?"

"My place is with my lord. Certainly, there is no

longer a place for me in Faerd." She bared her teeth again. "Perhaps we will meet again someday, Madam Pilot."

Rys bowed from the waist, intending no mockery, but when she straightened, only Ursul's scent lingered. At the thought that the effects of this journey would continue to be felt in Elbie's household for many years to come, Rys smiled to herself. She did indeed hope to see Ursul again. It would be very instructive.

The rising sun had melted the frost when the lord's household somberly disembarked. Travel trunks and carpetbags filled the wagon. Passengers gathered at the rail, shouting a confusion of farewells and curses. The dark figures at the smoking campfire on shore stood up to watch as the horses strained in the traces, and cursing, leather-dressed men and women leaned their shoulders into the back of the wagon. Rys spotted Mardi waving farewell. She lifted a hand briefly and then put it back into her pocket. The wagon wheels turned. The whip, wielded by a man with a leg in plaster, cracked in the cold air.

"It's a hard thing to start a journey on an empty stomach." Lindy Airhome, his hands black from engine grease, had joined Rys at the rail.

"They are no hungrier than we are. We don't have enough steam yet, but soon."

On the shore, Ash's brother-son walked toward the boat. He looked white and drawn in the cold light of morning. He stopped to look after the lord's household which, with many fits and starts, toiled up the first hill. He stepped onto the landing stage, preoccupied, stumbling as he paid no heed to where his feet were set. Rys walked over to greet him as he stepped onto deck. "We embark as soon as we've built up our steam. Where is Zara?"

He looked up at her, his face burned white by sleeplessness, his eyes staring with bleak expression. "Have you seen Ash this morning?"

"What has happened?"

"Why, nothing."

Rys laid her hand upon his shoulder. He glanced at her, startled. "Your aunt is asleep. She was up half the night."

"I think she would want to be awakened."

A parent drew near, complaining about the lack of food. Rys took Kaz by the arm and dragged him into the passenger's lounge. She went in to shake Ash awake. When she came out, Macy had come in from the gallery and convinced Kaz to sit while she expostulated with him as adults do when they fear that a young person they care for has done something disastrous. She threw up her hands as Rys approached. Beneath Kaz' sullenness, an enormity lay.

He has felt his power, Rys thought, her heart sinking.

Ash came out, tousled and groggy. Kaz stepped forward to take Ash's hand. "I don't know how to tell you," he said. "Just come with me."

Ash jammed her shapeless hat onto her tangled hair. Her battered boots were black with age. Her trousers sagged from her hips, crumpling at the stained knees. She gazed at her brother-son, eye to eye, unblinking. He looked away, and pulled on her hand like a child. "Rys," Ash said. "Macy. Come with me."

They fell in behind, glancing at each other with raised eyebrows. Kaz led them down the landing stage and onto Vaterian soil, where Macy hesitated and then stepped forward, looking around herself in astonishment. The melted frost had left water dripping everywhere. The tree trunks were black against the pallid sky. The departing wagon had dug gouges into the wet soil; Rys could still hear the cursing from afar, and the crack of the whip.

Smoke trailed from the camp in the midst of the rocks. Seven figures rose from around the fire as the four of them approached. Rys counted again, and then paused, frowning. Ash, too, had paused, her shoulders squared. "What have you done," she breathed, neither question nor accusation.

"I don't—it happened—I didn't know . . ."

One of the men stepped forward. He wore only the blanket that wrapped his shoulders. His hair hung to his waist, like that of the others, but it was brown, streaked with gray and with gold. Rys had never set eyes on him before: a big, aging man, square-faced, with a long nose and sensuous lips that seemed half inclined to sneer. Yet she knew him. "Ghost Dog," she said. But he was, of course, a dog no more.

The man's amused gaze did not waver from Ash. Something in his eyes made Rys want to grab hold of Ash and hold her back as she took a step forward, and then another. Zara, standing as erect as the others by the fire, stared at Ash with angry defiance. Ash stopped, her way blocked by burning coals.

"Cydna," the man said. He might have been dressed in furs and jewels, so proudly did he speak.

Ash lifted her hands, as though she would take him, and mold him again into the dog he had been. "How did this journey come to be so infested by the fallen mighty?"

"The fallen mighty? Speak for yourself, sorceress! I am still the king."

In confusion and shock, Rys realized she should kneel, but could not. Macy, too, stood beside her, head tilted, solidly planted upon her two feet. Ash, at their forefront, gazed gravely at the forgotten king. She did not seem surprised. Perhaps she had known all along who he was.

"Your sister rules now," she said at last.

"She rules badly."

Zara cried, "He is the rightful king!"

Anselm took Zara's hand. "I do not need your defense, my dear."

Zara's face was as transparent as glass. Exaltation flared there: Zara had transformed a king! At last, at last, her destiny had found her!

At Ash's side, Kaz shifted restlessly from foot to foot. Ash looked at him, and looked away. He flinched, as though she had struck him.

"Now what will you do?" said Anselm. Rys looked into the face of a king, and saw the dog he had been. The sight chilled her, but she could find nothing safe to gaze upon this cold morning.

Ash said, "I fed you and sheltered you for seven years. What do you expect me to do?"

"You might explain why the Ash of Ashland did not see fit to break the enchantment of one who came to her for succor."

"Explain? You should know better than anyone!"

Rys said, "Ash, his dog memories make no more sense to him, now that he is a man, than his man's memories did when he was a dog."

Ash took a deep breath, as though she needed to ease her heart before she could continue. "There are choices that cannot be unmade," she said. She addressed Anselm, but her words, Rys saw, were for the young man standing at her side, hanging in agonizing suspension between suddenly opposed forces: his love on one side, his common sense on the other. "Ten years ago, I saw that I could not endure what I had become, and I could no longer play the part that had been assigned to me. I chose to do it no longer, and in that moment I ceased to be Cydna. So I did help you, in the only way a poor farmer could help you. I sheltered you."

The king barked laughter. "Seven years you let me suffer, while my upstart sister snatched away my kingdom. Seven years, while the land fell to ruin and the army disintegrated and commerce came to a standstill because a weak ruler sat upon the throne. Seven years you tortured me, and you call it charity?"

"If I treated you like a dog, it was because you were one. I could not possibly have known you were the king. If you search your memory, you will see that I am speaking truthfully."

There was silence, and then Anselm said harshly, "You have made no attempt to renew my enchantment. I have to believe that it is because you cannot, for I doubt your charity to me extends this far."

"I would indeed immediately transform you into a dog again, if I could." Ash turned to Kaz. "Tell me what happened."

"It was an accident," Kaz said. "We were playing the drums, and—it just happened."

"You and Zara both use your power like children, without consideration or knowledge. You may destroy yourselves, or not, and there is nothing I can do to affect the outcome."

She laid a hand upon Kaz's shoulder, and gave him a gentle push. He stepped around the fire, to stand at Zara's side, bleak beside her exaltation. The Danae, too, had found in Anselm someone to follow; no doubt he had made promises that he could have kept—were he still the king. Anselm was born and bred to war. A fighting man uses whatever he holds in his hand as a weapon. Here, he had gathered his army of seven innocents. Rys feared for them.

"Now you have my children," Ash said. "Was there anything else you wanted?"

Anselm turned to Rys. "Madam Pilot, your boat."

"Neither I nor the *Amina* can serve you. The boat has just enough fuel to get us to the next village. After that, we are all at the whim of fate."

Anselm abruptly dismissed them with a gesture. "Then I have no further need of you."

Rys had to take Ash by the shoulder and physically turn her away from the sight of her brother-son, ensnared like a pigeon in a net, staring helplessly at her across the coals of the fire.

By the time they returned to the boat, all work had come to a standstill as crew and passenger alike crowded the rail, peering at the shore, arguing excitedly, and listening to an astonished, half hysterical old man insist that the naked man on shore was the King of Faerd. "Is it true?" they cried, rushing forward as Rys came on board. "Where did he come from? Has he been a prisoner here, all this time?" They stepped back in baffled amazement as she ordered them to prepare to embark.

"But you can't—"

"How can you—"

"—leave him?"

"It is not the king. Do as I say." She stared at the crew members, until they were reminded, by the sun-

light glaring from her guild pin, what would happen to
them if they were convicted of disobeying a pilot's orders.

They loosed the mooring lines and lifted the landing
stage. From the pilothouse, Rys watched the shore drop
away from them. Macy and Ash sat side by side on the
bench in dumbfounded silence.

The *Amina* steamed northward. Rys did not know
this stretch of river well, and she had to search her
memory for the name of this bend, though she remembered where the channel lay. On either side of the
river, rocky banks rose steeply into sparse woodlands:
a ragged, barren land, too rocky to farm, its trees too
gnarled and spindly to be worth cutting down. But the
Amina would reach a village by mid-afternoon, where
they could restock their fuel and supplies for the trip
south.

That was what needed to be done, king or no king.

Ash got abruptly to her feet. "Let me off here."

Rys clenched both her fists upon the helm. "It's too
shallow," she said. "There's a better landing up ahead."

On a narrow, rocky beach Rys set Ash ashore. Her
old satchel slung from a shoulder, and her bedroll hung
crossways upon her back. One of Macy's dancing jacks
hung from the satchel's shoulder strap like a good luck
charm. Weaponless, penniless, without even a mouthful of food to eat, she stepped briskly onto that hostile
shore and did not linger. By the time the landing stage
had been secured again, Ash was gone.

Macy spoke, for the first time since reboarding the
Amina. "You could have kept her from going."

Rys backed the boat out once again into the channel.
Through storm and flood and fog and every disaster
imaginable she had piloted her boats to safety. She
could do this, too, though her hands were less than
steady and her vision was less than clear. "You don't
understand," she said to Macy.

She shouted below for full speed. In another sweep
of her pocket watch's hand, the rocky beach would be

out of sight. "I was born to watch her leave me," she said. "It is what I do best."

The pocket watch made its sweep. The *Amina* rounded the bend, and the rocky beach was gone.

Chapter 11: Ash

The sparse trees closed around Ash. She walked south, across uneven stone, weaving her path around the low-growing branches of the stunted trees. Once the riverboat had journeyed out of hearing, she traveled through early spring's silence. No insect buzzed or bird sang. The cold breeze that came luffing through the trees' bare branches uttered an occasional sigh. Her own feet found no dry twigs to snap or crisp leaves to crush. She stepped from soft mold to hard stone without a sound.

As she walked, she began to chuckle, and then to laugh. She sat upon a stone in this stunted wood and laughed until she was weary, then caught her breath in the silence. Spring waited here, just beyond the threshold, and soon these barren stones would be scattered with frail flowers.

She got to her feet and continued southward, sober now, until, as morning reached afternoon, she saw the river turning back toward her again. A rabbit strangled in a snare warned her that those she sought could be nearby. She took and dressed the rabbit—she was hungry, and only expected to get hungrier—then continued cautiously until she could see Kerlin Point through the trees. No one moved upon that rocky shore. She crossed the stones to stand beside the scattered coals of the cold campfire.

The refitted riverboat would pass this place again on its way south. If Ash was not there to hail the pilot, the *Amina* would continue on. That was the way of the river.

Ash settled her satchel more securely upon her

shoulder and started off in the tracks of Lord Diggen's heavily laden wagon.

The lord's party had not traveled far before stopping to lighten the wagon. Travel trunks, valises, and loose clothing lay in a scattered pile at the foot of the tree. Hopefully, someone would stumble by this wealth before the next rainstorm spoiled it. Ash continued on.

The rocky land continued to rise. The wagon tracks followed a winding path around the stands of trees and mounded piles of stones. The breeze which had sighed in the barren twigs of the trees became, by evening, a raw, face-burning wind. Ash, legs aching from the afternoon's long climb, laden with firewood that she had gathered as she walked, made camp on the leeward side of a hill, in a hollow rimmed by stone. She started a fire and spitted the rabbit over it, then scouted around her campsite searching for anything more to eat. It was the barren time of year, in a land whose wealth was sparse even in the heat of summer, and she found nothing.

The sun set. She ate a few mouthfuls of charred meat from the rabbit's bones, and drank stream water. In the darkness, she climbed to a high point on her hillside, from which she could see the land rising before her. Not too far in the distance, another campfire burned.

She thought about the *Amina,* turning her prow into the current and letting it carry her homeward down the dark river. She returned to her camp, and lay down on her bed of stones.

Three times she awakened to darkness, with the cold stars winking in a cold sky, and once the curled horns of the moon floating past. She threw more wood onto the fire without unwrapping herself from the blanket. Although cold had numbed her feet, the rocks on which she slept had bruised her bones, and her belly grumbled with hunger, she fell asleep again. The earth, solid and unswaying, held her.

She awakened again to early dawn. With no breakfast to eat and no baggage to gather, she scattered the coals of her fire and took up her journey again. At least, with morning's advent, the wind had ceased to blow. Soon, the voices of Diggen Elbie's band, weary and complaining after the miserable night they must have spent, carried clearly across the dead silence of the countryside.

Ash journeyed cautiously among the trees. By sheer luck she stumbled across another campsite which had been hidden, like hers, in a hollow among stones. Until now, she had not even been certain that Anselm, the Danae, and Kaz and Zara had followed Diggen Elbie. The ashes of the fire still smoked.

She heard a startled shout and a shrill cry, very close by. She ran up a gradual hill through a stand of trees, then ducked into cover as a strange tableau came into sight. Diggen Elbie's wagon lay askew, with one of its wheels dislocated. The baggage seemed to have been thrown wildly about in a monstrous fit of temper, while several people who'd been picking through the debris stood frozen in shock. Anselm, rightful king of Faerd, with two plague orphans and five homeless tribespeople as his courtiers, stood face-to-face with Lord Diggen and his own haggard and hungry band. Ash would have found it hard to say which of the two men looked more like a rooster proudly displaying the manure of his chicken yard kingdom.

With everyone's attention distracted, she could slip hastily closer until she huddled in the bracken, only a few paces from the dislocated wagon. Up close, she could see Lord Diggen's stiffly smiling, shocked white face. His traveling clothes were muddy and torn after only one day of tramping through the woods. The king, dressed in a fur coat no doubt taken from the pile of discards, reminded Ash with every gesture and motion of the proud dog he had been.

"Come, let us converse," said Anselm. "By the gods, I had given up all hope of ever seeing the face of a friend again."

"And I had long since given you up for dead. Your Majesty—" Lord Diggen knelt stiffly, and many of his band also followed suit, in some confusion. Those young enough to have known only the rule of Queen Lynthe seemed not to know what to do.

"Rise up, rise up." Anselm gave Lord Diggen his hand, and the two walked together out of hearing. Ash could draw no closer to them without drawing attention to herself, but the physical attitudes of the two men told her more than enough. Perhaps the two of them had never been friends before, but circumstance would force them into friendship now. When they separated, Lord Diggen announced to his band that the king and his followers would join them in their journey to Tastuly.

Anselm called on Kaz to repair the wagon, and told Zara and the Danae to prepare a meal for Lord Diggen's band. The six of them picked up their carry bags and digging sticks and fanned out into the woods to search for food. Ash followed. The thinly scattered trees offered little shelter in which to hide, but Zara seemed eager to put a distance between herself and the great lords parleying in the clearing. Soon Ash could follow her without taking too much trouble over concealment.

Zara stopped to dig angrily in the wet ground with a stick. Her efforts turned up several tubers, which she separated according to size, gathering the large ones into a cloth bundle, and replanting the small. She sat back on her heels, glaring at her small hoard.

"The weak must serve the powerful with gratitude," said Ash. "So it was ordained by the gods."

"No gods of mine!" snapped Zara. She turned to Ash more in anger than surprise. "What are you doing here? We are free to do as we choose!"

"I have done nothing to impede you." Ash picked up Zara's makeshift bundle and offered her a hand up. "I will help you look for roots. This is a skill I wish you would teach me, before I starve to death."

Sullen, Zara turned away. With Ash following her, she took a wandering path through the woodland, pausing here and there to dig in spots that were likely to be shaded in the summer. More often than not she uncov-

ered a cluster of roots, and carefully separated and re-
planted the smaller ones.

They had worked together in silence for some time
before Zara asked, "Why did you follow us?"

"I don't know," Ash said.

"We're not going with you to Ashland. I was not
born to live out my days in some muddy potato field."

Ash shrugged. "Go where you like."

They walked to another spot. Ash glanced back to
make certain they could find their way back again. A
banner of fresh smoke marked the clearing.

"Kaz is unhappy." Zara dug her stick into the
ground, but nothing turned up. They moved on, and
she tried again. Some tiny birds were busy in a leafless
thicket. Their breast feathers were red as jewels.

"The king looks like he wants to eat him up." Zara
tried to smile, but it came out all wrong. "He seems
half crazy, the things he expects us to do for him. Last
night, there was no salt for his rabbit. He looked at
Kaz and said, 'Make some.' "

"He will use whatever tool he has to get what he
wants, and right now Kaz is what he has."

"But salt?"

"He is testing Kaz."

"Testing him for what?"

"For how much force he will have to use. He must
know that Kaz is . . . less than enthusiastic."

Zara blindly handed Ash some tubers. The sack was
nearly full. "What does he want from him?"

"Maybe he wants another Cydna. It worked for
Naiman."

Zara stood up. Ash lifted the sack to her shoulder. "I
doubt you can carry much more than this."

"They'll be wondering what happened to me." They
had taken only a few steps when Zara said, "King
Anselm will ask the King of Vateria to help him wrest
his kingdom back from Lynthe."

"Vateria and Faerd can ill afford a war."

"The queen will abdicate rather than fight, King
Anselm says."

"Indeed. What do the Danae hope to gain?"

"King Anselm will convince King Bartyn to give them back their land."

"What will Anselm give King Bartyn in exchange for his help?"

"Oh, I don't know." Zara banged her stick at a passing tree trunk.

"When Anselm looks at Kaz, what do you think he sees, that makes him look so hungry?"

Zara beat another tree. "Why don't you ask him!"

Ash set Zara's bundle on the ground. "I dare not come any closer."

Zara hunched her shoulders, as though she were cold. "The night before last, everything seemed simple." From the clearing came the strained sound of polite laughter. "Maybe it's because I was a simpleton."

Ash said, "You have not yet learned to let Kaz anchor you."

Zara looked away. "I seem to get him into trouble, that's for certain. Is the *Amina* gone?"

"I don't know. We might still be able to intercept the boat at Kerlin Point."

Zara picked up the bundle of roots, grimacing at the weight. "I will fetch Kaz and meet you back here," she said. She turned and started back toward the clearing.

Instead of waiting there, Ash returned to the clearing by a separate route. While she and Zara wandered the woods, Kaz apparently had mended the hopelessly broken wheel, and the wagon was now being loaded with a few battered and nondescript trunks and valises which probably contained gold and valuables.

The Danae sliced *ankhu* roots into pots of water at two cookfires. Zara delivered her load and walked up to Kaz. Perhaps Zara gave him a signal, for he rapidly ended his conversation, and the two of them casually walked off together, holding hands, heads close together as Zara talked and Kaz nodded. He was not smiling, but he looked relieved. They did not notice what Ash could see clearly from her vantage: Anselm, who sat with Diggen Elbie and some of the lesser nobles in his retinue, had started suddenly to his feet and strode briskly across the clearing.

When he was a dog, he had hunted like this. He looked elsewhere, pretending he did not even know his prey was nearby. Then, suddenly, he pounced.

Kaz and Zara had drawn near the edge of the clearing when the king inserted himself between them, taking Zara by the elbow and putting his arm across Kaz' shoulders. They stopped short, dismayed. They had been speaking so quietly, Ash had not heard even a murmur, but now she heard the king's voice clearly. "Come and be presented to his lordship and his lady. They do not even remember who you are."

It was Zara who looked desperately backward as Anselm half dragged them up to the privileged circle. Ash settled down in the bushes, but she did not need to observe the close watch Anselm kept on Kaz and Zara to know that the slender chance they could still intercept the *Amina* had evaporated.

When the travelers took up their journey once again, Anselm kept Kaz or Zara always at his side. Ash could do nothing except follow.

At mid-morning, the woodland gave way to stony, rolling country, with an occasional sheepfold or shepherd's hut hidden between the knees of the hills. A stream wound among the folds of land, bright and chuckling in the sunshine, gray with ice and silent in the shadows. Beside this stream, a track had been beaten into the ground by the hard hooves of passing sheep. The wagon followed this old track. Ash, walking in the footprints of those she followed, and often within hearing of their voices, kept out of sight within the land's sharp-edged pleats.

On the southern slopes, where vivid grass had begun to spear forth from stones and mud, white-footed hares gathered. They were wary and wild, and scattered in frantic disarray when Ash drew too close. Hawks hunted them overhead, and gray foxes melted into stone as Ash passed.

Of sheep and shepherds there was no sign. At mid-afternoon, when the north wind began to blow again, Ash understood why. Scented with pine and snow, it howled down from the mountains that loomed to the north. The hills, rather than offering shelter, seemed only to channel the bitter wind which soon silenced the chuckling stream under a cover of ice and broadcast white hoarfrost across the shady sides of the hills. Ash's clothing could not protect her from the wind's frigid raids. She tied her hat onto her head with a piece of string, drove her fists deep into her pockets, and tramped grimly through the assault of cold, chilled to the bone.

Before sunset, she took shelter in a shepherd's barrow, which was dug waist-deep into the ground, then walled with stone and roofed with trimmed tree branches plastered with mud. A large rodent had made its winter nest upon the hearth. Ash collected dung from the nearby sheepfold to use for fuel, and spent the remaining daylight filling chinks in the wall with stone and mud, so that the wind's greedy fingers would not snatch away the heat of what she knew would be a poor fire at best. Once the sun had set, she used the rat's nest for tinder. She had gathered *ankhu* roots before they left the woods. She set these to bake upon her stinking, smoldering fire.

She wrapped herself in a blanket for extra warmth, but when she crawled out the barrow's door, the wind's vicious cold nearly dove her back into shelter. She set her jaw and dove into the pitiless night. Down the hill she hurried, and along the icy silence of the stream, around the bends and folds of the black hills. She gasped and shivered as she walked, with tears from her wind-burned eyes freezing upon her cheeks and the wind-blown stars shimmering overhead.

These past two days had been solitary enough, but in this miserable night Ash felt the depth of her loneliness. Like a homeless ghost, bowed and crushed by misery, she wandered the howling darkness, until a bright and wavering light blinked at her. Following that signal's direction, she crept up a hillside to another shepherd's lodging much like that in which she had

sheltered. Lord Diggen's empty wagon stood beside
the barrow, but the travelers had all taken refuge in the
sheepfold. Ash put her eye to a gap in the basketweave
wall. Blanket-wrapped figures, indistinguishable in
their suffering, huddled around three small fires. The
Danae tended the cookpots. Each of their faces bore
the same grimly impassive expression.

Kaz sat by one of the smoldering fires, arguing with
the king. He looked exhausted and angry. Ash could
not see Zara. She moved around the perimeter of the
wall, looking through one peephole after another, until
she spotted Mardi standing beside Zara, who huddled
on the ground, far from the warmth of the fires. She
looked as white and angry as Kaz, but her eyes caught
too much of the red flames' glitter. The rope which
bound her by the wrists to the wall of the fold was
nearly invisible in the dim light.

Ash fell back from the sheepfold and stumbled down
the hillside again. Confused by cold and weariness, she
could think only of the fire smoldering in the barrow's
shelter. But its warmth was small, when at last she
squatted beside it and reached into the coals for the
charred roots. A bland and unsatisfying meal they pro-
vided her. She wrapped herself in blankets and lay
alone in the frigid night, listening to the wind howl.

In the deep of night, she awoke. The wind had fallen
silent at last, but bitter cold settled into its wake. She
got up, shivering, to follow the dim glow of coals to
the hearth. She sat by its weary warmth, blanket-
wrapped, feeding it sheep's dung piece by piece until
flames smoldered again, red and flickering in the darkness.

Peaceful Kaz and his headstrong Zara were accustomed to hunger and cold, and probably endured the
night in more comfort than Ash. After their years on
the streets, they were no more innocent or naive than
the hares Ash had seen today, who thrived in this hostile land despite the many predators stalking them. But
they had never been preyed upon by a man like

Anselm before. She feared for them, and she raged at herself for being able to do nothing.

Her belly ached with hunger. The fire's warmth could not seem to chase the cold from her bones. Restless, she stood up and cracked open the barrow's square door, to see how far away was the dawn.

The sky was clear as black ice, embedded with frozen stars. The hills huddled in stolid silence under the torment of the cold. The frozen stream glimmered like molten silver in the starlight. Along this shimmering pathway walked a jerky and misshapen shadow.

Too large to be a wolf, too silent to be a horse, it seemed, impossibly, to be four-legged and yet winged. A person walked on two legs before it, stumpy and bowed like a peddler under a pack. Ash's vision blurred in the cold. She rubbed her eyes and blinked, icy tears running down her cheeks. She could see nothing, now, except for the faintest of glimmers where the stream had before seemed afire with starlight.

She took a deep breath, the skin prickling across the backs of her shoulders, as though the poor fire had experienced a sudden fit of generosity. Now she heard something thin and faint in the chill night: singing, she finally realized, and a squeaking, clashing sound that accompanied the song with an irregular rhythm. A shadow walked through the darkness. "Treasures here," Ash heard. "Girls and boys."

She caught her breath again, as startled as if any icy bucket of water had been emptied over her head.

The night walker sang, "Won't you come and buy my toys?" And then, a summons: "Ash."

She heaved herself out of the barrow. The mystery of shadows below her resolved itself into a sight which, while scarcely ordinary, she had seen before: Macy, her peddler's pack upon her back, and the clockwork toy frozen in mid step. A third figure lay upon the ground as though deeply asleep. "Rys," said Macy, and the figure stirred. "Help her up, Ash. She hurt her ankle."

Rys still seemed only half awake as Ash dragged her to her feet. But she yelped with pain when she set her injured foot upon the ground and leaned heavily into Ash, gasping. "Did we catch up with you at last? What is this place?"

Ash half dragged her up to the barrow and helped her through the door, then lowered Macy's tremendously heavy pack before climbing in herself and taking the clockwork toy that Macy handed her. Rys had made it to the hearth, where she half reclined with her foot out in front of her, pallid and tightlipped, but with a brave passion smoldering in her eyes. Macy dragged the crude door shut. "Oh, it's warm!"

And it was: warm as a farm kitchen, warm as a summer day.

Rys said, "Creesil Village lies on the inward curve of Creesil Bend, between Junil and Arvil Crossings. The river has not shifted more than a foot or two since I first studied it for my pilot's license, because it winds between hills. I have not seen any children there in six years, but the village was deteriorating long before the plague years."

"Tell her about the mountains," said Macy.

"The Madeena Mountains rise above the hilltops, even though they are far away. It is—spectacular. That a village could be so destitute among such spectacular scenery has always seemed to defy logic."

"It was beautiful," said Macy. "Rys says the mountains are flowing with water at this time of year, and the river draws so close to the base of the mountains that it passes through the spray of the waterfalls. Tastuly sits on the opposite shore."

"A city of towers, as though trying to rival the mountains that overshadow it. Seven Bells City looks like a farm town in comparison to Tastuly's grandeur."

"What happened at Creesil Village?" This tale had already veered far off course, and Ash, though she was still eating the bread and cheese and pickles that Macy had produced from her pack, had begun to fear that she might sit here all night and never hear the tale's end.

Rys said, "Only a half-dozen people came out when I sounded the whistle, and by the time we had landed, only three of them remained. But I had their attention soon enough: a good many years must have passed since last a gold piece was seen in that miserable place. So a wagon was found, and a horse to pull it, and a guide to the nearest prosperous farm for supplies, and even some bread and milk for the riverboat's children, to tide them over while we waited for Lindy to return with the wagon. I sent north to the nearest woodlot to have a wood barge floated down to us, for only a few sticks of wood remained in the hold and we could have gone no farther. All of this took time, and it was nearly nightfall before we embarked. By then, Lindy and Kiva had talked me into going after you."

"Lindy and Kiva?"

"The mates," said Macy. "The three of them had quite a discussion about the oaths pilots take and what would happen if pilots started putting their personal needs before the safety of the boat."

"Ethics," said Rys, implying by the tone of her voice that it had been a dull conversation, scarcely worth the effort of recounting. "But we do need to train the passengers to act as crew, and there are some repairs to make, and in the end Lindy and Kiva convinced me that it made sense for the *Amina* to tie down for a few days before starting the trip south. The two of them are entirely competent to do what needs to be done, so—"

"They terrified you into it," said Macy.

Rys had drawn her knees up to her chest. She shut her eyes, as though suddenly exhausted. "I had them up to the pilothouse for tea. Macy had taken over the galley from Grelling—"

"—at least until they have tasted my cooking the first time—"

"—so she was the one who brought up the food, and I asked her to stay. As we argued, Lindy and Kiva both set their teacups down upon the bench. They both looked at me, half solemn and half smiling, one hand full of food and one hand empty. I felt . . ." Rys opened her eyes, blinking in the firelight. "I felt as though I was in the grasp of something."

"Both of them bought dancing jacks from you,

didn't they?" said Ash. Macy shrugged as though she could not remember and could not imagine why it mattered.

"What could I do?" continued Rys. "From the beginning, I have not been in control of this boat's destiny. So we tied the *Amina* down once again at Kerlin Point, and Macy and I started out by starlight. My ego took my first blow when I realized that she is a far sturdier traveler than I. Then I stepped in a rabbit hole in broad daylight yesterday."

"You found a way to keep traveling," said Ash.

"Well—" Rys looked confused, as though she could not quite remember how she had gotten here. Macy shrugged again, and Ash decided to pursue the topic no further. Some enchantments are so fragile it is better not to discuss them.

Ash said, "Do you know, I have never seen you wear anything other than a pilot's uniform?"

"You have never seen me on dry land, either." Rys sat up, rubbing her face. "It is an unimpressive sight, is it not? Almost enough to make one wonder why I ever get off a boat at all."

"Are you all right?"

"It hurts," she said wearily, "like the dickens. It was so cold out there, I could hardly feel it. But now that I'm warm—"

"Let me see."

They had wrapped her unbooted foot in makeshift bandages torn out of what had probably been a spare shirt. Underneath, Rys' foot was ugly: purple, grotesquely swollen. Rys shut her eyes, sweat popping out on her forehead. "It's not broken. Too bad—I hear breaks heal faster."

Ash cradled Rys' foot in her lap. She realized she was stroking the swollen flesh lightly with her fingers and stopped, for even so light a pressure could cause pain.

Rys opened her eyes. "Don't stop . . . it feels better. We told you our end of the tale, such as it is. Now you tell us yours."

Macy began laying out their blankets as Ash talked.

She set the clockwork toy by the doorway. Ash, talking
of Kaz and Zara, had to stop because of tears. Macy
said, "If that child learns to think as a result of this
mess, it will be well worth it."

Rys had fallen abruptly asleep. Macy covered her
with a blanket. "Finish your supper," she said to Ash.
She lay down herself, murmuring like a bird settling itself to sleep in the evening.

"Macy—"

Macy, arms folded behind her head, peered at Ash
from her nest of blankets, eyes bright in the shadows.

"In the end, we all become what our life demands of
us, whether that be great or small. My life has made
me into a farmer who talks to ghosts, just as yours has
made you—something you are reluctant to discuss.
Now that I need to be greater than what I am, I feel—I
am—small. But what can I do? I have become what I
had to."

"Rys has Pilot's Sight," said Macy. Ash thought that
was all, for Macy had closed her eyes. But she spoke
again, a nearly inaudible murmur. "You know she is
not reckless. She would never waste her heart's love on
something small."

❧   ❧   ❧

Daylight: blinding, white, blazing, gone suddenly as
the door closed. Ash lifted her head, startled. Macy
still slept. Rys was gone. Ash stumbled to the door and
crawled out into the midmorning blaze of light. Rys
strode into the sun, an erect shadow, scattering hares
before her. Their white feet burned, kicking the air behind themselves as though they were swimming
through the day's intense light.

Ash followed Rys down the hillside, wondering
why, if this were a dream, her eyes ached with sleeplessness. Rys knelt at the stream's edge, and lifted her
hands, dripping with daylight, to her face. She gasped.
"Oh, Ash," she said.

Ash knelt beside her. The water shocked her with its

cold. She ran wet fingers through her hair, easing out its sticky tangles. "Your foot?"

Rys grasped her arm. "What did you become, when you ceased to be Cydna the Sorceress?"

"What?" said Ash. Had Rys not actually been asleep, when she and Macy had their brief conversation earlier? Or was physical exhaustion making her stupid?

"What did you become?"

"A farmer."

"You hold things together, you break things apart. You restore and rebuild, you make things grow, you make things change. Is that it?"

Ash turned her face to the sun. It outlined Rys in a halo of light, catching in the coarse wool of her jacket, flaring in the white linen of her intricately tucked shirt. "Look," said Rys. "Yesterday I could not walk at all. And I was there, when you kept the *Amina* from breaking up in the storm. I know what I saw."

"That was good piloting!"

"A dozen times we would have sunk, if not for you! Do you think I do not know when my boat is in desperate trouble?"

Ash tasted the water. It was sweet; it made her mouth ache. "I don't remember doing anything."

"No more than I remember breathing or making my heart beat. I watched you heal my foot. I watched the swelling shrink; I felt the pain ease. You were not even paying attention. You did it because of who you are: the Ash of Ashland."

"The people of Semel named me Ash against my will and against my desire."

"Nevertheless, they named you, and you have become what they needed." Rys stood up, her hands making fists in her jacket's deep pockets. "I let you walk away from the *Amina* because of my despair, and I needed to be forced to come after you. But now that I am here, I think I understand why. When Faerd is in need, a hero comes. Perhaps Anselm thinks that hero is him. But I think it is us."

Chapter 12: Rys

Walking with Ash and Macy between the barren hillsides of that cold and abandoned land, Rys felt too lighthearted to fret about the abandoned riverboat behind her, or the restored king and the hostage children before her. Ash acted as if she had forgotten that she was no longer alone, but Rys and Macy sang old folk songs, until the track began to rise steeply and they had to break off, gasping and laughing.

They had reached the road, a sorry and undistinguished sight, where potholes gave way to quagmires, and only an occasional roadstone had survived to suggest that once this had been an important artery. Ash reached into the leafless bushes which grew here in unkempt abundance and pulled out a wooden box which nestled there. "I gave Kaz this box in Fortune. It is the only precious thing he has, besides his drum."

They stood around looking at it. No one asked Ash how she had known to look for the box in the bushes. When Ash raised her bowed head, her face had changed, like a dark room changes when a lamp is lit.

"Is that a roadhouse up ahead?" said Macy. "I could use a hot meal."

It was, or once had been, but now the roof had fallen in. The travelers ahead of them had also paused here, long enough for their wagon's wheels to sink into the muck. "Imagine their discouragement," said Rys. "To finally reach civilization, and still go hungry."

"You must have known that they would have been better off taking the riverway to Tastuly." said Macy.

"I admit I am a vengeful person," Rys said without remorse.

"I doubt we are far behind them anymore," said Ash.

"Not far at all," said Macy. "Look there."

Five slender shadows separated from the undergrowth and stepped into the road, their long black hair woven with twigs, small animals strung across their backs, rattles and whistles hanging around their necks: the Danae. "Aunt of Kaz, he said you would come."

Ash stepped forward, holding out her hand. The old man clasped it and bowed over it, like a lord greeting a treasured friend. He named himself, A'tin, and the other four, two men and two women. "We are not impressed with your lords and kings," he said.

"Neither are we," said Ash. "Tell me what has befallen my children."

A'tin gestured, and they all squatted in a circle, except for Macy who began handing out food from her pack: boiled eggs and oatcakes and dried fruits. A'tin said, "Once, the Danae had sons and daughters like Kaz and Zara: children of fire and earth, strong and foolish and brave-hearted. Now, our children are weak and spiritless, because they are born in a broken land. Most of them die, but those who live have no heart in them. Perhaps it is too late for my people."

"There are no children at Ashland either," said Ash. "But I do not think it is too late."

"The man who was a dog wants to claim them for himself. All treasures belong to him, he thinks. We followed him because we thought he was a king. But he is like the land of stones: he has no soul. He has captured Kaz and Zara, and now he seeks to break their spirits to his will. He is no king." A'tin leaned forward and took one of Ash's hands in his. "Their spirit has given us strength. We will not let them be eaten by a dog."

"Then come with us," said Ash. "There must be something we can do."

After the Danae had eaten, they continued after the king. They passed vacant farms, where the windows gaped and the wind blew through the bared ribs of the barn walls. Along this only escape route from Tastuly,

plague had raided and pillaged every household. Now
the trees took the land back, and sometimes a quick
shadow ran along the sagging rooflines: squirrels,
awake at last after the long winter.

Rys said, "Do you hear something?"

For some time, the wind had been keening through
the rattling bones of the trees. Shouting voices now
chorused in accompaniment. They hurried forward as
quickly as the road would allow, then ducked into the
roadside undergrowth as the king's party came into
sight. The wagon had gotten stuck axle-deep in mire.
The weary horses stood with their noses in the mud,
not even flinching at the crack of the whip. Part of the
wagon's load had toppled into the muck, and more
than one member of Lord Diggen's party stood by the
side of the road, muddy to the hip, with the boxes and
chests they had recovered from the mess unrecognizable on the ground beside them.

"Where is Kaz?" breathed Macy.

"There." The king, white-faced with rage, dragged
him forward.

"Zara?"

Two of Lord Diggen's strongarms had cornered her
between them, with a bare blade at her throat.

The king flung Kaz at the horses, where he landed
on his knees in the mud. He struggled to his feet and
slogged through to the wagon wheels. He leaned
against one, and pushed. The king shouted at him. Kaz
turned to him helplessly, protesting. The king gestured,
and the strongarms brought Zara forward, fighting like
a wildcat, so that the strongarms' greatest worry
seemed to be that her throat might be cut by accident.

The king shouted again. Kaz gave a panicky heave
at the wagon. The mud sucked hungrily at the wagon
wheels, drooling rivulets of brown-stained water that
dribbled across the road. Not even a stream bed, but
more a path that water followed to get to the stream,
this place must have been waylaying travelers every
spring since the first wagon rolled along this route.
Zara screamed ragged curses, and Kaz slipped and fell
into the mud, but none in that grim audience laughed.

Several, in fact, moved as if to help, but stopped, seeming afraid to counter the king's will.

Kaz got to his feet again, rubbing a muddy face upon a muddy shoulder. His face had turned white under the mud. His eyes had a hard, polished look. He put his shoulder into the wagon once again.

Beside Rys, Ash put her hand against a tree, and pushed. The horses jumped. The wagon spit out of the quagmire's grip, leaving Kaz once again sprawling. A ragged cheer went up. The king stepped back, smiling with satisfaction. Ash held the tree, trembling.

Kaz sat in the middle of the road and put his forehead against his knees. The muted travelers loaded the wagon once again. Lord Diggen, who had stood back from this distasteful scene, spoke quietly with Ursul. Leather-dressed, with a bow and arrow slung across her back, now she looked like his lordship's woodsman. She frowned at what he said, but nodded and beat her hand against her tunic to shake loose some of the dirt.

When the travelers started forward again, heads bowed, trudging wearily, Ursul remained behind with Kaz. He waved her angrily away, but she insistently held out to him the dry shirt which she had taken from the bundle she carried upon her own shoulder.

Macy had taken the clockwork toy out of her pack and held it under her arm, as though she had been about to set it down upon the ground. When she let go of the key, its legs began to move jerkily and its wings to flap. Rys had never heard her turning the key.

Macy tossed the toy into the air. The trees shook in a sudden wind, and there was a clattering of pinions among the dry branches. Up ahead, Ursul tipped back her head as a wide-winged shadow cut off the sun. Macy gave a gleeful laugh and clapped her hands like a child.

They stepped out of hiding. Of all those gathered here, only Ursul had a weapon, but her bow was unstrung, and she did not reach for it. She stood quietly, with the dry shirt in her hand.

Kaz got to his feet. "Ash! He's hurting Zara!"

Ash stroked the water out of his shirt with her hands. Rys stepped forward to wrap him in a blanket, but by then his clothing was dry.

"Are you hungry?" said Macy. She handed out another picnic, and even the Danae ate again. Rys approached Ursul, who ate ravenously, keeping a nervous eye on the sky.

"He is still waiting," Macy said, as the winged shadow once again crossed the sun.

"Madam," said Rys to Ursul.

"Well, you have had your revenge," said Ursul. She looked as though she were about to start up the road after her lord, but was stopped short by Macy, who used a paper-wrapped honeycake to take her prisoner. "Where did you get this food? I have never seen a land so barren!"

"Indeed? Parts of Faerd are this bad. The food came from Creesil Village which is, I grant you, a poor place. All the more reason for the people there to be inspired by the sight of gold."

Ursul sputtered. "Gold!"

Rys offered her the clean kerchief out of her pocket. Ursul dabbed at her mouth daintily and handed it back, her eyes hard and bright as a blacksmith's fire. The food seemed to have done her good.

Rys said, "Five gold pieces I've carried with me, sewn into the seams of my duffle, ever since my early days behind the helm. I wanted to be ready with bribe money, in case Cydna ever was taken prisoner. I never thought I'd use the money to provision and fuel a boat!"

"Well, you have done a good many things on this journey that you never thought you would do, just as I have. Since when did a pilot leave her boat to go chasing across land on an errand that should be none of her business?"

"The world has changed, madam, and this is something that you, Elbie, and Anselm all need to learn. Though I am a lowly commoner and my cohorts are but a poor farmer and an even more impoverished toymaker, history's direction is in fact up to us."

"You sound like Naiman the Poet."

"Do I? He was my friend, too, though not many remember it. Can I bring you some more food?"

"No, thank you." The pinioned shadow once again crossed the sun. Ursul eyed it speculatively. "I think none of you three is actually as common as you would have me think."

"It depends, I suppose, on what you mean by common."

"I think that we are defeated already. Defeated because we have lost hope and you have found it."

"I think that someone with your insight is wasted on a man like Elbie."

"Perhaps. What are you going to do?" Ursul did not sound as though she cared particularly.

"Does Lord Diggen regret any of the choices he has made?"

Ursul gave a bitter laugh. "No man on earth loves the queen as much as he. What do you think, Madam Pilot?"

"Well, his vengefulness is ever stronger than his self knowledge. But I want to think he realizes he cannot live with himself if he betrays the Queen of Faerd to her enemies."

Ursul gazed at Rys, cautious, offering no disagreement.

"Anselm and King Bartyn have never been friends. Without the support of Elbie, I do not think that Anselm will continue to Tastuly. I think he will choose another journey—one which need concern you no further. If you can convince Elbie that he need not support Anselm, Elbie will not be forced to betray his queen any more than he already has, and you can continue to Tastuly and start your new life. We will let you go."

"And when Anselm returns to his rightful throne, do you think he will forget that Elbie abandoned him in a strange land?"

Ash said, "Anselm will never again sit on the throne of Faerd." She had been speaking with Kaz, holding him by the hands to keep him from rushing down the road after Zara. Rys did not think she had even been listening to the conversation with Ursul. But the sound of her voice left a silence after it, like the silence between lightning's flash and the thunder. Ursul opened her mouth, as if to ask, but said nothing. Ash must have been invisible to her before today. No one notices a stone until it has become an avalanche.

Rys said, "At the next crossroads take the left fork, until you come to a wagontrack that goes toward the east. Follow that a short distance, and it will take you to a farm which is known to take in travelers. They will feed and shelter you and show you an easier way to Tastuly and not charge you too much for the service."

"Better hurry," Macy said. The winged creature had begun to spiral languidly earthward. There was a squeal of frightened horses. The creature banked and stalled, and then dropped down below the line of trees. It had been the size of an infant child when Macy launched it. It had grown, as it flew, to the size of a small house.

Ursul looked down the road and looked back again at Macy. Macy shrugged, as though she did not understand either how such an amazing thing could have happened. The screaming shrilled, a peculiar sound in the silent spring. "Good-bye, then," Ursul said, holding out her hand. One by one, Ash, Macy, and Rys clasped her hand. She turned away and started down the road. She walked lightly for someone with so long a journey ahead of her.

"That woman makes my knees weak," Rys said. "She'll be ruling Vateria in another ten years, just you wait and see."

"She's something," said Macy. "Have a honeycake."

Ash turned Kaz's head with her hands. "Look."

The winged creature had launched itself again in a climbing spiral above the trees. A slender figure rode upon his back, waving a mocking farewell to those out of sight below. Even at such a distance, they could hear Zara's laughter. It had been a long time since this sorrowing place had heard so joyful a sound.

When the creature landed her, light as thistledown, in their midst, Zara could scarcely speak for laughter.

"If you could have seen!" she gasped against Kaz' shoulder. "Oh, oh—I will never forget!"

Macy carried the clockwork toy under her arm until its works ran down, and then she stowed it in her pocket.

❦   ❦   ❦

Ten of them traveled together now. Dusk found them sheltered within the ruined walls of the roadhouse, roasting the Danae's kills over a reluctant fire on the crumbling hearth of what had once been the kitchen. The falling-down chimney would not draw, but, with all the gaping holes in the roof, it scarcely mattered. The Danae squatted around the fire. Sometimes they spoke to each other, but mostly they were silent, gazing inward as though they could not tear their attention away from their people's protracted tragedy. Zara lay in a corner, asleep in a drift of wool blankets.

Kaz joined Ash and Rys on the bench in the doorway, where they had been sitting for some time without speaking. The door had fallen flat upon its back, and stars appeared between the pillars of the doorjamb. Macy's creature patrolled the perimeter of the ruin. Sometimes, Rys heard it wander past, creaking and ticking like a clock getting ready to chime the hour. Kaz sat with his hands folded, his elbows upon his knees, just as Ash had always sat on the bench in the pilothouse, when she was young and known by another name. He said, "In the stories, kings are always wise. I thought I was in a story, I guess. Zara thought she had found someone worthy of her allegiance. Like with the drum-dancing: she always thinks that this is the one thing that will ... save her, somehow. I am not like that, am I? Everything she had died in the plague. But I always had a home."

Ash put her arm around him. She said nothing, but Rys saw that it was a peaceful silence, though the peace was not without its cost.

"You are always sitting in the cold, Ash," said Kaz.

"I like to see out. Look at all the people who are willing to join me here, in the cold."

"I left the box for you to find. I thought, if the king does consume me, at least Ashland will be safe. He bragged about me, as if I was his. He commanded me to do things, and when I told him I couldn't . . . it became a kind of war. He thought I was just defying him. But truth is—" Kaz paused, frowning. "I don't know why I didn't, or couldn't. I just knew it would be wrong, to give in to him. Did you get the box?"

"Yes. It's in my satchel. I'll give it back to you before you leave."

There was silence. "So you know," Kaz said. "I was working up to tell you."

"When you offer to go with the Danae, it will give them their hearts back. Anselm never cared what you are, only that he could use you. But the Danae—they are a wise people, and you cannot help but learn from them even as you call down the stars from the sky for them. I think they are what you and Zara need. As for me . . ." Ash sighed. "Your children must be born at Ashland, Kaz. When the day comes, tell Zara that I am a good midwife. You might be surprised at how important such things become to her."

Kaz leaned his head against her shoulder as though he were still a young child. Rys, keeping silent witness to this quiet conversation, marveled at the trust the young man had remembered through all the nightmare years that separated the two of them. Ash had been more of a mother to him than the woman who birthed him ever had been. No wonder it came so naturally to Ash, to call him hers.

Kaz said, "Do you remember when the people of Northern Semel started calling you Ash? You told me the title should never be given to a ghost. You always seemed like a ghost—a kindly one, but still not entirely alive. After the plague, all the people who survived seemed like hollow shells. Sometimes, they just sat down and died out of sheer emptiness, it seemed. You were like that, before. But when you walked through

Macy's door in Fortune, I saw . . . you had come back
from the dead."

Macy's creature walked past, creaking and clashing below the brilliant stars. Come summer, Rys
thought, the night would be filled with song: crickets,
cicadas, birds, and frogs, a cacaphony of reproductive
magic. Though the fields lay abandoned for years to
come, and the farmhouses collapsed into mere piles
of debris, life would continue in this blasted land.

Ash said, "Every time you alter the world, you alter
yourself. Remember that, next time you have a choice
to make."

"I'm sorry about Anselm—"

"I knew his enchantment would wear out, someday.
I am surprised it lasted as long as it did. It was not
your fault. I certainly do miss my dog, though."

"What is going to happen now?"

"I don't know. Ask the seer."

Kaz lifted his head. "Rys?"

Rys began to laugh. "The seer!" But then she found
it was not funny anymore. "We have to talk with the
queen," she said. "We cannot act on her behalf without
her consent."

They sat together until the Sun People took supper
from the fire and Macy began producing boxes and tins
out of her bottomless pack. Kaz awoke Zara, and all
ten of them ate together, sitting in a half circle around
the fire, burning their fingers on the hot meat, and
passing the tins from hand to hand until they were
empty, much to Macy's satisfaction, since that gave her
less to carry. Kaz told the Danae that he and Zara had
decided to return with them to the land of stones, if the
Danae would have them. A'tin took Kaz by the hand,
as he had done with Ash earlier that day. That was all.

Rys took A'tin aside later, and offered to arrange for
supplies to be delivered regularly at Kerlin Point, so
that the Danae—and Ash's only child—would not
starve to death while they waited for their harvest. She
saw no reason to tell Ash, suspecting that she would
feel obliged to object to the expense.

In the morning, Macy told them that Anselm had passed that way during the night. He was alone, she said, but he rode a horse, and was well supplied for a journey. Smelling the smoke of their fire, perhaps, or merely guessing that they had taken shelter at this place, he paused on the road, until Macy's creature stalked forward to challenge him. He continued southward. The shod hooves of his mount cast sparks through the darkness.

Macy, who had been asleep, saw none of this herself. The creature had told her about it, when she went out to wind his key at sunrise.

PART III:

Dancing Jack

Chapter 13: Rys

Rys traveled the Madeena's entire length several times a year, past Allhaven's walled towns and orderly nut groves, all the way to the sea, where the wind turned salty and sweet. She would walk the streets of the port town, reveling in the languages and accents of far countries, fingering the texture of alien cloths. At dockside public houses she shared tables with pilots who made their living following the pathways of stars across the sea. Many a strange tale she heard there, of trees rooted in air and dragons winding through the sea, of lands where the rain never fell and lands where the sun never shone, of icebergs large as continents and islands born of volcano's fire.

Rys recounted some of the stories she had heard, on the long nights she and Ash spent together in the pilot-house as the *Amina* returned to Faerd. One tale she told was of a people who slept the day through in darkened caves, then emerged like bats at dusk to hunt through the night.

"We have nothing in common with them," said Ash.

"Indeed? How long has it been since you saw daylight?"

"I saw the sun at sunset, just as you did."

Ash had fetched supper and taken over the helm while Rys ate. Because they traveled a clear stretch of river, Rys loitered in the window opening with the empty tin plate upon her knee, paying more attention to the rising moon than the river. Ash gazed steadily forward at the distant sightmark at which she had earlier aimed the boat. "I don't know how you endure it," she said.

"I think I am not as burdened by worry as you are," said Rys. Ash did not disagree.

Ash had been assigned to be Rys' helmswoman. Macy, who operated the galley with the help of the ship's children, joined them every evening on the storm deck to watch the sun sink to the horizon. Macy's creature, which she launched at dawn as Ash and Rys stumbled to their bunks, always landed at the exact moment the sun's bottom edge rested upon the edge of the earth. The creature told Macy that Anselm had been set upon by thieves, who took his horse and food and even his shoes, and beat him besides. The next day he turned thief himself, though it nearly cost him his life when the farmer whose cart horse he had stolen chased him with a musket. He was turned out of one town he went into; perhaps they thought he was a madman. Perhaps he would indeed be one, by the time he reached Faerd.

Even though the twists and turns of the river meant the *Amina* had to travel farther than he, the boat's engines soon outpaced Anselm. Macy's creature spent more and more time journeying back and forth, and less and less time observing Anselm, until finally he could not complete the journey at all. "No point wearing him out," said Macy, and she packed the creature away.

They had reached the borderlands by then and had traversed a second time the stretch of new river that had nearly laid claim to the *Amina* on her northbound journey. With Lindy as her helmsman, Rys made that trek by daylight this time, with a drawing board on the windowsill in front of her and her watch in hand, using time to measure distances as she sketched a preliminary map of the new channel.

A storm caught up with them that afternoon. They tied in at a sheltered cove, and played cards by lamplight as the wind buffeted the trees and rain poured down out of the sky. Travel weariness and boredom had brought out the worst in everyone's personality. Rys was called upon to settle several squabbles, and at one point ordered all the children confined, each to a different cabin.

Macy coaxed a half-dozen dried apple pies out of the galley's oven. Some of the passengers went early to bed. Others sat around the salon in melancholy moods, shuffling cards aimlessly, dosing their teacups from someone's long-husbanded whiskey flask, and talking about the plague years.

All of them had lost someone they loved. Some, like Rys, had nearly died themselves. As the whiskey took hold, they told each other things they would be ashamed of in the morning: of the sick they refused to help, the children and lovers they could not save, the insanities in which they participated. They had brawled and looted and attempted suicide and worshiped dark gods. One woman baked while her family died. One man washed his front steps every day, as he always had, though corpses awaiting the death wagon littered the street.

Rys put on her oilskins and went out to inspect the boat. When she came back, they had all gone to bed. Only Ash remained, with an empty teapot beside her. Rys sat beside her and dealt out a card game upon the table, then gathered up the cards and dealt them again.

"Dyan wanted a puppy," said Ash. "For an entire season, it was all she talked about. Ghost Dog had come by then, but the small children never trusted him. He was such a strange dog—I never thought I would miss him so much." She looked at the cards. "Did you want to play a game?"

"Not really." Rys gathered up the cards. "I usually bring some sewing with me on the long boat trips, but I had no idea this one would last so long. There's a half-finished shirt in my sewing basket back at home; I must have wished a dozen times I had brought it with me . . . I am glad those people all went to bed."

"I did not really want to hear what they had to say about the plague. It was excruciating enough to sit at home as I did, trying to convince myself that somehow my kin would be safe. I wanted to believe that there is a limit to the pain we are expected to endure in one lifetime. After I heard they were all dead, I probably could have chosen cousins or other kin to become Ashland's heirs. But I could not face the possibility of having someone else to lose." Ash shook the empty teapot absently. "Do you ever regret having had no children?"

"I always have regrets. But I never saw a man I wanted, and I never loved anything more than the river. You wanted Naiman's children, I remember."

"And a bitter mother they would have been cursed with, the poor things."

"I will fetch some more hot water."

Ash set down the teapot. "Don't bother."

The *Amina* creaked and sighed, tugging upon her moorings as a gust of wind shoved her aside. Rain rattled loudly upon the windows. The lamp swung upon its chain, and all the shadows in the salon rocked rhythmically with its motion. Ash reached for Rys' hand. Their fingers interfolded.

"The river does go by your Margo's door," said Ash.

"Indeed the river does. It is a most convenient arrangement. The entire relationship is convenient." Rys lifted Ash's hand and held it to her cheek. Even the skin at the backs of Ash's fingers was scoured rough by hard work. Rys touched one of those strong fingers with her lips.

All the tales told this night of people whose lives had cruelly and abruptly ended had made Rys desperate. She kissed another finger. "Would you share my bed this night?"

When she looked up, Ash was smiling. Lately, Rys had seen that expression frequently: respect and affection and a wry amusement all mixed together, the loving look that one old friend gives another in the midst of an intimate conversation. Ash said, "I suppose Kiva and Lindy thought they were doing you a favor by subjecting you so much to my company. What about your ethics? What about being chosen?"

"I don't care anymore."

"I had better go in my cabin and lock the door, then. When we part, I want to part friends."

Chilled by this reminder of their imminent separation, Rys let their hands return to the tabletop. "On the other hand, I could use this night to do my laundry." Yet she would have remained, except that Ash helped her along by letting go of her hand and bidding her good night.

Alone in the galley, Rys bathed herself and washed everything except the clothes she needed to wear. By the time she finished, the storm had begun to abate. She hung her clothes to dry, and climbed to the storm deck. Ash already stood at the rail, soaking wet, with the rain misting down around her, and the moon's face peering through the ghostly clouds. She could have been standing there for hours. "The storm is breaking," she said.

Once, the river had been a mystery. Every bend revealed unexplored territory; every crossing contained a hundred secrets to be unpuzzled. But as Rys learned to cipher the river, the mathematics overwhelmed the wizardry. She learned its winding list of a thousand names, and the river was no longer a stranger. Its dangers became known, and mostly predictable, and even its changes became part of the pattern. A love affair had become a marriage, though not a marriage without romance.

This night, carried by the current down dark, moonlit waters, with the sky shattering into stars and the moon dropping down like a sliver of gold from a smith's hand, Rys and Ash journeyed into the river's silence, side by side at the *Amina*'s helm. From storm break to sunrise, Rys breathed in the stars' fire and breathed out the stillness, and within her heart she saw the clouds parting.

They traveled south into spring, which dropped its petals upon the *Amina*'s decks and filled the night with the din of amorous frogs. In Fortune, many of the passengers disembarked. Rys used her authority to close the river to northbound traffic, citing the extreme dangers posed by its altered course. If Anselm hoped to return to Faerd by riverboat, she meant to keep him waiting. The *Amina* took on new crew, some cargo, and passengers for Saltertown. With the current friendly, the river well-behaved, and the weather holding clear, the journey from Fortune to Saltertown, past Faerd's half-abandoned towns and greening fields, took only four days. The strangest part of the entire journey was its ending: after so much fear and hardship, such dull predictability.

The *Amina*'s crew gave a great hurrah when they rounded Salter Bend, for two of their number had not lived to see home port again, and the rest of them certainly must have wondered if they would share that fate. Rys had forgone sleep that morning, to pack her gear and bid farewell to the crew. She stood at the rail with the passengers now, dressed in shore clothes, watching Saltertown draw near. The river's commerce was Fortune's lifeblood, but more boats and riverfolk called Saltertown home than any other place upon the river. People crawled over half a hundred riverboats still tied down to a maze of winter docks, polishing the brass and covering the winter's neglect with a coat of white paint. They shouted in disbelief as they identified the *Amina*, crying the news from boat to boat faster than the *Amina* could wend through the maze, so that a crowd had already gathered upon the landing when Lindy sounded the incoming whistle.

Ash and Macy joined Rys on the deck. Ash's satchel and bedroll lay at her feet and she held her battered old hat in her hand. Sleeplessness cast her face with shadows. Macy's pack, little more than an empty bag with a single dancing jack pinned on the outside, sagged from one shoulder.

They disembarked in the first wave of passengers. A red-faced man raced up to the landing, muddied by his heedless race across town, coat flapping like a flag. "Captain Garvin," muttered Rys, and Ash and Macy crowded close to her to shield her from recognition as they passed. They might as well not have bothered, for the captain's eyes were only for his beloved boat. He shouted hoarsely and incoherently at Lindy in the pilothouse, tears in his eyes, reaching out with both arms as though he could embrace the entire river. "He always was a demonstrative man," said Rys as they hurried past. It was to avoid him and the celebration dinner that he was sure to host that she left the boat in disguise. They had no time to spare.

A rush of townspeople, probably the families of the missing crewmembers, hurried down the road. The three of them stepped into an alley between warehouses to let them pass, and Rys looked back at the *Amina*. Many a larger boat plied the Madeena, but none sturdier. Lord Diggen could not have chosen a better boat to hijack into a storm. For over thirty days, that brave boat had been Rys' home. Now steam, released from her boilers, settled down around her bows. *Another journey ended,* Rys thought, *and another journey begun.*

The plague had made two passes at Saltertown, but it had not lingered long. Those who were at home when the plague hit fared far better than those who were abroad; many were the riverfolk who never came home that year. According to rumor, the taverns never closed, even at the height of plague. Today, a giddy market day crowd shared the streets with horses and wagons, confused sheep and shrieking children. Rys changed some of her gold for smaller coin. They hired a wagon at a livery stable and had soon left the furor of the busy town behind.

Between Saltertown and Seven Bells City flows a quiet river with a road beside it where the barge mules walk up and down, towing their loads of grapes, wine, apples, cider, and brandy to the Saltertown docks. Ancient apple orchards and vineyards filled the valley, flowing over the creases in the land like a pattern woven into a blanket. Today, the sun shone through a haze of mist beyond which the hills lurked, sometimes mysterious shadows and sometimes illuminated visions of verdant green, with the white-frocked trees standing in rows like farmgirls at a dance. They passed a wagon that had broken down on its way to the Saltertown market. Ash climbed down to buy a penny's worth of

peas from the hapless farmers, which they popped out
of their shells and ate raw. They tasted of spring: green
and unfinished, sweet at the core.

"We will not have peas in Northern Semel for another month at least," said Ash. She and Rys, who both
knew how to drive a cart, sat side by side on the
wagon seat, talking to keep each other from falling
asleep in the gentle sunlight.

Macy reclined on the bedrolls in back, waving languidly at the farmworkers who walked among the
grapevines in their red felt hats. Ash had taken off her
baggy jersey, and rolled up the sleeves of her
workstained shirt to the patched elbows, revealing
muscular forearms still brown from last summer's tan.

"The best potatoes come from Northern Semel,"
said Macy. "They keep best, too."

"Oh, it's true. But a long, hungry winter we endure.
It must be hot here in the summertime."

With the sun high in the sky, they came to a roadside
tavern where they lunched on brook trout, dipped in
ground corn and pan fried, and raisin dumplings sprinkled with brown sugar. A garrulous bargeman and his
mule were the tavern's only other patrons. "This is a
fine place," said Macy. "Forty-six years in Fortune,
and look at all I've missed."

It was after sunset that the steep roofs and seven
towers of Seven Bells City appeared around a curve of
the road, sunset-gilded black slate above steep stone
walls, with narrow, cobbled roads ducking between
them like rabbit paths through a hedge. The city sat at
the edge of a wide flood plain where horses and cattle
grazed in the dusk. A lamplighter hurried ahead of
their wagon, lighting the major intersections of the narrow road with the deep orange flames of burning oil.
Although for every lamp that was lit a dozen more remained quenched, it was not so dark that Rys could not
see the boarded-up windows.

During King Anselm's time, this road would have
been crowded with night revelers from sunset until
sunrise. Now, the clattering wheels of the wagon
echoed down the abandoned street. When Rys last vis-

ited here at the height of the plague, the streets had been frenetically, desperately busy. Inured though she had already become to the sight of death, there had been more of it to see here than she cared to remember. But this echoing silence was the stillness of a mausoleum, even more eerie when the vineyards and orchards through which they passed all day had been so well maintained and populated with busy workers.

"Eh, another dead city," said Macy. She shifted restlessly in the back of the wagon.

Rys, her own backside thoroughly bruised by the jolting journey, peered ahead into the light-punctuated darkness. "There used to be inns here. Perhaps we should have lodged with farmers outside town."

The echoing rattle of their wagon wheels started to unnerve her, and she halted the horses gladly when they passed a shuffling figure. "Pardon me, can you tell us where to find lodging?"

The figure paused, head tilted. Rys shouted, thinking the person might be deaf, "Lodging! A place to rest!"

Lamplight shone upon a bald head, but it was a woman's face that peered up out of the many layered wrappings, blankets and shawls seven or eight deep, like a turtle peering cautiously out of its shell. Very strange she looked, without even eyebrows or eyelashes and one hand plucking all the time at her face as though to pick out even the fine, downy hairs growing upon her cheeks. "Rest?" she said, cackling a laugh, hollow and empty as a rock demon giggling in its cave.

"I doubt she can help us," muttered Macy in the back, though not uncharitably. Enough plague madness she must have seen in her own home town.

Ash, the closest to her, leaned down and offered a coin. The bald woman eyed it suspiciously in the gloom. Ash said, "Food and drink, a bed. Where can we find it?"

"Ask the queen," she said. "Oh, yes, ask the queen. Where has it all gone?" She tottered forward to take the penny. Ash, always kindhearted, let her have it. Rys clucked to the horses and slapped their rumps

gently with the reins. Wearily, they started forward
again.

"What now?" said Macy, but no one replied. Rys
wished they had even one weapon among them; the
spring twilight had not lasted long enough to suit her.

Somberly, Ash leaned her head upon her hand, staring down the dimly lit street, turning to glance down
the dark byways as they passed. "This is the only road
with lamps lit. Why is that?"

They passed a corner where the road's name was
glazed in tile embedded in the wall. "Briary," read Rys.
"This is the road to the palace, I'd wager: it's famous
for its roses. A dozen shuttered inns we must have
passed by now, and not one with the welcome lamp
lit."

"Perhaps we should ask the queen, like the woman
said," muttered Ash.

Rys urged the horses into a weary, clopping trot.
Though they passed a few other people, shuffling and
even striding through the shadows, she did not stop
again to ask their way, or allow the horses to slow until
the road entered a startling blaze of light and opened
up into a wide courtyard, where a dozen iron gateways
gave access to the marble entryways of fine town-
houses. Three carriages stood at the curb, and Rys
heard the sound of a trained voice singing sweetly to
the tinkling of a concertina.

Ash peered into the shadows for a better look at the
fine stonework of the wall on the far side of the yard.
Climbing roses badly in need of pruning clothed the
top of the wall and drooped over its sides, pale flowers
budding in a jungle of wicked thorns. The stone arch-
way had no gates, and the hospitality lamps were lit, so
Rys turned the wagon through the entrance and up a
beautiful carriageway overhung by blooming trees.
The drift of blossoms underfoot muffled the horses'
hoofbeats. Lamps of polished brass lined the roadway,
casting light and shadow upon a lush, overgrown garden. At the top of the carriage way stood the formal
entryway of a pretentious building: columns and arches
at the top of a broad flight of steps, and a dozen stone

towers looming overhead, spiking the stars. Here, too, lamplight blazed, and at the sound of their humble wagon rattling over the roadstones, an ancient man in servant's livery came down the stairs, leaning upon a cane.

"This is no inn," said Ash, as Rys drew up to the foot of the stairs.

"Madam Pilot," said the old man, recognizing her even though Rys barely remembered him from her visit six years ago. "Welcome, in the name of the queen."

"If you would tell Her Majesty that the Master of the Pilot's Guild begs her hospitality—"

"Enter, enter. No, leave your bags."

Wide-eyed, Ash and Macy climbed stiffly out of the wagon. "I was just making a joke," Ash said.

"I could not think of what else to do. Be at ease. You will not be the first farmer to guest here."

They followed the old steward up the stairs, through a gigantic carved door, and into a magnificent entryway. Here, lamp oil did not burn so profligately, but two more aged servants appeared at the ringing of the old man's bell. One bustled to light more lamps, and the other climbed upstairs on creaking knees to prepare guest rooms for them. "Her Majesty begs you to join her for supper," said the steward, though he certainly had not had the opportunity to consult with the queen.

Rys was the least shabbily dressed of the three of them, but six days tamping through Vateria's woods had left even her shore clothing somewhat the worse for wear. "Of course," she said, shrugging at the others' dismay. Lamp in hand, the old man showed the way down an echoing hallway, past the formal dining room which was dark and cold as a vault, down a flight of stairs, and into a gigantic, noisy kitchen, where he bent over abruptly to snag by the shirt a chortling toddler who seemed poised to tumble headlong into a bucket of soapy water with the mop still in it.

"Even Evie's house is not this bad," muttered Ash.

Children ran amok among the dangers of hot stoves, sharp knives, and blazing fires as a dozen elderly servants stirred and cooked and chopped busily, uttering cries of appreciation as the first of the bubbling pies came out of the oven.

"This way, madams," said the steward, unruffled, as the toddler tucked under his arm uttered a shriek of protest. In a corner of the kitchen, a middle-aged woman with puppets on her fingers held a youthful audience enthralled. A bowl of half-shelled peas sat beside her on the tabletop, forgotten. The steward gestured at some empty chairs, where the table had been partially set for supper. They all sat down, but first Ash collected the bowl of peas so she could finish shelling them. When the woman had finished telling her tale, Rys stepped forward. "Your Majesty."

"Madam Pilot!" Queen Lynthe plucked the puppets hastily from her fingers and set the child on her lap onto the floor so she could stand up and take Rys' hand. "What a delight to see you again. I fear I was not expecting you—oh, dear." She looked around the kitchen. "I gave Mister Donil a list of people who do not stand much on ceremony, and I fear you were one of them."

"I cannot tell you what a relief it is to sit in this kitchen. May I present my companions, Macy, a toymaker of Fortune . . ."

Macy had paled and leapt to her feet when she realized that the puppeteer was the queen. Lynthe took her hand. "A toymaker? Upon my word, I thought there were none left. And from Fortune, no less, where there are so few children!"

"Ash of Ashland, a farmer of Northern Semel."

"Thank you for shelling the peas," said the queen graciously. Ruler of a land of ghosts, her glamour was fragile at best, but it dissolved suddenly in the silence. The gracious hostess, the doting mother, these roles also gave way, revealing the heart-weary woman within, and the paralyzing guilt which held her in thrall, and the unsteady burning of a newly ignited hope. She had taken off all her masks at the sound of Ash's name; never had Rys, or perhaps anyone, seen her so clearly. *So this is the queen,* thought Rys, and understood much in the course of that long silence.

After supper, warm fires, wash basins filled with warm, scented water, and plates of sweetmeats in their opulent if somewhat dusty rooms demonstrated that the servants' age did not prevent them from knowing their business. Rys found Ash seated tentatively in a carved and upholstered chair, working with one hand at the laces of the booted foot crossed upon her knee. "It is a feather bed," Ash said. "Do you know, I have been sleeping on the floor for six years? I couldn't fit a bed into the kitchen, and I couldn't chop enough wood to keep a second room warm."

Rys sat on another chair and felt her bones seem to collapse within her like sticks falling over in a sack. She could no longer endure sleeplessness with half the grace she used to have. She asked, "Why do you suppose the servants are so old? And where did all those children come from? The queen only has three."

A voice spoke from the hallway. "The able-bodied servants have all been given farms to manage. They have sent their children to be reared in royal service, for their families have served the House of Nilan for many generations."

Both of them rose hastily to their feet. Queen Lynthe stood in the doorway, robed in Faerd's royal blue, with a circlet upon her head. Rys bowed without realizing it. Ash seemed nearly as surprised to find herself upon one knee, with the queen's hand in hers. "Ash of Ashland," said the queen. "In my library is an ancient, illuminated book—three hundred years old it is, or older. In that book your name is written, one of the hundred names of the rulers of the land."

Ash had bowed her head over the queen's hand, but now she lifted her face. Not more than two or three years separated their ages, but in that light Lynthe seemed far older. Ash said, "The Ash of Ashland never was a ruler, though by custom the people of Semel turned to Ashland for leadership when it was needed. My people swore fealty to your father's mother, along with all of Semel."

"My book says there is power in Ashland, ancient as the earth. It is just legend, my advisors say."

"It is both legend and truth, your majesty, like most things in Semel."

"Well, I will not have you bow to me." Lynthe lifted Ash to her feet. "Why is your face so familiar to me?"

"Perhaps you saw me many years ago when Anselm was still king. I was known then by my given name, Cydna."

"Cydna? Twice welcome, then. Surely it has done Rys' heart good to find you alive after all these years."

Ash, who certainly had been expecting a less courteous response, seemed taken aback. Rys said, "Indeed it has."

"Madam Pilot, the prince consort and all my counselors are in Allhaven renewing a trade treaty, but I expect their return sometime tomorrow. However, your unannounced coming suggests to me that perhaps whatever brings you here may be best discussed in their absence."

"I think so. If you will excuse me, I will fetch Macy."

Macy, who had heard the voices next door, stood indecisively in the center of her room. The night the *Amina* landed for the second time at Kerlin Point and she had to set foot again on foreign soil, she had looked like this: delighted and desperately afraid. When they returned to Ash's room, the queen's elderly servants had come and gone, leaving behind them a tray where cups of a hot beverage steamed. Ash, holding an exotic flower which she had plucked from the arrangement on the tray, discussed hothouses with the queen.

"Now," said Lynthe, when Rys had served them all with what seemed to be hot milk, except that it smelled like nothing she had ever scented before. "I wish you would not mince words; every year that passes I have less patience with long speeches."

"Your brother Anselm is not dead," said Ash.

Lynthe sat in a chair. She looked around blindly for a place to put her cup, and finally set it at her feet on the floor.

Ash said, "He has been under an enchantment, and

for most of these seven years has lived with me, though I did not know it, in the form of a dog. By an accident of fate, both of us became passengers on the riverboat *Amina*, along with Rys and Macy and ... many others. As you no doubt know, that is the boat Lord Diggen hijacked to flee northward, out of your reach. In Vateria, Anselm's enchantment was unintentionally broken. We left him there. He is coming back to Faerd, traveling by horseback."

"It will be a difficult, if not impossible, journey," said Rys, for the queen so far seemed unable or disinclined to speak. "He has no money, and no one in Vateria recognizes him. If he tells them who he is ... the people of Vateria are not kind to madmen. Perhaps he will never even set foot upon Faerd's shores—"

"He will find a way," said the queen. She rose to her feet, white-faced, and walked aimlessly across the room, heedlessly knocking over her cup and spilling its creamy contents across the priceless carpet in passing. "He will find a way," she said again. "Anselm gets what he wants."

Rys said, "You are not as surprised as I expected, Your Majesty."

Lynthe stood at the window, the heavy draperies crushed in her hand. The windowpanes broke the sky into black diamonds, each one scattered with starlight. "Surprised? The land's best woodsmen could find no blood, no body, no evidence of an attack at all. I have always expected Anselm to return. One would think, after considering the matter for seven years, I would know now what to do." Stiff and queenly, she gazed out at the remote stars.

Rys sipped from her cup, and the remarkable flavors it contained could almost distract her for a time. It was the hardening of the queen's face and the deepening of her silence which brought Rys once again to speech. "There are others who have seen him. There will be rumors. But only we three know for certain, and we have vowed to keep Anselm from the throne. Your Majesty, we are your friends. Each of us is more than

we seem. Perhaps we can help you. Dissemble to others, if you feel you must, but not to us."

Rys thought it a poor speech, but it proved enough
to turn the queen from the darkness outside. "Dissemble?" Her laugh was more harsh, perhaps, than she had
intended. "There are some in the world who serve their
own self-interest in every decision they make, and it is
they who sleep peacefully at night, while we who think
we serve a higher master are condemned to suffer from
a tortured conscience. We do what we think is right,
but in the end we, too, must ask ourselves if what we
see as right might be, after all, only our own self-
interest. If I kill my brother so that I can remain
queen—that is what we are discussing, is it not—
whose interests do serve? That of Faerd, or that of its
queen?"

Ash said, "If you need a pilot and a toymaker and a
farmer to tell you what you already know, then we will
say it. It will only harm Faerd to have Anselm as king.
The future of this land cannot be served by returning to
the past."

"And it will not harm Faerd to have as its queen the
kind of woman who would murder her own brother?"

Reluctantly, though she had given Lynthe plenty of
opportunity to speak the truth voluntarily, Rys asked,
"Has it harmed us these last seven years?"

Queen Lynthe said quietly, "How can you have lived
through the plague and ask such a question? It has de-
stroyed us."

Chapter 14: Ash

Ash awoke before dawn. At midsummer, in Ashland, she sometimes jerked awake like this, with the day already too short, though the sun had not yet risen. But she had reconciled herself to a year without a harvest; it was not her abandoned farm which burdened her now.

The palace servants had taken her clothing away, tutting over the ragged, stained, and oft-mended cloth, shaking their heads in dismay at the rotting workboots. They had left her a robe large enough for someone twice her size. She kilted it up and laughed in the mirror at her weatherbeaten face swathed in so much velvet.

Barefoot, she went out into the hallway where sunlight spilled across the frowning portrait of a long-dead king. The window here looked out upon the rose garden, where, in the pale light of dawn, a few budding roses glowed like jewels. At the far end of the garden, a gray woman walked slowly, carrying a basket on her arm.

Ash found a stairway, another hallway, and a door which led out into the garden. The cobbled path she followed glistened with cold dew. Her feet were wet and numbed by the time she stood before the Queen of Faerd, who lifted a hand in greeting. Ash turned and walked beside her. Queen Lynthe wore an old leather apron, with a pair of silver scissors hanging from the waist by a ribbon. She clipped the unopened rosebuds one by one and laid them in her basket.

The walls of the rose garden had been pieced together out of a rich golden stone, each piece fitting into the next like fingers of a folded hand. The stonemason had long since died and been returned to earth, but the mason's magic still survived in these stones. These enchanted walls separated the garden from the anguish and chaos and crying needs of the land. This Ash saw, with a vision so newly resurrected that she kept rubbing at her eyes like a bedazzled infant. Had the forgotten wall builder known what he was doing, any more than the first Ash had known, when he planted his seeds in the aftermath of the devastating fire?

The night before, Queen Lynthe had left her guests to stare at each other over their unfinished drinks, as though, having told them something she had never told anyone, she could no longer endure their company. Ash had slept deeply and peacefully in her feather bed, even though she had entrusted too many precious things this spring to the careless inattention of fate. Her soul had grown deep roots during its long winter.

There was much she needed to say to the queen, but she did not know how to begin. They paced together through the silent, enchanted garden, and gathered up the roses as they opened. Lynthe bowed before the ancient plants and placed her fingers gracefully between the thorns. Ash watched, recognizing a kindred soul. The queen must have often walked here, from first bud to last blossom and on into the winter, until she became the garden, and it bloomed inside her.

"I have lost my entire family," Ash said. "Now I am finding a new family, one member at a time."

"Shall I call you cousin?" said the queen.

It took Ash a moment to remember that fellow regents call each other cousin, whether they are related or not. She laughed.

Lynthe reached for another rose. "There is such irony in this: that the Ash of Ashland, about whom I have long wondered, should bear me such terrible news; that you were once Anselm's worst enemy and yet you gave him shelter; that you have been blamed these seven years for the plague which I caused . . . and now that you seem to know me on sight, as I feel I know you. I scarcely know what to do: if I laugh, it is bitter; if I weep, I smile through my grief."

"Then you understand," Ash said. "You understand as much as I do."

"This is understanding?" Lynthe had bloodied a finger, but seemed not to notice. She had come directly from her bed to the garden, it seemed, with her hair uncombed and a pillow crease still etched into her cheek. "I have been trying to remember why . . . I did what I did. It is like trying to see through a warped piece of glass. I had lived my life upon the shore of history, watching, often without much interest. How was it that suddenly the current swept me up and bore me forward?"

"This his how it happened to me: I walked down a street in Fortune with a basket of potatoes in my hand, and saw a man standing upon the corner, reciting poetry with his eyes closed."

The queen shaded her eyes as the sun suddenly breached the wall. "So simple as that? I paid little heed to the Poet's Revolution. I was busy with my children. Yet, when we heard that King Bartyn had killed Naiman the Poet, and Anselm called for a celebration, I was stunned. I came out into this garden and walked here—for hours. I knew that Anselm would challenge the new law. For a year already, he had delayed the formation of the parliament, with one excuse and another. Now that Naiman was gone, I knew that Anselm would not be afraid anymore. He would wage war against his own people for the rest of his life, rather than give up even a drop of his power."

Lynthe carefully added another rose to her collection. "I found an enchanter to help me, and so the spell was cast, and I never saw Anselm again. It appalls me still, that it was so easy. Do you know, I did not do it to become queen, but to rid the land of its king. When the lords of the land begged me to take the crown . . . well, what did I expect? Oh, I do not even remember anymore. A long time ago, it was: a different age, a different world."

They stepped into the shadow of the garden wall. Here the rosebushes had not yet broken their dormancy. The tines of a rake had scratched a wavering artwork into the damp soil. The queen said, "And then there rose up the plague, and everything I had done and hoped to do became meaningless. So the gods make fools of us all."

Ash said, "During the *Amina*'s journey north, three people were lost overboard, another six were badly hurt, and the boat was nearly sunk due to Lord Diggen's obstinacy. When he castigated Rys for nearly losing the boat, she lost her temper and hit him. Afterward . . ." Ash paused, for the queen had laughed despite herself, ". . . I overheard some of the passengers saying that Rys was wrong to hit Lord Diggen because she is a commoner. I never thought that the queen herself would say something even more absurd."

"Indeed. And what was it that I said?"

"That the plague was a punishment, visited upon all the people of Allhaven, Faerd, and Ashami, because you were, as you put it last night, the kind of woman who would murder her brother."

Queen Lynthe dropped her scissors and made a gesture as though she could not bear to hear her terrible secret said so openly. Ash spoke on ruthlessly. "When I plant seeds in my garden and they are eaten by birds, do I blame myself for what the birds have done? Do I say that they have eaten my seeds because I deserve it? Do I lose all hope and never plant another seed? My neighbors would laugh at me for doing such a thing, and advise me to give my farm cats less milk, so they will not be such lazy hunters."

"It is not the same thing at all."

"Do you truly believe that ill fortune is visited only upon those who deserve it? If it were true, then Anselm would never have survived childhood, and you would be queen anyway."

"You take a farmer's view of the world. But I am the Queen of Faerd, and I am responsible to the gods."

"And you think I am not?" said Ash softly. Perhaps Lynthe did not hear. They walked together among the rosebushes sleeping in spring's cold shadows, until suddenly they stepped out into a blaze of light from the newly risen sun, and Lynthe reached for a rosebud whose green overskirt could no longer conceal the scarlet beneath. Ash said, "You are the queen, and yet you hesitate at the very moment you know you must act. Are you reluctant to protect Faerd from Anselm because you are afraid of causing a new plague?"

Lynthe abruptly set the basket down upon the ground. "I am weary."

Ash looked into the queen's face, as though she were peering at herself in a mirror, and then looked away. She bent over and chose a flower from the basket. It was red and richly perfumed. She shut her eyes, asking herself what to do. She knew about weariness and loneliness and the crushing weight of guilt. Yet what presumption was this, that she thought she could advise a queen?

She opened her eyes. On the far side of the garden, Macy and Rys stepped through a doorway. The rising sun haloed Macy's frizzed head. Rys' white shirt blazed with light. "We ought to go greet them," said the queen.

Neither of them moved. Ash said, "It is not an accident that the three of us have come to you. We have brought you a choice, and you must make it."

Queen Lynthe said, "I realize this." She was polite and cold.

Ash, who had been so ready to call this benign and well-meaning woman her kin, suddenly remembered that Queen Lynthe had only recently exiled a man she had loved since childhood, when he came too close to her long-hidden secret. Despite the sun shining on the rich cloth of Ash's velvet robe, Ash shivered in a chill of prescience. What did Rys see when she gazed upon the queen? Lynthe had many faces; had Rys ever even seen this one?

Her two friends were coming, chatting idly as they followed the winding pathways among the flowers. What would happen, Ash asked herself, if in panic or ruthlessness the queen decided to rid herself of the three of them? Did even Rys, who had said so seriously that they were the heroes, completely understand what they had put at risk here? Not just their lives, but the flames they kept protected within the shelter of their lives.

Macy and Rys came up to them, bowing, offering morning greetings and compliments on the garden, responding politely to the queen's inquiries about how well they had slept.

Ash waited for the right moment. She took a breath, and said, "Macy makes wonderful toys. She still has one left, I think, a dancing jack. Perhaps she will offer it to you ... for your children."

With confused pleasure Macy dug the dancing jack out of one of her pockets. In this short month the toy had journeyed from spring to winter and back to spring again, but it shone like new, its paint unchipped. Upon its head it wore half a crown and half a fool's cap. Macy shook her head apologetically, but Queen Lynthe seemed amused, and reached out to pull its string, as innocently as a child running eagerly forward to pet a dragon.

Ash felt Rys' gaze, piercing her to the heart. How recently had she sworn anew that she would never take a hand in altering anyone's fate? Well, in this moment she had foresworn the luxury of cowardice; whatever was to happen now, she never again could choose not to act, to hide behind Ashland's thickets, to be only a hard-working, fate-afflicted farmer. Rys gazed at her, solemn and unsmiling, and Ash wondered if she had lost her or found her, and whether, in the end, it would even matter.

The queen took a ring from her finger to offer in payment. Macy put the dancing jack into her hand.

Ash watched. Even as she smiled, a tear drew a freezing line upon her cheek. One hand curled at her side into a fist. The other hand held a budding red rose. One foot was rooted to the earth. The other lifted lightly, as though music played and it was time to dance.

🌿   🌿   🌿

The Queen of Faerd came to Fortune on a magnificent, balmy day, with white clouds piling upon the hilltops and peach trees blooming in the abandoned orchards. A half-drunk stevedore, the only person upon the landing as the boat came sweetly in, stared in disbelief at the silken banners snapping in the wind and the blue ribbons and white paper roses decorating the *Amina*'s railings; and then he took to his heels, shouting and waving his arms. Before the landing stage had been secured, a noisy, cheering crowd had begun to gather, and no few of the people carried armloads of roses hastily snatched from the city's wilderness of gardens.

Standing on the storm deck, waiting for Rys to be free to speak with her, Ash watched the crowd gather. During the entire seven-day journey from Saltertown to Fortune, she and Rys had scarcely exchanged more than a brief greeting in passing. The *Amina* carried a full crew, including a second pilot and two helmsmen, and Rys, dealing with the unceasing distractions of her dual role as captain and first pilot, never worked alone.

The last time Ash and Rys spoke privately was in Seven Bells City, the same day they walked with the queen in the rose garden. Rys had knocked on Ash's door after breakfast. "I hardly recognize you," she said.

Ash patted self-consciously at the new wool trousers, the crisp cloth of a never-worn shirt. "This shirt is not half as fine as yours."

"It takes time to sew a good shirt." Rys carried her duffle across her shoulder. "They are bringing our wagon around. Are you ready to go?"

"How could I be ready so soon for another journey?"

Rys sat on the edge of the bed and cupped her chin in her hand. "We'll have a day in Saltertown before the queen comes."

"You'll be busy."

"You could go shopping."

Ash laughed. "Do you think I remember how?"

Rys smiled with her mouth but not her eyes. "We are parting ways."

"Not for—"

"—days yet, I know. But every step we take now will draw us farther apart. By the time we say our last good-bye, we will already be gone from each other. The river will own me again, and Ashland will own you, and Macy will again belong to Fortune."

"As it should be," said Ash.

Rys said nothing. Soon she would put on her uniform and become again the master pilot, the Guildmaster, the devoted servant of the queen. She would go home to her Margo, complaining of what a wearisome journey it had been, and never tell her—

"No," Rys said, as though she could actually read Ash's thoughts. Ash sat beside her with her arms around her, until they heard the sound of wagonwheels in the courtyard below. Rys washed her face with cold water. She had been weeping, but now her eyes had the look of polished steel. They went down to begin their journey to Saltertown, where Rys left Ash and Macy at an inn while she found Lindy and Kiva and then hijacked the *Amina* again, this time in the name of the queen.

On this journey, Ash and Macy had too much time on their hands. They ate every meal with the queen, and played cards with each other until the day Macy threw the card deck into the river. Macy took to standing at the rail, watching the riverbank. Ash read the book and newspapers she had bought in Saltertown, and braced herself for another parting. Now, as Ash stood on the storm deck, looking out once again at the plague-devastated city of Fortune, she watched Macy, her empty pack sagging from her shoulders, walk briskly ashore and shoulder her way through the crowd. Without looking back, Macy stepped into a passageway between two buildings and disappeared from sight.

The *Amina* sighed. White steam drifted across the bright sky. "The queen will not disembark for a while," said Rys, coming out into the sunshine. "I can't tell you what a relief it will be to have her safely ashore and no longer my responsibility. What's the matter, Ash?"

"Macy is gone, without even a farewell."

Rys looked from Ash's face to the satchel and bed-roll slung over her shoulder. "And you, too, are going ashore."

"I'm going to wait in Fortune while you continue north."

"Did the queen ask you to keep her company here?"

"There is something I have to do here, something which concerns no one but myself."

"I wish you would stay on the *Amina*."

"I have nothing to do, and no one to keep me company. You do not need me getting in your way."

By late summer, most farmers looked like Rys: too worn to smile, too tired to take pride in the pending harvest. She said, "It could be as long as ten days before I return."

Ash said nothing.

"You'll need money. Don't argue." Rys took Ash by the elbow and escorted her to the mud clerk's tiny office, where she wrote a letter authorizing Ash to charge her expenses to the Pilot's Guild, and put a purse into her satchel which weighed it down substantially. "Tell the dockmaster where I can find you."

Ash was tempted to retort angrily that she followed no one's orders but her own. She smiled instead and took her beloved friend's hand in hers. "Do not linger upon the river," she said. "I will be waiting for you."

❦   ❦   ❦

Eight days later, the roses of Fortune were spilling over the crumbling walls, filling the ruins with their sweet fragrance, and blossoming everywhere in such profusion that most people wore a white rosebud tucked into a ragged buttonhole, to recognize the presence of the Queen of Faerd in their city. Ash used her pocketknife to pick a bouquet of roses as she walked in the evening to Macy's cellar workshop.

She did not miss Kaz as much as she hated his absence, but the silence where Rys and Macy's voices had been never ceased to trouble her. Macy, at least, was in the city. Ash had visited her one other time, to ask her to store some things for Kaz. Already, a hundred dancing jacks hung from her workshop ceiling. Ash doubted Macy would remember their brief conversation; she worked in a frenzy the entire time they talked.

She reached for Macy's door just as a man and a woman came out. She did not know them, but they seemed to recognize the dancing jack hanging from her satchel, and one of them said, "You must be Ash. We just brought Macy some supper and more paint; perhaps you can make her eat."

"I will try," said Ash. She had asked Macy how she was managing to survive when she was so busy making toys that she had no time to sell them. Macy had told her not to worry. The basket on the man's arm, which had probably come in filled with supplies, was now filled with dancing jacks, their wry, eager, laughing and weeping faces peering out from around the edge of a napkin. So it seemed other people were selling them for Macy. At the rate she was making them, there would soon be a dancing jack in every household in Fortune.

The man said, "Are you going to remain in Fortune? You would be warmly welcomed."

At least once a day, and sometimes more often, total strangers came up to her like this, and invited her to make Fortune her home. Kaz and Zara's drums had created a community, one or another of them told Ash. Though they did not know of her kinship with Kaz, they recognized Ash on sight as one who would be at home within that circle.

"My place is in Ashland," she said. "Every day, I regret it more."

The man and the woman nodded solemnly and bowed from the waist as Ash passed them on the steps. She did not bother to knock, but opened the door and went in.

Macy sat upon a stool, frowning absorbedly in the dim light of a lamp whose wick she had forgotten to turn, painting a dancing jack's face. Ash did not disturb her. She turned up the wick and gathered up the paint-clotted brushes to wash them in a pot of warm water. Macy's visitors had left a meat pie upon the hearth, and a steaming pot of soup, and a flat cake sprinkled with sugar. By the time Macy began looking around distractedly for another brush, Ash had served up the food on the tea table by the fire.

"I washed all your paintbrushes. Come and eat some supper while they dry."

"Ash," said Macy in some surprise. "How are you?"

"Lonely. Leave off your work for a quarter of an hour and eat with me."

"Goodness, is it dark already? Well, I suppose I am a little hungry." Macy grimaced as she got stiffly down from the stool. "What day is it?" She laughed out loud when Ash told her. "Is it still spring?" she asked. "Is it still the same year?"

They sat down together by the fire. Ash had been working hard all day and was ravenous. Between the two of them, they emptied the soup pot and the pie dish, and quibbled politely over the last slice of cake, until they finally split it between them and washed it down with the teapot's dregs. "Are you still waiting for the *Amina*?" said Macy.

"Still waiting."

"And the queen?"

"She goes out riding every day, up and down the streets of Fortune. She visits shops and homes, she wanders the burial ground. No one knows where she will next appear. You never saw such house cleaning as she has inspired in this city."

"It is about time she came to Fortune." Macy swung the kettle over the fire to heat water for another pot of tea. "How goes your work?"

"So you were listening to me last time I was here!" Macy grinned. "I may be a crazy old coot, but my hearing is still good."

"My search is going badly," said Ash. "I found nothing today. Nothing at all."

"That's too bad. Maybe tomorrow your luck will turn." Macy's hands were covered with paint. Her face

was drawn, her cheeks hollow, her eyes bright and blue
as the spring sky. "I have been thinking about your lost
children . . . what are their names again?"

"Dyan and Lisl," said Ash. She thought she had bid
them a last farewell; she thought her grieving was
done. But lately the children had been rushing through
her dreams of Ashland, filling the farmhouse with the
noise and chaos and debris of young life. When Ash
spoke their names out loud, it shocked her to remember that they were dead.

"You brought me some of their toys, to save for
Kaz. A rag doll, and a wooden rattle. You made those
toys for them, didn't you? As I put the toys away, I almost could see the children. You should take the toys
with you when you go home to Ashland. You need to
remember, not that the children are dead, for this you
know too well already, but that your love for them is
still alive. It was grief that brought winter to your
heart, but it was your love for them that finally brought
the spring. I know."

Half in dark and half in shadow, the dancing jacks
hung from the cellar's low ceiling, rank upon rank,
each one as bright and fresh and new as a mother's
love for her infant the first moment it is put into her
arms.

"Every day I say their names," Macy said. "Every
day."

When Ash left, the hour was late. Three toys she
took with her, besides the dancing jack she always
carried: the rag doll and the wooden rattle, and Macy's
clockwork creature. "Fortune has grown too small for
him," Macy said. "He wants to travel."

Ash awoke in the dead of night to the scent of
roses, and to the faint hooting of an incoming steamboat's whistle. In darkness she dressed, and splashed
her face with cold water from the basin. Though she
had lived in this hired room for nearly nine days now,
she had only to throw soap and comb into the satchel,
and her packing was done. The two baskets, though
awkward to carry, were a light enough burden. She

left her room empty, taking even the roses from the tabletop, tucking them into one of the baskets.

She reached the landing before the riverboat did. She had counted the other riverboats as they came in: three in ten days had arrived in Fortune on their northbound run, only to be stalled here by the closed river. Three others stood at port as well, packet boats, taking on cargo, passengers, and mail for the regular run south to the sea. One packet boat embarked each day at first light, and one arrived each day, sometime between noon and sunset.

The incoming boat wended between these docked boats, huffing white steam in the darkness, coming into the landing in eerie silence, until at last she had drawn near enough for Ash to hear the throbbing of her engines and the splashing of water spilling from her buckets.

Ash did not need to read the name ornately painted on the boat's wheelboxes. She had lived on the *Amina* long enough to know the sound of her whistle. The boat nosed into the landing and hovered there while the stage was lowered and the crew rushed ashore to tie the boat down. Ash stood with her baskets on the ground beside her, listening to the mate shout her orders, watching the crewmembers rush here and there through the shadows. The engines fell silent suddenly, and the boat heaved a sigh. Here and there along her decks, a few lamps were lit.

A lone figure came down the landing stage. "Ash."

"These are for you." Ash held out the roses. "You enjoyed them so much in Seven Bells City."

"Ouch." Rys sucked a finger.

"You are back so soon."

"It seemed long to me. We marked and mapped the new stretch of river. We also found what we were looking for. Do you want to come on board?"

"Not yet. Can you leave the boat for a while?"

Rys called someone over to bring Ash's things aboard, and gave him the roses, too, to put in water in her cabin. They walked together along the dark landing, then turned down a side road, where a dockside

tavern had just lit its lantern. Within, a yawning
tavernkeeper with a burning taper in his hands waved
them to a table and asked what they would have. Rys
ordered supper and tea, and gave him a message to be
delivered. She held Ash's hand across the tabletop. In
the lamplight she looked drawn. She had inkstains on
her fingers. "Tell me what is wrong."

"Nothing, it is so silly."

That rare, sweet smile crossed Rys' face, and the
deep smile lines fanned out from the corners of her
eyes down the sides of her cheeks. "The oddest things
seem to turn out to be the most important. Toys and
dogs and drums, for instance."

"Well, this is important only to me. Tell me about
the hunt for . . . him."

"It was hardly a hunt at all. He made himself easy to
find. He was camped by the riverside, perhaps a day's
journey south of the border. He built a signal fire, and
begged for help when I sent the yawl over with a couple of new crewmembers who were too young to recognize his face. They told him to stay where he was
and we would pick him up on our return journey, after
we were done with the mapping. It would be ten days
or more, they told him. They gave him some food, but
he was not in too desperate straits . . . he had plenty of
meat. My guess is that he killed and butchered his
horse for food. On our return journey, we slipped past
him in the darkness. He should not even be getting impatient yet, though the latest rainstorm might have
ruined his food supply."

Rys ceased her narration as the tavernkeeper reappeared with bread and cold sliced meat. He had put an
apple pudding in the oven to warm, he said, and the tea
would soon be ready. Rys spread her meat with mus-
tard and put it between two slices of bread. "Do you
want some bread and butter?"

"It's the middle of the night. What do I want with
food?"

The tea came. Ash poured cups for both of them,
and dosed hers with milk and sticky sugar. "I thought
about you constantly. Now I don't have anything to

say. People—total strangers—keep coming up to me, begging me to stay in Fortune. Something is beginning here, they say, and I should be a part of it. If I did, I could meet you at the landing like this, every time you came into port."

Rys said softly, "How could I let you do such a thing? Every day you are away from Ashland, you blame yourself."

Ash folded her hands upon the tabletop. Rys finished her supper, but did not seem to take great enjoyment from it. Another riverboat pilot appeared at the doorway of the tavern, youthful and sleep tousled, but with that grim look about the mouth that pilots all seem to acquire after a while. Rys waved him over and showed him the contents of a dispatch bag: a carefully drawn map revision and a set of instructions for running the new stretch of river to the north. He would oversee the printing and distribution of the revisions, and in a matter of days the passage to the north would be open again.

"I suppose the next thing to do is send for the queen," Rys said when he had left.

Ash said, "Do you really want her on this journey? Better to tell her after it is done, is what I think."

Rys stared at her as though shocked, but then she smiled suddenly. "I hate to say anything bad about the queen . . ."

"She may not have the resolve. She may change her mind despite the dancing jack. Macy's magic is slow."

"Well, then." Rys seemed relieved.

"Can we embark before dawn?"

"Probably, though refueling always takes more time than it seems it should." Rys took the watch out of her pocket and examined it. Reading the time upside-down, Ash concluded that the sun would not rise for several hours yet.

Rys said, "There is nothing to do but wait, then. Shall we return to the boat? You could finish your night's sleep."

Ash unfolded her hands. She remembered again the

stone wall in the Queen's rose garden. "I have not finished what I had to do in Fortune."

Rys sipped from her teacup, silent, watching Ash.

"I don't know how to explain—"

"This is how I see you, Ash: You ride a river you cannot see, so you have trouble believing it is there."

"Perhaps I need Pilot's Sight."

Rys set down her cup and gestured to the tavernkeeper, who stood against the far wall with a cloth in his hand, half asleep. He came over with an account book for her to sign. Ash and Rys went out together into the empty city.

Ash wished for a lantern but had to settle for starlight and Rys' hand, reaching out from time to time to steer her around a bad place in the road. The city might have been a forest, waiting to unfurl its leaves when day dawned, silent now. In the darkness, Ash could not distinguish between ruins. One overgrown garden blended into the next. The crumbling chimneys seemed one with the sagging rooftops, and the walls gave way to roads like streams flowing into rivers.

The ghosts were out. They gathered in patchy groups, whispering. She heard their whispers behind, and turned to find that they streamed down the road behind her and Rys like a river of gauze, following them. Ash had spent one day in the burial ground, returning to Hala and her kin the dignity they had lost in death. There had been many other burials going on, but it would be a long time yet before the last ghost was laid to rest.

"What is it?" said Rys.

"I thought I heard something."

Rys turned. "There is something restless about the darkness, but I see nothing following us."

"I must be imagining things."

They walked on, with the ghostly entourage increasing behind them. Ash took Rys by the hand. Its warmth demonstrated through contrast how cold was her own. "This is a desolate place," said Rys.

"This part of the city has been given over to the ghosts. These houses are full of bones."

Ash stopped to open a gate. From dawn to dusk she had spent her days here. She imagined what Rys saw: the raw wounds of the harshly pruned garden, the clean stoop, and the washed windows. The door glided open on oiled hinges. It no longer smelled of death within, but of the herbs that Ash had strewn everywhere. The trailing ghosts stopped at the gate; this small piece of the city was no longer theirs.

Indoors, with the starlight blocked out, she could see even less. But she knew her way by now. Rys followed more slowly behind her, her steps slowed, perhaps, by wonder, as she examined the emptied house. Some of its contents Ash had salvaged, giving away what retained its usefulness, storing with Macy a few things which seemed unique and valuable. The rest she had loaded into a borrowed wagon and carried away to the city dump.

"I ripped open the upholstery and emptied out the stuffing. I took every single thing out of the cupboards. I cleaned everything, even the chimneys. But still—"

Ash opened the door of the nursery, where she had first found the remains of her brother's children. She had left the window open, and faint light spilled in, glittering on the clean and waxed floor. "Most of their bones were still here. I found some out in the garden, in a rat's nest I uncovered, and others scattered through the house, here and there. With every bone I found, I thought, 'this must be the last one.' But no."

"You would know when you had found them all?"

"I don't know, perhaps. Yes, I would."

"So long as you're certain," said Rys.

"The next step," said Ash, "is to take down the house, board by board."

"That seems extreme. What's this?" Rys stepped forward to pick something up from the floor. "Someone must have loved this once." She rubbed it on her sleeve, and Ash saw a faint gleam in the starlight. "It's a pretty brooch—silver, I think: a crescent moon, wound about by vines. The clasp is broken."

"It was not there this afternoon. The rats are always rearranging things. Perhaps they got tired of having cold silver in their bed."

"A rat could not have carried this very far." Rys took something from her pocket and placed it on the floor in place of the brooch. "Now, let us stand watch."

"What did you put there?"

"A piece of dried apple."

They went out into the hallway and closed the door. On her knees, Rys peered through the keyhole, but the view did not satisfy her. She lay down and put her eye to the crack underneath the door. Ash sat down in the hallway with her back against the wall, and listened to the faint, rapid ticking of Rys' pocket watch. *This is absurd,* she thought.

The difference between sleeping and waking blurred. Ash dreamed of children racketing down the hallway, chasing a cat who, in turn, chased after a mouse. Lisl, a baby, just able to walk, tripped and fell over her own enthusiasm. She began to scream, but when no one came to pick her up, she got up on her own and continued after the others, into the darkness. Ash wanted to call out after her. The effort awoke her.

Rys had tensed. Ash held her breath. She heard a faint scuttling, a sound she had almost forgotten, it had been so long since Ghost Dog wiped out Ashland's rats. Rys heaved a sigh and got stiffly to her knees, and then to her feet. She helped Ash up. "The rat came from under the closet door."

"I searched the closet."

"Let's have another look."

The closet had six shelves, which had contained the remains of the children's clothing, much chewed and fouled by rodents. Ash had found a missing rib bone in there, in the debris. Rys crouched on the floor to peer at the closet floor. Ash had cleaned it thoroughly, but tonight there were fresh droppings. Rys looked on the next shelf up. "More droppings. Phew! It smells worse than it should."

It did smell distinctively of rat in that closet. Ash

said, "If I never need to tear down the house, perhaps here is the place to start."

"I don't suppose you have a pry bar."

"There's one in the garden shed."

Ash went out alone into the back garden, which she had shorn even more cruelly than the front garden. A loud banging began in the nursery. By the time she returned, Rys had taken out all the shelves, exposing a rat hole which even Ash could see in the darkness. Ash crawled into the closet and began tearing out its paneling. Soon they both were coughing in the dust. "It's a glamorous business, being a sorceress, isn't it?" said Rys. "Aren't you glad you wore your clean shirt?"

Ash hacked away at the paneling, while Rys cleared the debris and helped her get the bar properly wedged. The interior of the wall was packed with rats' detritus: shredded cloth, droppings, and a miscellany of unidentifiable objects. Ash raked it out with the pry bar and put it in a pile on the floor for Rys to go through. "Your debt to me is increasing," Rys muttered as she began to pick squeamishly through the pile.

"We'd better visit a bathhouse before we board the *Amina*."

In order to tear up the floor, Ash had to first remove the closet door and the walls which boxed it in. In the process, she found a place where the floorboards had gone rotten. She started her removal there and soon uncovered another cache of debris. A half-dozen rats climbed out of this pile to glare at her. "Ware, Rys," she said, standing ready with the pry bar. Rys got hastily to her feet. Ash pounded the bar on the floor, and the rats all disappeared under the floorboards.

Rys said mildly, "I'd rather face a bad turn on a stormy night, actually. Those are big rats."

"Did you find anything?"

"Looks like a stuffed toy." Rys held it up, looking like she wished she were touching it with a pair of tongs rather than her fingers. "It appears that even rats get lonely. Otherwise, just trash—no bones."

Ash began lifting nesting material out of the hole under the floor. The heavier debris had sifted to the bottom. Ash had Rys look to see if any more rats remained, then she reached in with her hands, encountering more than one thing, as she felt blindly in the darkness, which she would rather not have touched. Rys picked through the uncovered treasures. "Button, needle, what is this, a feather? A piece of something, I don't know what, it makes me sick to look at it."

"Spare me."

"A wheel from a toy wagon, the bowl of a wooden spoon, more buttons, a little finger ring, heavens! a metal cup, a shard of glass . . . a bone. Another bone."

Ash took them: a curved rib, and the round disk of a vertebra. One belonged to Dyan, and one to Lisl. Rys was looking at her; she shook her head and slipped the bones into her pocket. She finished emptying out the hole, and went back to tearing up floorboards.

"Shoe buckle, seashell, seed pod, broom straw, button, something heavy, maybe a clock weight. Rocks . . . no, one of these is a bone."

It was tiny; amazing how small a baby's toes are. Once again, Ash shook her head and put the bone into her pocket. She leaned into the pry bar, and Rys prowled through the debris one more time in case she had missed anything. Ash reached into the hole she had uncovered. Her fingers brushed something dry and frail. She picked it up, a slender twig of a bone, part of Dyan's hand.

"Rys," she said, "we can go now."

Scrubbed clean with rough bathhouse brushes, their wet hair braided at their necks, the two of them stood on the *Amina*'s storm deck, watching the sun rise over Fortune, as the second pilot sounded the embarcation bell. At a tower halfway up the hill, the queen's flags lifted and flickered in the rising breeze. Light glimmered along the rooftops of the city, then suddenly came cascading down the hillside.

"Look," said Rys.

Gold paved the streets of Fortune.

Chapter 15: Rys

This was the sweetest time of year, with balmy days and the gentle spring sun bringing the land to life; the farmers busy in their fields, the fishermen casting their lines, the birds flocking home to nest and sing, and everything in bloom. With the storm season over, only the usual snags, fogs, collisions, accidents, and fires threatened the *Amina*'s safety.

After fifteen days without a single day ashore, another ten to go before they saw Fortune Landing again, and no passengers to keep them busy or diverted, the crew suffered most from weariness and boredom. Lindy and Kiva, who had accompanied the *Amina* willingly this time, kept the crew in line and did not pester Rys with questions. Not one person besides Rys and Ash understood the purpose of this journey, and Rys often wondered if even they truly understood.

This was the third time in thirty days that Rys had piloted the *Amina* along the stretch of river between Fortune and what had been Gelsin Bend. By daylight, Ash joined her more often than not, and Rys left the helmsman unsupervised as they watched the blooming land together from the rail. It was at night, as she served her second watch from midnight to dawn, that an elusive truth taunted her. Deep in her awareness, it flickered from shadow to shadow like a fish in still water. She knew better than to ignore its presence, but although she considered everything which had happened on this strange journey, enlightenment evaded her.

She considered Ash and her basket of bones, as though she were a riddle to be answered, or a puzzle to be taken apart. She considered whether she truly loved Ash herself, or merely the idea of her; whether she truly saw her, or only an image; and if her old passion were only an old habit. She considered whether Ash, in questioning the queen's resolve, should also have questioned her own.

So Rys went fishing for this flickering truth, but it lived in deep water and would not rise.

One night, a couple of hours before dawn, Ash came tousled and distressed from her bed, with her hair all in a tangle and her shirt only half buttoned. Rys sent the helmsman to bed. Rather than sitting on the bench as she usually did, Ash paced from window to window, straining to see the shoreline. Rys said, "We are at Japa Bend. Perhaps that is why you could not sleep."

They did not speak again until the *Amina* started the next crossing, and the night sky dropped down to glaze the forward rail with stars. With Japa Bend behind them now, Ash turned to gaze forward, but Rys knew that her compass heart would always point steadily homeward. "Look," Ash said, pointing at the sky. "The Hunter slays the Beast of Winter. The storms of spring are over."

"Do you remember lying on our backs on the roof of the pilothouse, when I taught you the constellations?"

"I remember." Ash sat on a windowsill, still gazing out at the stars. "What did I ever teach you in return?"

"You taught me that it is not always dangerous to be rooted."

"I doubt it was as useful to you as knowing the stars has been to me." Ash folded her hands around one knee, and they finished the crossing without speaking again.

"We are close," Rys said then. "We'll be tying down in four hours or so, at an easy landing on the western shore. We'll have to hike up from there, but better to go on foot than risk alerting Anselm to our coming."

"I'm going alone," Ash said.

"No, you are not."

"You have been a pilot for too long. I am not one of your crewmembers, required by law to serve your will!"

"I will not let you go alone."

"I don't want you to see—" Ash took in her breath. "How could you still care for me, if you watched—"

"I know what you have to do. You will not do it alone."

"I do not want you to come with me!"

Rys said softly, "You have no choice. You will not be able to stop me."

Ash stalked outdoors. Until day dawned, she paced the rail outside, near enough that Rys could hear her footsteps, far enough that she could not see her face. Perhaps Rys could force her company upon Ash. But she could not break her solitude.

Still, the elusive truth would not rise.

The sun still hung close to the horizon when the *Amina* landed. Rys told the second pilot to bring the boat back to Fortune if she and Ash did not return by sunset, and gave him a letter to deliver to the queen.

Neither road nor path had ever cut through this wilderness of forest. They had to battle their way, step by step, through a resilient, nearly impenetrable thicket. Rys struggled through as though she were swimming, using her arms to part the way for her head and shoulders. The bushes closed in behind her. She lost her footing and fell; the plants captured her and she flailed, entangled.

Ash was gone. Rys struggled, entrapping herself further. She called in a panic, "Ash, do not leave me!"

"I've broken through," Ash said nearby.

Rys heard the sound of her coming back through the thicket, indomitable. She plucked Rys' entrapped arm free and steadied her as she disentangled her feet. The plants parted before her. Rys followed behind, keeping a hand on her shoulder until, with a last pluck at her sleeve, the thicket let her loose into the open forest.

"A fish out of water," Ash said, smiling.

Rys examined her torn sleeve, embarrassed. "I'm surprised you came back for me."

"Well—" Ash looked away. "I've been haunted by enough angry partings."

They walked through the woods in silence. Birds flashed from sunlight to shadow, and Ash pointed out a wide-eyed dappled fawn. Without Ash to guide her, Rys would have felt like an alien in this verdant forest. They walked side by side, until the cool morning gave way to early afternoon, and they found a path that the deer had beaten through the thickets to get to the water.

Once they could see the river again, they realized they had walked past the rocky point where Anselm had made his camp. They had no choice but to work their way through the bracken, keeping the water within sight so they would not lose their way again. Ash broke the path and Rys followed, until suddenly the undergrowth cleared and they found themselves in the open woods again, with the water glittering off to their left. It was a beautiful sight.

Rys pointed toward a streamer of smoke, a gauzy smear across the blue sky. A stand of trees grew between them and river, their trunks clustered together, their slim branches clothed in budding green. As they started forward, the man who had been king stepped from behind those trees. He wore woodsman's leather now, with the skins of small animals tying his waist. His teeth bared in a predator's smile. He turned sideways and came dancing toward them. From his right hand he launched a spear.

Ash seemed unable to move. Rys stepped in front of her. The spear floated like thistledown upon a soft wind. Its slow, soft flight gave Rys forever in which to realize that the blade would take her in the heart, yet somehow there was no time left to reconsider or regret. So this was that cold and glittering truth she could not seem to tease out of its deep places.

It is yours, my Cydna, she thought, for she had no time left to speak the words out loud. *As always, my heart is yours.*

There was no time, even, to feel the pain, though she did feel a blow that jarred to the bone. Then she plunged into an empty, echoing silence, as though she had leapt into a river and sunk to the bottom like a stone.

Chapter 16: Ash

Rys uttered a surprised grunt and took a step backward. She fell against Ash and hung in her arms, a dead weight, with the spear rooted deep into her chest. She was too heavy to hold. Gently, Ash laid her down.

Anselm turned and bounded among the green leaves of spring, his hair flowing behind him, thick and gray as the fur of a wolf. Birds rose up from under his feet, crying, "Tragedy! Travesty!" The forest took him into its dark-limbed embrace, and Ash could see him no longer.

She pulled the spear blade from Rys' heart. The bed of moss and twigs crackled and sighed under the pilot's weight. On her knees, Ash ripped frantically at the blood-soaked shirtcloth, and pressed both her hands against the deep wound. But the blood had already ceased to flow.

Rys' lips were parted as though there were a last thing she had wanted to say. She would never say it now. "Why did you have to come!" cried Ash.

The forest gave voice around her. Birds whirled overhead.

She stood up. She felt cold and silent as a stone whirling in a slingshot. She took a small thing out of her pocket and turned the key in its back, then set it down upon the ground. Macy's clockwork creature took a step, and another. With the first step it grew to the size of a squirrel, with the next to the size of a fox. Ash picked up Anselm's spear.

In seven more steps, the clockwork creature had grown to the size of a small pony. "We are going hunting," Ash said.

* * *

The forest striped the creature's back with shadows. It bounded ahead, nose to the ground like an eager hound, crashing through thickets and bracken, leaving a wide, broken swath behind it. Ash ran full tilt down this trail and still could not keep pace with the creature. It drew farther and farther from her, until she could no longer even see it. A bramble caught her by the ankle. She stopped to disentangle herself and realized she could run no more. She rubbed her eyes with a shirtsleeve, to keep her vision clear, and walked steadily onward.

A sweet and metallic voice sounded up ahead, like the ringing of a clocktower's bells. Had Macy's creature spotted its prey? She began to run again. She heard an angry bellow and a harsh, battlefield clashing. Ash looked toward the sound. *How glad Anselm must be to have an enemy at last.*

By the time she caught up with them, the creature had been dismembered. Anselm beat savagely upon its remains with a tree branch. Pieces of metal and fine-toothed gears flew through the air, spinning and shining in sunlight, disappearing in shadow. "Stop!" Ash cried.

The king turned upon her, teeth bared. Dirt and sweat blackened his shirt. Sunlight glimmered in his black and gray hair, and shone upon the polish of sweat on his face. Panting for breath, ecstatic with the joy of battle and the chase, he began to laugh. "You will pay," he said. "Oh, you will pay dearly. That boy of yours . . . your fields to weeds . . . the end of Ashland. And you. I will tear your throat out, for what you have done to me."

Ash remembered the spear in her hand and hefted it. He hefted his own branch mockingly. She could not possibly throw true, and he knew it. Ash lowered the spearpoint. "I forbid you," she said.

He laughed, and started toward her.

"I know you," she said.

He crouched to leap. His eyes were like the stones polished in a dark river, tumbled so long in that ancient journey that they could no longer remember where their journey began.

"I know who you are," she said. "At your secret heart."

He sprang at her, his hands curled, reaching eagerly for her throat.

"You are a dog!"

He struck her, snarling, slashing at her with his ivory teeth. She hit his head with the butt of the spear, knocking him to the ground. He came at her again, slavering, maddened. There was velvet inside his ears. He had a wide forehead. Perhaps he could have someday become wise. Ash took the spear, still red with Rys' blood, and pierced him through, and pinned the flame-shaped blade deep into the earth.

She stayed while he died, for he had been, for seven years, her only friend. Then he left him there, pinned to earth. In time, the forest would claim him.

Seeking her way, Ash walked through the woods' bitter beauty. Every time she thought she had made her final choice, yet another lay before her. Which way should she turn now?

Her mighty strength bled out of her, until she could scarcely walk at all. She continued, stumbling, until she saw Rys lying on her bed of moss, gazing without squinting into the bright sunshine. Ash sat down beside her, empty as an old pot. She took off her hat and propped it up to shield Rys' face. It was all she could do, she was so tired.

The torn, scarlet-stained shirt gaped around Rys' only vulnerable place, that pierced heart which she never would protect: a dancing jack's heart, forever choosing pain so that she could also choose joy.

Nothing other than death could bring Ash to this crossroads. She had been here before and had chosen bitterness and solitude and the paralysis of self blame. The choice had taken her away from Ashland even as she returned there. It had taken from her the spring, the joy of the harvest, the companionship of her friends. It had taken the children she loved and given her ten years of emptiness. Now Rys was dead, and Ash could spend the rest of her life in bitter regret. She could choose this way again and let her life be like this love of hers: destined to be forever unconsummated until death ended it.

When she closed her eyes against the tears, she saw Rys only more clearly: honed and weathered by the years on the river, somber and grim at the helm of the boat, facing down the hurricane, and then turning, and smiling that sweet smile.

"This time I choose joy," Ash said to her. "I choose the drums, the wild night, the dangerous throb of passion, the shout: Aha! I know the truth! I choose joy so I can always love you. I choose joy so I can be your heart for you."

The forest caught its breath. Ash opened her eyes as the pierced heart beneath her hand gave a startled thump, as though a drumstick had come down suddenly upon a drum. "It is yours," Rys said. Then she gasped, and lifted a startled hand to her chest, where a red scar marked the site of her death wound. A beam of sunlight slipped past the shade of Ash's hat. Rys squinted, looking profoundly puzzled.

"I will always love you," Ash said, fiercely and hastily, lest Rys be snatched away from her again, leaving her with those words still unsaid. But Rys took in her breath, and let it out, and Ash lay down beside her, and put her head upon her shoulder, and wrapped her arms around her to warm her. They lay so still that a crowd of young hares came up to peer at them, and some chattering birds landed within arm's length to forage for worms. Ash wept, and then fell silent, and listened to the steady rhythm of Rys' heartbeat. When she lifted her head, the birds started up in a panic, and the hares bounded away.

"I doubt I can walk far," said Rys. Already, she was thinking about their predicament and how to solve it.

Ash managed a smile. "You look much better than you did."

"I can imagine."

"We'll go to the shore and wait. Sooner or later, there will be a boat."

Ash helped Rys to her feet. Leaning together, they walked the short distance to the river's edge. There they sat side by side and watched the sun set.

Ash built up the fire Anselm had left burning, and went out in the darkness to gather more wood. She returned to find Rys on her feet, leaning against the support of a strong young sapling. Rys pointed downriver, where a spark of light bobbed in the darkness. "Boat's lantern," she said. "It will be a while before they get here, for they're against the current. But they've seen the fire."

She stripped off her ripped, blood-soaked shirt and dipped it in the river. She used it to wash the blood away, then she threw it into the fire. Ash took off her jersey and gave it to her to wear. They walked down to the water's edge and waited there until the boat landed. Kiva lifted the lantern to shine on their faces. "Madam Pilot, I'm sorry—but we're more than your crewmembers now; we're your friends. We had to disobey you." She lifted the lantern higher, revealing Lindy, who sat at the oars behind her. "By the river, what happened to you? You look like death!"

Rys convulsed with laughter. Lindy and Kiva both stared at her, baffled and alarmed. Ash said, "Not death. Not this time."

They got into the boat, and the loyal mates rowed them out into the current of the dark river. The frogs raised an ecstatic chorus and the stars laughed their light down upon them. Rys, leaning wearily in Ash's embrace, continued to chuckle until suddenly she fell asleep.

Ash held her closely, grieving. With every dip of the oars, Ashland drew nearer. Soon, much too soon, they would part.

The river flowed: from sky to earth to ocean and back again into sky. The current carried them back to the *Amina,* and the *Amina* carried Ash to Japa Farm, where she disembarked the next day with her baskets of bones and set her feet, at last, on the road home.

Chapter 17: Ash

Ashland had bloomed without her. The orchard still wore its festival clothes of pink and white. In the potato field, neatly rowed plants pierced through to the sun. In the hay field, a wall had been repaired that she had always meant to mend. Pea plants climbed the trellis in the vegetable garden, and onions grew like grass. Swallows nested in the eaves of the old barn, swooping and calling in the bright afternoon sun. Someone had even dug the old flower bed, and now seedlings grew there: red broom and blue button and hollyhock. By midsummer, for the first time in many years, the old stone wall would be abloom.

The kitchen smelled like home. Ash set down her satchel and her blanket roll and the two baskets, then went out again, to Katleree, where Evie's older children boasted proudly of all the work they had done, and All-Red baked a cake to celebrate their return. Bewildered by their kindness, Ash thanked them until they laughed at her for repeating herself so often. It was a good thing that neighbors did not keep accounts, or she would be too deeply in debt to ever extricate herself.

She returned home late, after nightfall, and lit a lamp on the tabletop. Never had the old house seemed so quiet, or so empty. She sat in an old rush-bottomed chair, thinking about Kaz, Zara, and Rys. How much longer, she asked herself, would she struggle alone to keep the fires of Ashland burning? Something had changed in her absence, or, rather, she had changed, and Ashland had changed with her. But her solitude remained: a solitude no longer natural or even tolerable, when the journey's many reunions—and even the separations—had left her heart so full.

She got up and opened one of the baskets. One slender bone she took out, and laid it upon the tabletop. She laid down another beside it, where it belonged.

In the morning, the Katlerees brought her sheep and her ox and a bag of chickens, including a dozen yellow chicks, and a couple of piglets to raise. There was work to be done, and Ash set to it, but in the evening she sat at the table, putting together the puzzle-piece bones.

Night after night, she dreamed of her lost children. They demanded that she feed them and tell them stories. They brought flowers, stolen from the blooming meadow. They slept in her arms. She dreamed of herself, harried by their idiocies, delighted by their delights. Day after day, she awoke to a kitchen table covered with bones.

A man found the way to Ashland, despite the thickets choking the road, and asked her why the wild geese had not returned to his pond this year. She told him to fence in his cows, for they had fouled the water, killing the fish and leaving nothing for the geese to eat. He spent the afternoon clearing some of Ashland's brush before returning to his own home, well satisfied. There would be others, Ash knew. The people of Faerd were hungry for answers.

On the seventh night, she put the last bone in its place. She contemplated the skeletons by lantern light. Had she cherished her brother's children like this when they were alive? She could not remember. There had been no peace, no silence, no contrast of loneliness to make the deep, hot, bright fire of love all the more vivid. Only now, with everything stripped away, could she feel the essence of that brave, persistent joy.

Alone in her empty kitchen, Ash smiled at the bones of her lost children. She lit a candle against the darkness and put it in the middle of the table. She could not remember the old songs, so she paced around the table in solemn silence. As her feet wore a circle in the dust on the floor, the old tunes began to come to her. She hummed until she remembered the words, and then she began to sing.

She sang the ancient carols of Winter-turn, though the day of the winter solstice was long past. She sang because it was during this spring that she had turned her back upon her heart's winter. She kept the Long Watch, in peace and solemnity, as it was meant to be kept. She sang and clothed the bones of her children with her song.

She sang until dawn light revealed the battered table, the burnt out candle, and herself, sitting in stunned weariness, watching the children sleep. In the silence she heard the sounds of their breathing. In the gray light, she saw them quiver in their dreams.

She got up after a while and went to take the toys out of the baskets: the rattle and the rag doll. She put the toys into their hands, to comfort them in case they felt afraid when they awoke from their long sleep.

She built up the fire and put a pot of water on the stove to heat for porridge. Suddenly, sunlight came pouring in, and the woods pressing in upon the house rang with a chorus of birds. On the tabletop, the sleeping children began to stir. Any moment now, they would open their eyes.

Epilogue

An exuberant summer marked the rebirth of Faerd that year, with heart-lifting balmy days giving way to gentle showers that soaked deep to the roots of the crops in the field. Lambs frolicked behind their dams, tree branches broke under the weight of ripening fruit, babies fattened in the cradle, old people nodded and chatted in the sunshine, and everywhere stone walls, cobbled roads, and entire buildings were repaired and rebuilt. When the first freeze came, late and long expected, the farmers of Faerd hung sheaves of wheat in their doorways, decked their children in crowns of crimson leaves, and stared, amazed, at the winter stores set by in their root cellars. In every vale and hamlet, Faerd rang with the sound of celebration.

In Vateria, the winds of change had begun to blow.

At planting time, the Danae, Kaz and Zara among them, had come down out of the land of stones and into the verdant land of their ancestors. They traveled by night, and planted corn and squash and other vegetables in darkness. By day they hid in the woods. The settlers did not even realize that the Danae had returned until the corn had reached knee height and could no longer be mistaken for grass.

Rys' first shipment of food had arrived at Kerlin Point by then. With their bellies full, the Danae's spirits lifted, and when the settlers came to burn the crops, they stood their ground against them. Though their numbers were much reduced, still they were many, and the settlers were few. The settlers became afraid and decided to send to the king for help.

Kaz and Zara played the drums that night, now that there was no longer any need to keep their presence a secret. From sunset to sunrise they played, and the people sang and danced. They cared for their crops in daylight now. Every night, all night long, they played the drums and waited to see what would happen next.

They played the rhythm of storm, the rhythm of tides, the rhythm of the river's current rushing to the sea. They played the drums, and the king's army did not come.

The settlers grew restless and worried. They had a few guns, but none of them seemed to work. Their sheep began to fall ill; they worried that their children might be next. They sent again for the army.

Only one person came, riding a wild-blooded horse, bearing a document with King Bartyn's seal. She spoke to the settlers, then left them shouting angrily in her wake. She rode into the encampment of the Danae and took off her hat. Her hair was tied up in a knot, but Kaz and Zara had already recognized Ursul.

"Lord Diggen is now steward of this land," she said. But everyone gathered there could see who was the true steward.

A'tin bowed to her. "This land has always belonged to the Danae."

"I have told the settlers to let you be. A dozen armed men are camped nearby. I will send for them if I must."

A'tin bowed again. "How can we live like this? How can we care for our crops and our children when we must always be looking over our shoulders?"

Ursul said, "I will stay here tonight, and tomorrow I will stay in the settlement. The day after tomorrow, your elders and theirs must come together and agree on how to share the land. You must agree together, or I will decide for you. The choice is yours."

Night after night, Kaz and Zara played the drums. The sheep recovered from their illness. Some of the settlers left in a rage, but the rest began herding their sheep more carefully, to keep them out of the Danae's fields. The settlers and the Danae continued to look suspiciously at each other across the distance that separated them. Their children began playing together.

In the first month of summer, Rys personally delivered a second shipment of supplies at Kerlin Point. There, two dozen people and as many pack animals camped among the stones, patiently awaiting the steamboat's arrival. When Kaz and Zara spotted Rys coming ashore they hurried over to greet her. She looked tired, they commented to each other later, and preoccupied. She had not heard from Ash, she told them, but she offered to bring a letter to Fortune in the hope that it might eventually reach Ashland.

"Ask her to send us some potatoes," said Zara.

"We won't need them, really," said Kaz. "We'll have our own vegetables before her potatoes are harvested."

"Potatoes would grow well here, wouldn't they?"

"Well, yes."

"Ask her to send us some potatoes to grow."

Kaz boarded the boat to use the pen and paper in the mud clerk's office, leaving Zara and Rys alone to watch the unloading. "Will you be writing to her also?" Zara asked.

"I think so."

"Will you tell her—will you thank her for me?"

"What am I to thank her for?"

"For helping us." Zara's hands made fists in her pockets, but then her hands relaxed. "I want her to like me. For when we come . . . home."

"What has happened with the Danae?"

"I think it will work out. It was all because of the drums. The drums, and Ursul. Do you remember Ursul?"

"How could anyone forget her?" Rys and Zara sat side by side upon a rock. "Is she Queen of Vateria yet?" Rys asked.

Zara laughed. "I don't think so!"

"It will happen," Rys said. "Mark my words."

❦   ❦   ❦

When the leaves began to turn color and the first cold winds to blow from the north, Rys traveled to Seven Bells City on guild business. Her seven years as Guildmaster had not been easy ones, but this day's simple work proved the most painful of her tenure. She remained in town only one night and left early the next morning in the guild's open carriage. Traders, farmers, and business people crowded the streets. She watched the activity in amazement, asking herself where all these people had come from. A housecleaner, busy upstairs, shook out a dustmop onto Rys' head as she passed below.

In the countryside, donkeys pulling wagonloads of grapes and apples crowded the road. Rys had her driver stop at a cider mill. The cider man, busy and breathless with his assistants rushing frantically around him, stopped to pour Rys a cup straight from the press. When she commented on the harvest, he shook his head in disbelief. "Who would have thought it would be such a good year?"

The carriage driver had been a pilot until he lost the use of a leg in a boat accident. He turned to Rys when they were underway again, and asked diffidently, "Are you comfortable, madam?"

"Yes, thank you."

"Madam, if you'll forgive me the impertinence . . ."

"Goodness, you'd think I was the queen! Say whatever you like!"

"The guild would never have survived the plague years without you. It's not right, to treat you like this."

"Thank you for your kind words." Rys settled into the cushions and gazed out over the countryside. The first frost had not yet happened here in the warm south. Summer green had not yet given way to autumn's gold and scarlet, but the air had a bite in it, and she was glad of her warm coat.

She said, half to him and half to herself, "Have you ever sat and talked with an ocean-going pilot? Sometimes, out on the ocean, they can go from cold to warm, winter to spring, in an instant. That is what is happening here in Faerd: a seachange. But there is no change without cost. The old must step aside—or be forced aside—to make way for the new."

"Philosophy doesn't make it right," said the driver, stubborn in his outrage. "What will you do now? Where will you go?"

"There will always be a boat for me."

In Saltertown, she caught a boat to Marlestown. She had returned here only one other time this season. Then, she came bravely, thinking that perhaps something might still be reclaimed: her friendship with Margo, if nothing else. She told Margo everything that had happened, but Margo did not comprehend, even when Rys showed her the scar over her heart. Gazing into Margo's calm, kindly face, Rys first understood what had happened to her when Ash healed her heart. "Nothing can continue as before," she said. "This is not my old life given back to me. It is a new life." But Margo shook her head, half laughing, half bewildered. To this day, she did not understand.

Now, although Marlestown had served as winter port for Rys' entire life, and she had even served as interim mayor during the summer of the plague, the town no longer felt like home to her. She met Margo at a lawyer's office, where she signed over her half ownerships in the house and the store. Margo insisted on giving Rys part of the profits for the next ten years. They parted amicably. Rys had conducted her business so efficiently that she was able to arrange passage to Fortune on the same boat that had brought her here from Saltertown.

In Fortune, she lingered. The boats would continue to run the river until it iced over, but Rys had decided to sit out the rest of the season. She stayed in the Guild House the first night, but none of her fellow pilots could be comfortable in her presence. They avoided her or spoke stiffly to her, as if to a stranger. She moved into a public inn the next day, to give them time to get over their guilt.

Here in the north, autumn had gilded the trees with gold and copper. The roads of Fortune had been repaired for the first time in seven years. New flags flew on the ramparts of the fortress. A stranger handed Rys an autumn rose to put in her buttonhole as she went shopping in the merchant's district. By the time she reached her inn, delivered purchases filled half her room. She had never done anything like this before.

She hired an agent to purchase a sturdy wagon and a pair of horses to pull it. He bought a wagon, then took it back to the wagon builder to have its wheel bearings repacked. He rejected several pairs of horses. The whole business seemed to take much longer than necessary. In the morning, Rys sat by the window of her room, eating sweetbread and drinking imported tea. In the afternoon, she went out walking. Someone had moved into the house where she and Ash had searched for bones. An old man worked out in the street, cobbling a pothole.

The sun was setting, and the air tasted of autumn: smoky and crisp. A cart horse trotted past, harness bells jingling. Rys found Macy's basement workshop and ate supper with her after her assistants had left for the evening. Half finished toys piled the tables. A stack of packed crates stood by the door for the freight wagon to take away in the morning. Rys told Macy that she had spotted dancing jacks in taverns, private houses, inns, and even hanging around people's necks all the way from Tastuly to Sandros. Macy insisted on giving Rys a toy wagon with a clockwork horse to pull it, and a mysterious, intriguing construction of wooden disks on a stick that made peculiar sounds when turned. "You'll have a need for these," she said.

Rys walked back to her inn and told the innkeeper this would be her last night. "I put a bunch of roses in your room," the innkeeper said. "It's been quite the year for roses." A dancing jack hung in the inn's entryway, beside a portrait of the queen.

Rys left Fortune at dawn. In her breast pocket she carried a letter from Ash. But the weight of sadness did not begin to lift from her heart until she had traveled more than half the distance to Semel.

After two days' journey on the main road, she began asking her way to Ashland. On the third day, a farmer riding a cartload of potatoes pointed Rys up a wagontrack. The way looked newly cleared, the pruning scars only partly grown over, the road repairs still raw. The track wove crookedly up the forested hillside. The trees had clothed themselves in scarlet, but white flowers still bloomed in the shadows. The horses mounted the road slowly. The reins lay slack upon Rys' knees. She caught a whiff of woodsmoke, and lifted her head.

Atop a crooked fence, a barefoot girl perched, tangle-headed and leaf-crowned, dirty to the knee. A half-grown puppy rolled in the dirt at her feet. Rys halted the horses. "Is this the way to Ashland?"

The girl lifted her chin loftily. "Is it advice you seek?"

"Advice? No, I am a friend. Would you ride with me and show me the way? I was just going to open this bag of toffee . . ."

The girl hopped down from the fence and scooped up the puppy. After she had settled onto the wagon seat, Rys offered her some candy. The girl hesitated. "It's just ahead."

"That's all right, have some candy. I appreciate the company."

The girl took a piece for herself and a piece for the dog, who promptly lost his and went scrabbling under the wagonseat to find it. "Are you a peddler?" she asked.

"A riverboat pilot."

"I thought you might be a peddler, with your wagon so full."

"I went shopping in Fortune."

"All of that's for you? You must be rich!"

The trees thinned, and the crooked fence marked a clearing. An ox and two horses stood with their noses to the fence, chewing their cud sleepily. An oxcart half full of potato sacks stood at a break in the fence. A crowd of children worked in the wake of a half-dozen shirtless adults, sorting the potatoes that were turned up and tossing them into sacks. Younger children, one just barely walking, played at one side of the field. Rys gave her young guide the sack of candy, admonishing her to share.

The adults all stopped work to fix Rys with cautious, measuring gazes. The potatoes glowed in the black loam, some red, some white, some purple. One of the men was red too, and several of the children matched him. Ash stood among the other farmers, with a potato fork in her hand. She drove it into the ground and left it there. Her shirt hung from the fence. She paused to put it on, but did not button it. She walked up to the wagon and put one foot on the running board, and glanced back at the full wagon. "What's all this?"

"My dowry," Rys said. "I will never come to you empty-handed."

Ash turned her callused palm up on the wagon seat. Rys laid her hand down on top of it lightly and felt a shock, as though she had grasped hold of a lightning bolt. Ash lifted her head, startled. She took in her breath and said, "This is my field. I have to keep working."

"Tell me what to do with my things. I'll come back and help."

"Keep going uphill until you reach the house. Park there and I can help you unload later. There's plenty of pasture for the horses, and a watering trough." Her fingers tightened on Rys' hand. "You picked a good day to come. There's a harvest party tonight, at Katleree's."

Both the barn and house were newly thatched, golden haired, and crowned by the thatcher's symbol, a crane made of reed. Flowers bloomed by the kitchen door.

A fat, heavy-uddered cow grazed near the barn. Rys filled the trough for the animals, then walked back down the wagon track, rolling up her sleeves. The potato diggers were hard at work, the children all happily sucking on toffee, the girl who had guided Rys earlier busy in their midst. She called Rys over and showed her how to sort potatoes. The large, unblemished potatoes were for market. Those that were about the size of a hen's egg were set aside for next year's seed. The rest were tumbled willy-nilly into bags, "for eating." The sun shone kindly on the potato field. Rys fell into the rhythm of the work, turning her head from time to time to watch Ash dig.

Suddenly, they were tying up the sacks and heaving them onto the oxcart, and the children began rushing about. Rys joined the adults for the first time, as they walked behind the oxcart up to the barn. They had harvested more potatoes than they had wagons to transport to market, and were discussing whose wagon they could borrow.

"You'll take my wagon, of course," said Rys. That seemed to solve the problem.

Ash walked beside Rys with a sleeping toddler in her arms. At the barn, Ash's neighbors all bid her farewell. "We'll see you at Katleree," they said.

When they had all gone, Ash handed the sleeping child to Rys. "Will you take her up to the house? Dyan, you go with Rys and start washing up. I'll be there as soon as I've milked the cow."

The girl waited while Rys figured out how to hold the baby in one arm, then took her hand. They walked up the hill to the house. "You'll be staying with us," Dyan said.

The child sleeping against Rys' shoulder was warm, and heavy. Confused, Rys looked down at the small hand clasping hers. "You live here?"

Dyan let go of her hand and ran up the hill to hold the door open. "I'll show you my bed. It's up above the kitchen, like sleeping in a tree."

"Ash said you were to wash up," said Rys. Being around children always made her feel rather stupid. She put the baby in the cradle by the fire, and followed Dyan up a ladder to peer into the warm loft where she slept. It was indeed a cozy nest up there, with a half-dozen bright quilts piled up, and a rag doll holding court on a windowsill. "Very nice," Rys said.

"You can sleep up here with me, if you want."

"That's very kind of you."

Rys expected that she and Ash would talk when she came in from milking, but by then the baby had awakened. Rys had never realized how much attention children demanded. At last, she and Ash went out together to unload the wagon. Rys said cautiously, "I did not expect to find children."

"I know I should have warned you. But I didn't know how to explain."

"You didn't think I would understand?"

Ash looked up, arms laden with burlap-wrapped hams. She set the hams down again, and put a hand to her face.

Rys said, "Dyan and Lisl and I have a great deal in common with each other, don't we?"

Ash shook her head slowly, laughing at herself. Rys put her arms around her, and they stood, rocking each other in the late afternoon sunlight, until Lisl came barreling out the open door and Ash snatched her up, one step away from a head-cracking fall. "Sorry," she said to Rys.

"We have all winter."

They all rode in the wagon to nearby Katleree, with a crock of pickles and one of Rys' hams in the back. Rys drove, and Ash wove autumn leaves into crowns for each of them to wear.

At Katleree, the clans of Northern Semel had already begun to gather. Wagons lined the road and people hustled busily about in their holiday clothes. They rushed forward to greet Ash and help unload the food. Rys drove the wagon away and tied the horses to a fence. When she came back to the crowded barn, she could not find a single familiar face. One stranger after another came forward to introduce herself or himself to her: Merriam of Calter Farm, who raised horses; Roser of Alin Orchard, Claril and his three children, all of the nearest village; Anto and Gian of Sith Farm, who raised potatoes and were both pregnant. At last, a familiar face: Evie of Katleree, who asked her to dance.

The sun had not even set yet, but the fiddlers in the barn had already struck up a tune. Rys did not know the dances of Northern Semel, but they were not too hard to learn. When they stopped to rest, Evie said, "Ash and I grew up together. You've known her a long time, too."

"Not as long as you."

"Ash reads to us about you, from the papers. You've had a bad year."

"Difficult. Not bad." Someone came forward to ask Evie a question about the food preparation, but she brushed him away. On a riverboat, Rys thought, Evie would be a pilot. "I will make her happy," Rys said.

Evie looked at her. "You'd better."

Someone else asked Rys to dance, a man this time. He asked whether the conflict in the Pilot's Guild meant Rys might find herself out of work. "I doubt it. The new Guildmaster and I are on good terms so far, and I am still one of only six master pilots on the river. I am also a friend of the queen."

"Are you?" he said. "That certainly can't hurt!"

She danced: line dances, circle dances, couple dances, square dances. The sun set, and still they came to her, one partner after another, a hundred polite inspections, a thousand probing questions. The people of Semel keep the old ways, and this testing of the stranger is the oldest of rituals. Rys dared not beg off a single dance, lest she fail the test.

The dance over, her last partner left her alone. She pretended not to gasp for breath as she leaned surreptitiously against a wall for support. The trestle table groaned with food, but the far wall seemed too far to walk. She spotted Dyan, frowning with concentration as she danced with the red man from the potato field. She braced herself as a man came up to her, but he just offered a cup of cider, grinning with amusement.

The sweating musicians drank deeply from their mugs of beer. Someone shouted for a couples dance. The musicians tuned their instruments, and the leader shouted hoarsely, "Choose your partners!"

Rys saw her, coming through the crowd. A blaze of scarlet leaves crowned her head. Upon her shoulder

was pinned an ivy-wound silver moon. The lanterns
overhead cast her shoulders with fire.

"Choose your partner!" shouted the leader again.

Ash did not belong to Rys: she belonged to Ashland,
to these gathered people, to the land and the harvest, to
the children of her rich and deep-rooted soul. Rys had
always known she could never claim her. She could
only be claimed. Ash lifted her face, and a spark ignited deep in her eyes. Rys took both her hands. There
was a silence: the raucous shouts, the stamping and
shuffling of feet, even the plucking of the violin strings
fell quiet.

Ash said, "I choose you."

There was a clap and a shout. The music began.

DAW

Laurie J. Marks

THE CHILDREN OF TRIAD

☐ **DELAN THE MISLAID: Book 1** UE2325—$3.95

A misfit among a people not its own, Delan willingly goes away with the Walker Teksan to the Lowlands. But there, the Walker turns out to be a cruel master, a sorcerer who practices dark magic to keep Delan his slave—and who has diabolical plans to enslave Delan's people, the winged Aeyrie. And unless Delan can free itself from Teksan's spell, it may become the key to the ruin of its entire race.

☐ **THE MOONBANE MAGE: Book 2** UE2415—$3.95

Here is the story of Delan's child Laril, heir to the leadership of the winged Aeyrie race, but exiled because of an illegal duel. Falling under the power of an evil Mage, Laril must tap reserves both personal and magical to save the Aeyrie people from the Mage's deadly plans for conquest—plans which if successful, would set race against race in a devastating war of destruction.

☐ **ARA'S FIELD: Book 3** UE2479—$4.50

For many years, members of the Community of Triad have been striving to make it possible for the four primary species of their world to coexist. Now, the sudden, ugly murders of many high-ranked Walker and Aeyrie officials have shattered all hope of peace. Caught in the chaos of imminent war, the children of Triad must discover who is playing this deadly game of death and somehow force them to stop—before their world erupts in a genocidal war of species against species.

DAW
Tanya Huff

VICTORY NELSON, INVESTIGATOR:
Otherworldly Crimes A Specialty

☐ **BLOOD PRICE: Book 1**   UE2471—$3.99
Can one ex-policewoman and a vampire defeat the magic-spawned
evil which is devastating Toronto?

☐ **BLOOD TRAIL: Book 2**   UE2502—$4.50
Someone was out to exterminate Canada's most endangered species—
the werewolf.

☐ **BLOOD LINES: Book 3**   UE2530—$4.99
Long-imprisoned by the magic of Egypt's gods, an ancient force of evil
is about to be loosed on an unsuspecting Toronto.

THE NOVELS OF CRYSTAL

When an evil wizard attempts world domination, the Elder Gods must
intervene!

☐ **CHILD OF THE GROVE: Book 1**   UE2432—$3.95
☐ **THE LAST WIZARD: Book 2**   UE2331—$3.95

OTHER NOVELS

☐ **THE FIRE'S STONE**   UE2445—$3.95
Thief, swordsman and wizardess—drawn together by a quest not of
their own choosing, would they find their true destinies in a fight
against spells, swords and betrayal?

Buy them at your local bookstore or use this convenient coupon for ordering.

PENGUIN USA P.O. Box 999, Dept. #17109, Bergenfield, New Jersey 07621

Please send me the DAW BOOKS I have checked above, for which I am enclosing
$_____ (please add $2.00 per order to cover postage and handling. Send check
or money order (no cash or C.O.D.'s) or charge by Mastercard or Visa (with a
$15.00 minimum.) Prices and numbers are subject to change without notice.

Card #_____ Exp. Date _____
Signature_____
Name_____
Address_____
City _____ State _____ Zip _____

For faster service when ordering by credit card call **1-800-253-6476**
Please allow a minimum of 4 to 6 weeks for delivery.

Mercedes Lackey

The Novels of Valdemar

THE LAST HERALD-MAGE